I worked in warehouse distribution before joining the aviation and radar field for many years. Having retired, I joined a local writing group where, after a couple of years, I entered and won a competition with a four thousand-word short story, my idea for this novel. The following year I was third-placed with another four-thousand-word story. I have also had a full-page short in my local newspaper, besides having a novel published in July of 2020: *Hidden Intentions*, by Dave Flint, which is being rewritten under a different title: *Blackwater Wood*

I may be retired, but the brain is well and ticking the way I want. I have other stories, some completed, others in work progress.

I lead walks in my area with a group of similar-aged people.

BECOMING BROTHERS

Dave Flint

BECOMING BROTHERS

Best Wishes

Dave Flint

Vanguard Press

VANGUARD PAPERBACK

© Copyright 2023
Dave Flint

The right of Dave Flint to be identified as author of
this work has been asserted by him in accordance with the
Copyright, Designs and Patents Act 1988.

A CIP catalogue record for this title is available from the British
Library.

ISBN 978 1 80016 634 9

Vanguard Press is an imprint of
Pegasus Elliot Mackenzie Publishers Ltd.
www.pegasuspublishers.com

First Published in 2023
Vanguard Press
Sheraton House Castle Park
Cambridge England

Printed & Bound in Great Britain

Also by the Author
Hidden Intentions

For Norma

'You had anything to eat today, Forest?'

'Not today, but I had some bread and dripping yesterday that the butcher gave me. Mum gives me some pennies when I'm hungry.'

Danny listened to his answer and put his hand on Forest's shoulder, watching him shy away. 'Where do you live?'

He pointed down one of the side roads, where most buildings lay in ruins after an earlier air-raid. 'We've got a flat down there.'

Danny raised his eyebrows. 'There are not many buildings left down there. Your dad live with you?'

'Mum – don't have a dad. But I've got lots of uncles. They're mostly in the Navy; that's why me and Mum moved here so that she could be with them more often.'

Chapter One

London, 1938

Walking home from a full day's work, Forest Grady felt the strain across his small body after handling all the different kinds of waste from the ships, besides the cruel interactions from the hardcore dockies who he worked alongside. Looking at his rough hands with cuts all over them, he wondered when this existence might end. At almost ten years old and undernourished, he felt all the hardships suffered by trying to help out with the day-to-day living. Trudging through the streets of London's dockland area, he listened as unsavoury language came through the walls of the houses he passed. The foul tongues of workers as they quenched their thirsts in the many alehouses, expressing their views of a bawdy woman. Journeying past the occasional fight, he hurried away, should consequences of it come his way. Any other ten-year-old boy, so his mum had told him, might not become a target, but being the colour he was, he applied caution whenever he came close to a disturbance.

Turning into a run-down, filthy street, he walked past the run-down houses, hoping not to step into anything nasty, as all manner of rubbish littered the neighbourhood. With the late evening drawing on, he reached another turn and saw the curtains pulled in his mum's bedroom. The cheerless building gave almost no sign that someone lived there, but it was home, and he knew his mum had a customer, which meant waiting for whoever it was to leave. He just hoped it wasn't going to be too long.

Stood in a derelict building opposite, he allowed his mind to wander as the evening turned colder and the night clouds gathered, sending shivers into his small body. Suddenly, a shadow appeared in front of him.

'What are you doing in there, you little shit? You up to no good?'

Forest edged further into the gloom as the man picked something from the street and aimed it into the building, missing him by inches.

'You in there, you thieving git?'

Another hard object hit a wall, and more abuse came towards him as he sunk onto his knees, trying to hide, yet ready to scarper if necessary. Another voice joined the man, and with talk of ale, they moved away. Forest peered out from the darkness and watched the two men curse as they drifted away. Looking across to the house opposite and up at the lit bedroom window, he wondered how much longer he would have to wait. His mind drifted to all the hardships he'd endured. His mum's sister, Betsey Addles, was a cruel woman. All he could remember when his mum left him with her at a young age was the pain and hunger he suffered where he had to wait behind her kids with food given out, besides the backhanders he collected when her kids told false stories on him. Two years ago, his aunt told him he should get a job, and Uncle Bronek, her Polish old man, got him one out of school hours. But at least helping out in the docks showed him ways he could look after himself. Then his mum, realising money was involved, hastened in bringing him back home, seeing a few shillings would come her way – and umpteen bottles of gin. Still stood there half-hour later, he felt his stomach moan. The bananas and tin of spam he had at lunchtime had helped, even though he caught a backhander from one of the men, who told him he was a thieving black bastard, but that went with the job. If he didn't take the opportunity to feed himself, he knew there wouldn't be much coming his way at home. Suddenly, the front door opened, and a rough-looking sailor came out of the house, slamming the door behind him. Forest was ready and anxious to get indoors as the cold gripped his small body, and he shivered. 'Come on, Mum, hurry up.' Feeling the ground through the holes in his shoes, he hobbled from one foot to another, wanting to get into the house as the November wind blew through the tumble-down building, while the oncoming darkness made him hug himself even more. Then the light went off. 'About time, Mum.'

Crossing the road, he knocked on the bare wood, waiting for the door to open.

'Who is it?'

'It's me, Mum. Who do you think?'

Gradually, the recognisable face showed through the opening as the door eased ajar.

'Mum, what's happened? Is that blood?'

'Get in quick, and don't say anything.'

He followed her into the kitchen and spread across the floor was the body of another sailor. 'Is he drunk, Mum?'

'And bloody violent. If he comes around, watch out for that fist of his; the blighter's got a whack on him. I managed to hit him with that pan.'

Forest looked at the heavy frying pan on the table. 'What are we going to do?'

'You watch him. He owes me money for what he's had.'

Forest stood there as his mum knelt, rummaging through the pockets of the legless individual. Finding money, she stuffed it into her bra when a hand shot out, grabbing her neck.

'You whore, thieve my money, will you?'

Forest listened to the drunken pronunciation as the man concentrated on his mum. Getting onto one knee, the sailor used force in trying to throttle her. Wondering what to do, Forest grabbed for the knife on the draining board and saw the fear in his mum's eyes as the sailor squeezed his hands tighter, turning her face red. Gripping the handle, he plunged the blade into the attacker's back without thinking. Straight away, the sailor disregarded the woman and turned. Trying to grab the penetrated weapon with one hand, the man gripped Forest's leg with the other, pulling him towards him. 'You little bastard, you'll…'

Without thinking, Forest kicked out with his other foot, almost toppling over as the man sneered at him. Looking up, Forest saw his mum swing the frying pan, hammering the knife deep into the sailor's back, and watched the man's eyes go up into his head, before he dropped to the tiled floor.

'I think you killed him, Mum.'

'You killed him, Forest. I just helped him on his way.'

'What are we going to do?'

'I tell you what we're going to do. We're going to get rid of this one when it gets darker. I want you to go back to the docks and bring one of those barrows and a cover to throw over him. We can tip him in the Thames. That bit of water can take care of him.'

'What about that other bloke that left earlier? Won't he know something's wrong?'

'That one's been sleeping off the drink in your bed. He never knew anything about this one.'

Forest stared at his mum's casualness of the situation. 'My room, Mum?'

'Go on, get going, and bring back what I asked. The sooner we lose this one, the better. Him lying there like that is costing me money.'

Forgetting about being hungry, Forest pulled his

coat together, knowing how cold it would be. 'I'll try and get a cart, Mum, but if any of the…'

'Just do it. Otherwise, the police will want to know what happened, and you know how that will affect you, doing what you did.'

'They wouldn't put a ten-year-old in prison. Would they?'

'Twelve, you are, old enough to know what's right or wrong.'

Forest hurried through the back streets, not only unsure if he was ten or twelve, but what might go down if the police found out what he'd done. Reaching the docks, he knew where he would find an old barrow and cover, but he needed to be wary of the night watchmen that roamed about the port. If they spotted him, his job wouldn't be around anymore, and his mum wouldn't be happy with that. Reaching the area, he sneaked into the open-doored sheds and made his way inside. Seeing one of the watchman's huts, he knew not to make a sound and moved forward to where several barrows stood, beside a rags bundle. Finding one that was easy to push, he tossed a cover onto it and ever so gently eased the cart back the way he had come. A shadow appeared within the watchman's lean-to where someone passed the window. Anxious about going further, he waited for the movement to stop. He stood there for what seemed like ages, until the silhouette eventually disappeared, and Forest continued into the approaching darkness. The empty barrow made a considerable racket on the uneven streets, but he knew he had no choice and pressed on, hoping no one would be nosey enough to look out of a window. Hurrying the barrow towards his back gate entrance, he took the heavy cover with him through into the kitchen.

'You took your time. What have you been doing?'

'I had to be careful; the night watchman was there, and I didn't want him finding me. You got anything I can eat, Mum? I'm hungry.'

'Forget your bloody stomach; let's get him out of the house. I've pushed the table out of the way; lay that cover over the floor so we can pull him onto it.'

Forest dragged the sailor onto the tarp with his mum's help and wrapped him in it, with the knife embedded well into his body.

'This will be the awkward bit, getting him onto this barrow you brought. I hope it's not too high to lift him. I'll need you to help me do this.'

Forest gathered that, and together they clumsily lugged the body outside into the backyard.

'Make sure nobody's around, Forest. I'll wait here.'

'All clear, Mum.'

Chapter Two

Lifting the body onto the cart was demanding, and it took several attempts to lay the sailor's body on the rickety wooden barrow. Eventually, they did it, while making it look as if they were moving something else, and with his mum going ahead, Forest pushed the handcart over the uneven ground once more. The sound was less noisy with the weightier load, but twice they needed to stop when someone came near, where they edged into a building's shadow until they passed. Nearing the River Thames, Forest became stuck when one of the wheels sat in a hollow, with the barrow unable to move. Calling his mum, they heaved backwards and forwards, when a group of drunken matelots came around a corner, almost colliding with them.

'Hello, love, what you got under there? A body!'

The five sailors edged around them with alcohol fumes breathing over everyone.

'Just moving to a different flat; can't afford the rent at the old one.'

'A moonlight-flit, love, is it? You want us to give you a hand?'

Forest could see all the sailors were well inebriated.

'I can't get this wheel out of this rut I'm in. Could you give me a push?'

After a lot of banter from the group, the barrow resumed its travels, and within a short distance, Forest's mum managed to dissuade the men from helping further. With a lot of emphasis on saying goodbye, the matelots continued on their way, heading towards another alehouse and more alcohol.

'Blimey, Mum, I thought we'd had it that time. Good job they were drunk.'

'Stop chattering and hurry up. I want to get this over with.'

Steering the barrow around another corner, the river Thames came into view.

'About time. Over there, where there is no wall; we can tip him in easily.'

Forest watched his mum check that they were on their own and called him over to the water's edge.

'Lift the cart. He should slide in.'

'This ain't easy, Mum. Give me a hand.'

Undertaking Forest's demand, the momentum took the body and barrow over the edge, with it all going under the water.

'Mum, what did you do?'

'Don't worry about it. No one saw you take the cart. Forget it; all we need to do is go home.'

Forest knew that the body would drift away in the dark moving water. He just hoped it stayed below the surface.

'Clean the floor for me, Forest, and I'll cook you something. You never gave me any money when you came in. Where is it?'

'I forgot, Mum, we were busy.' He passed over the few shillings from his Saturday and Sunday pay.

'This isn't as much as what you earned last weekend. Are you holding some back, or are those bastards trying to fiddle you down at that port?'

Looking at the scant amount, Forest's mum passed him back some coins and told him to nip to the pub on the corner and buy a couple of pasties or pies once he had finished. Forest guessed she wouldn't cook anything: she never liked cooking.

Lying in bed that night, he heard the creaking bed in the next room sounding already. Obviously, the gin his mum told him to purchase along with the pies was taking her mind off what had happened earlier, and he guessed her visitor wouldn't be the only one through the door that night. Unable to sleep, he lay there thinking. He had never really known his age; only what others had told him. Never having a birthday or Christmas present or celebrating any occasion, he pondered his life once more. Tonight, wasn't the only time a situation had happened with one of his mum's clients. She had cut a few when they tried to short-change her. After one of her episodes, the police called and warned her prison might do her some good if she did it again. He remembered hearing one of the policemen tell another that his mum was trouble and had always been from an early age. He thought long and hard about what he had done and should anyone find out about it: his life could end.

Looking at the clock on his bedside table, it showed three-thirty. He hoped that the noise outside might be the last caller. Suddenly, his bedroom door opened, and his mum came crashing in, fumbling with her nightgown.

'You asleep, Forest?'

Checking her unsteady posture, he thought if he had been, he'd be awake now. 'No, Mum, what's the matter?'

'We're leaving; a friend has a place we can live in. We're going to Portsmouth.'

'When did all this happen?'

'Never mind that. Next Saturday we are moving, so tell your teacher at school about it.'

'What about Aunt Betsey and Uncle Bronek?'

'They can whistle for all I care. They're nothing but trouble as far as I'm concerned. Now go to sleep, or you won't be able to get up in the morning.'

Forest knew sleep was out of the question. Where had this come from? Was it from the bloke she had in the next room, or what? Portsmouth – he wondered what the place was like and where they would live. Question after question ran through his mind as the night dawdled. Getting out of bed, he went downstairs and sat in the kitchen, looking at the spot where he had stabbed a sailor who was choking his mum. He pictured the sailor drifting with the current as it floated down the river. It would be far away before anyone saw it, and that's only if it surfaced.

Making himself a cup of tea without any milk in it, he sat on the kitchen chair, lifting his feet off the cold floor. Putting his finger into the mug, he scooped out umpteen dusty tea leaves and drank the beverage. 'Why are we going to Portsmouth, Mum?' He spoke the question to no one, but, deep down, guessed the reason. Finishing his drink, he pulled his coat off the hook on the back door, went out into the back yard and sat huddled in the privy. Removing a newspaper square beside the pan, he saw the movement as it came under the wooden-panelled door. The rat was a big bugger, as its teeth gnawed at the wood, trying to make its way into the lavatory. Screwing the sheet of paper into a ball, he aimed it at the creature and watched it bite into the thrown pellet, before deciding to seek another location. Ready to return to his room, he spotted a picture card showing warships, with sailors everywhere on the photograph. Guessing his mum's visitor was a sailor, he assumed there might be more customers for her in Portsmouth, which would mean he would need to fend for himself once more.

Chapter Three

Portsmouth

Nineteen-forty arrived, and the bombing raids as Hitler's planes found their targets. Forest's mum had moved two times in the last year and a half, and each time it was to get nearer to the Dockyard and its paying customers. Leaving the precarious building they lived in, Forest looked back, wishing they had stayed in London. The last year or so had been awkward for him, with people calling him names he hated. It wasn't so bad here in Portsea, but he still needed to watch out for himself.

Danny was cockling with his dad in the foreshore. Picking up handfuls of mud and cockles, he checked out this skinny, scruffy-looking kid doing the same, standing in the sludge not fifty yards away. Watching him knock and bash one of the molluscs before breaking it open and scooping the raw contents into his mouth. If he saw him, do it once, he saw him do it loads of times. It was unbelievable watching him. The day was going to be a warm one, seeing it was half-past-six in the morning, and some of the clouds were already starting to fade as the sun gradually dismissed them. With his bucket a good three-quarters full, Danny knew his dad was itching to finish and get home, seeing he was going out for a spot of fishing with his mates; but that depended on Adolf's bombers organising another air-raid. The last one two nights ago was scary, with many houses and the Dockyard taking hits. Watching the skinny kid again, he received a clout around his head, knocking him over backwards into a running creek of water that was beginning to fill with the tide coming in.

'Will you concentrate on what you're doing, Danny? I want this bucket filled and be home before eight. You know I've got a busy few hours with the lads coming up.'

'Sorry, Dad.'

'You're nearly twelve years old; now stop sodding about and put your back into it before the tide comes in.'

Danny saw the strange boy look his way. He knew he saw the old man clobber him but didn't show any expression as he continued filling his small tin while still chewing on the odd rubbery shellfish. Later that morning, having done some errands for his mum, Danny strolled over to one of his pals. Fortunately, the June day had stayed bright and warm, and he could imagine his dad sitting with his mates in a rowing boat anchored somewhere with them laid across the planking, their lines in the water, drinking beer that they had cooled under the boat in a net while catching fish: a busy day, he thought, yeah, right, even though it rarely happened.

Turning into the next street, the same skinny kid he had seen that morning was sitting on a high wall, facing the other way. Looking at him, he could see he could do with a good wash, his feet and legs still covered in mud, along with his torn shorts and vest. Keeping quiet, he continued past him, but he was sure the kid had seen him, although he never let on. Reaching the end of the road, Danny turned the corner and glanced back, but the boy was gone, and he wondered if he lived in the area. If he did, the kid was new to the neighbourhood, as he'd never seen him before.

Danny's friend Eddie was out in his garden, kicking a ball about, when he heard his mum shout something at him.

'Eddie, you there?'

The top of Eddie's head appeared by the fence.

'Are you riling your mum again, Eddie Button?'

Within moments, Eddie poked his head over, and a grin came back. 'I didn't think you were coming. I've had an earful kicking this ball around. You got Johnny with you?'

'No, I expect we'll meet him in the park. You ready?' Danny heard a few heated words coming from inside the house before Eddie stepped out of the front door. He stood on the pavement with his football, wearing the recognisable flannelette shirt and long trousers that his mum always seemed to make him put on, no matter what time of year it was. Eddie's trousers were forever baggy, covering his long, scrawny, pigeon legs, as his mum always called them. 'You got trouble, Eddie?'

'I forgot to clean the chickens out this morning. I've had it in the ear ever since.'

Danny shook his head, knowing what his mum or dad would do if he ever forgot to do a chore. 'You don't know how lucky you are, Eddie, especially having five chickens in the garden. Me or Johnny would love to eat a fresh egg.'

They soon reached the park, or what was left of it after a few bombs fell on it; but like any Saturday, it was full of people doing all sorts, unless there was an air-raid. They could play only in parts, as sections were cordoned-off, but it was good to be outside with kids kicking balls to one another and running about. It wasn't until after two o'clock before Johnny joined them.

'You're late,' Danny scolded him, but Johnny's face told them something was wrong.

Eddie piped up, 'Has something happened?'

Sitting on the grass, Johnny took his round-rimmed glasses off and wiped his eyes on his shirt sleeve as Danny and Eddie walked over to him.

Sitting down, Danny spoke to him. 'What's happened?'

Johnny looked up sheepishly. 'It's my dad; he's gone.'

Eddie piped up, 'Where, where's he gone?'

That brought a flood of tears as Johnny rolled over onto his side and hid his face in his arm. Danny glared at Eddie and shook his head should something serious have happened. They moved next to Johnny and waited for him to say something as the park endured its noisy inhabitants. It took a while, but, eventually, Johnny lifted himself from the grass and sat up.

'Are you okay?' Danny asked, knowing it was a daft question, but what else could he say?

Eddie put his hand on Johnny's shoulder. 'Sorry, was that the wrong thing to say?'

Johnny half-smiled at his friends and wiped his eyes again.

It was then that Danny saw the skinny kid he'd seen earlier. He was alone, hovering by the park gate. Then, Danny's attention returned to Johnny. 'Do you want to tell us?'

They waited for him to compose himself and listened as he began his story.

'Dad's left home; he's gone off with another woman, mum told me.'

Danny and Eddie kept quiet and waited for more news.

'Mum said he's been seeing some tart in the fire brigade who drives the fire engine with him; she told me he's not coming back.' Johnny wiped his eyes once more and continued, 'It's just me and mum now.'

Danny and Eddie gave up on the ball game they were going to play, and taking Johnny with them, returned to Eddie's house, which was one of the more decent ones with a proper garden, even though it wasn't very big. With Eddie's mum a bit more heartening, after listening to Eddie's account of what happened she allowed them into the garden. As they sat cross-legged in front of the hen house, his mum came out with glasses of orange squash, and the boys talked some more. The afternoon drifted by, with Johnny telling them that his dad was supposed to have gone fishing with Danny's dad, but his mum had told him he had packed his bags and fled. Eddie's mum must have overheard most of what was said, as she came out later with some rock cakes she'd made, something she had never done before. Leaving Eddie late in the afternoon, Danny walked Johnny home and realised he was reluctant to go indoors, but he told him his mum would need him now, and if there was anything he needed, to let him or Eddie know.

As Danny made his way home, he thought about what it must be like for your dad to leave. Sometimes, he wished his dad would, although he knew he never meant it. Turning at the end of the road, he spotted the skinny kid once more, who was hanging around the remains of the almost bombed-out Wellington pub. Standing there a moment, watching him, the kid saw him and went into the building. Danny knew the place was still functioning as a pub, with bits of corrugated tin and canvas hanging over parts of it, yet plenty of customers used it, even though it was a bit of a mess like the rest of the city. Danny waited in case the ragamuffin

– for that's what he looked like – was thrown out, seeing kids weren't allowed in those places, but he never showed, so Danny carried on wondering who he was.

Chapter Four

Eddie popped into a neighbour's house on an errand for his mum that evening, knowing she was having another off day, probably from having listened to Johnny's story. His dad had told him a couple of times when he got home from the sea that his mum hated him being in the Navy, but he realised his dad was a sailor to the core. He had no choice now with the war on, unlike Danny's dad, who was in the Home Guard. Walking home from his mission, he recalled the tales his dad had told him about different parts of the world, the scrapes he had got into, and the adventures he had while ashore with his mates. He decided that he would join up when he was old enough – that's if the war wasn't over by then.

After eating, he helped his mum wash up before settling in his bedroom. Studying the map of the world taped to the wall, he wondered where his dad was. The last time he had spoken to him, he said he would be somewhere in the thick of it with the enemy and Eddie could imagine how scary that must be. Every night he said a prayer for his dad to come home safe. The Navy had begun losing ships, and it worried him, and he guessed that was why his mum was like she was.

Hours later, pulling the bedclothes up and

snuggling down, he listened to his mum scolding him from outside his bedroom door as she readied for bed.

'You make sure you clean those birds out tomorrow, Edward, or that football will find its way into the rubbish. Are you listening to me?'

'Sorry, Mum, I'll make sure I do it tomorrow.'

'Just because your father is away at sea.'

Getting out of bed in the dark, he parted the heavy curtains and opened the window and leant out, feeling as though summer had arrived. Looking down, he watched a couple of passing wardens stare up, making sure there was no light showing, while still hearing the odd word coming from his mum. Taking in the skyline around him, he knew it would take years to rebuild, but at least Hitler had spared his house. A few slates had come down, and one of the chimney pots fell off, but their house was lucky. The blitz on the Dockyard and homes around them suffered terribly. Many of the still-standing places had massive cracks running through them, along with their windows blown out and roofs shattered. Bombs and incendiary devices had rained down all over the city. Several kids from school had died, but his mum said they had to get on with their lives and must not brood over what was happening. A friend of his mum's repaired their damaged roof and told them they were fortunate that was all that happened. Closing the taped-up window, he guessed the night would be quiet, seeing cloud was covering the moon. Back in bed, it took ages to go to sleep; all he could think about was

Johnny and wondering where his dad was.

Sunday morning, Eddie cleaned out the birds without being told and had a fresh egg for breakfast. With his mum in a happier frame of mind, he made his way into the back garden and kicked his ball up against the house until his mum gave him that glare from the kitchen window. Moving away, he pulled a few pieces of long grass out beside the fence and pushed them through the wire as beaks pecked at the tasty strands.

'What are you doing, Eddie? Wring one of their necks: our mum could do with a bit of fresh meat on the table.'

Turning, Eddie saw Johnny wringing his hands over the fence with a smile on his face, and Danny stood beside him. 'Don't let mum hear you say that about one of her birds. She'll likely wring yours, Johnny Wilson.'

'You coming out, Eddie?' Danny lifted his head higher over the fence.

'Let me tell mum, and I'll be with you.'

'Hurry up, Eddie, the weather seems okay this morning. I thought we could do a bit of mudlarking this afternoon. Me and Danny's game on for it.'

'Will we be allowed?'

Danny cut in, 'Our dad said they are working on the harbour railway station after the last air-raid, but if we stay away from there, we should be all right. We haven't done a bit of larking for a while; it should be good fun.'

Walking down Queen's Street towards Portsmouth harbour, the boys helped two wardens lift a massive wooden beam in one of the shops that had received a direct hit. Searching underneath, the rubble, one of the men turned over some debris and discovered a hand. Johnny shouted, frightening his mates, as the man threw the mannequin's hand at him, laughing and telling him not to be so touchy. Afterwards, as they walked to the harbour, Danny and Eddie creased up at what had happened. At the end of the road, the stink of the mud hit them as they surveyed the busy quayside. Over by the train station, men and machines strained, lifting parts of the damaged building, trying to get it ready to rebuild, seeing parts of it had fallen into the harbour waters.

Danny nudged the others. 'They'll need to get that back to normal sooner than later, especially with more troops coming in.' Then, as they were about to cross the road, he spotted the skinny kid once more. 'Eddie, Johnny, that's the kid I saw in the park and when I was cockling with dad. He's still got those muddy clothes on and nothing on his feet. I wonder if he's following me. Let's go over and find out.'

Johnny squinted behind his wire-framed glasses, watching the Dickens-type character in his dirty clothes sitting on the railings, studying the boats in the harbour. Getting nearer, Johnny tapped him on the shoulder.

'You following my mate around?'

The frightened expression coming back told them they must have worried him, as he jumped off the bars, ready to run.

'Danny here said you were cockling near to him the other day, and he saw you later in the park!'

They all saw how the kid attempted to run, and all three of them put their arms out, stopping him, with Danny getting closest to him.

'We're not going to hurt you: we just wondered who you are and where you live. We've not seen you around before.'

The skinny kid's eyes studied all of them as he gripped the top railing behind him, ready to leap over should he need to.

Eddie bent down to the urchin's height, that was about twelve inches shorter than him. 'My name's Eddie, he's Johnny, and that's Danny.'

They all waited for a response as the newcomer dithered, wondering what to do.

Eddie put his hand into his trouser pocket and pulled out a bag of tiger nuts. 'You fancy some of these?'

The eyes latched onto the exposed food offered to him, and before you could say Bob's-your-uncle, the urchin had them in his mouth, chewing on them like there was no tomorrow. Eddie checked the dirty imprint on his palm and looked at the kid's fingers, doubting if he had ever washed, before getting an unpleasant whiff from him as he moved.

Johnny squinted as the sun caught him once more. 'I think he's lost his voice, Eddie. Perhaps we ought to push off and leave him to it.'

'Guess so; we got things to do. Come on, the tide's on the turn, it should be getting ready to go out; that will give us time to go home and have a sandwich before coming back.'

Danny observed the kid as he listened to Johnny's words about food. Walking away, they all noticed the scruffy kid following. The clothes he was wearing could do with throwing out instead of putting on. As they neared the bridge that led to the ferry crossing the harbour, the three of them stopped when a voice called out behind them.

'My name's Forest!'

Johnny turned around first. 'Blimey, he can talk.'

They all stared at Forest as he stood there, nervous but holding his ground, looking at Eddie's sweet pocket. With his scruffy, tangled, curly hair and dirty face, you wouldn't have known if he had a bit of colour in him.

'You want to come with us, or do you have something else to do?'

Forest shook his head at Johnny's words.

'We're going to do a bit of mudlarking. You fancy coming along?'

Another nod came back.

Tapping Forest on the back, Danny got his attention. 'You can speak to us; we won't bite.'

Forest gave a nervous smile and shuffled his bare feet along the pavement, with the boys noticing how his hard-crusted feet splayed out, and that his grimy black toenails – like his fingernails – had probably never seen soap and water. Bringing his hands together, he cupped them in front of Eddie. 'Could I have some more of those nut things? They're tasty.'

Eddie held the bag of nuts above Forest's hands. 'You can if you say please.'

'Please,' came the reply.

Eddie emptied more into the waiting hands, saying, 'I think you might want to clean those mitts of yours. They look as though they need a wash.'

Danny and Johnny told Eddie to keep some back as they liked them.

Forest shoved the contents, along with anything else, into his mouth, not losing one of them. All the boys watched him chew and almost choke as he swallowed them down.

'I like those.'

Chapter Five

Danny marvelled how the nuts vanished and guessed he never had a lot to eat. The boys checked out the waters as they walked out onto the bridge and together decided it was time to leave and get back within the hour. Forest, still hanging around, followed them back to the road while looking at Eddie's pocket.

'You had anything to eat today, Forest?'

'Not today, but I had some bread and dripping yesterday that the butcher gave me. Mum gives me some pennies when I'm hungry.'

Danny listened to his answer and put his hand on Forest's shoulder, watching him shy away. 'Where do you live?'

He pointed down one of the side roads, where most buildings lay in ruins after an earlier air-raid. 'We've got a flat down there.'

Danny raised his eyebrows. 'There are not many buildings left down there. Your dad live with you?'

'Mum; don't have a dad. But I've got lots of uncles. They're mostly in the Navy; that's why me and mum moved here, so that she could be with them more often.'

Johnny gave Danny a fixed stare, while Eddie's eyes opened wide at the remark, knowing full well what his mum meant, telling him he had many uncles. Changing the subject, Danny suggested they leave; otherwise, the afternoon would disappear before they did anything. Wandering through the back streets, the boys followed Forest to see where he lived. Moving towards an almost ruined building, Forest pointed up to a first-floor window, telling them that it was home. The structure leant slightly, touching the adjoining building, or what had been a building, with cracks showing all over the place.

Danny spoke up. 'Is it safe to live in there?'

The other boys took in the unsafe construction.

Eddie couldn't believe his eyes, seeing someone lived there. 'Does the rain come in?'

'Sometimes, but it doesn't cost much. We've got a bedroom and a kitchen in there.'

Eddie looked amazed. 'Where do you sleep?'

'I got a mattress on the floor in the kitchen until we can get something better, but I'm all right. Mum needs the bedroom for when her friends come to see her.'

Astounded at Forest's remark, they all pictured something they couldn't rightly imagine before Danny questioned him about his room.

'Do you have any gas or electric in there?'

'No. As I said, mum gives me pennies should I need anything to eat. She don't like cooking, so we don't need any of that.'

All the boys realised he had to fend for himself.

'You come home with me, Forest; our mum will

give you something to eat.'

That statement appeared to grab Forest's attention straight away as he followed Danny eagerly. Carrying on, the boys went their separate ways, knowing they would soon be up to their knees in mud, and guessed Danny and the new kid would be joining them.

Johnny walked into the kitchen to find his mum chucking all his dad's left-behind clothes into a cardboard box. Still trying to understand why he left, he stood there, not knowing what to do when his mum spoke to him.

'I will take this lot down the market tomorrow with me and see what your father's clothes will bring. I've got a letter arrived saying your dad's coming back for them. Well, won't he be in for a shock?'

Johnny looked at the crack in the kitchen wall, noticing how it now went from floor to ceiling when houses further away were damaged in the bombing. Being the end house, his dad had braced the outer wall and taped the windows before leaving; that at least had helped. But like a lot of buildings around the city, it would have to be repaired one day.

Fetching an almost stale loaf from the pantry, his mum told him he'd need to earn some money now, or they would both starve. He knew she was worried about the future as she warmed a couple of slices of bread over the stove, trying to freshen them. He then told her he was going mudlarking with the others and would bring some money home. The bread had had its day, but with a bit of tinned condensed milk on it, it tasted all right.

After changing into his old mudlarking gear, he came downstairs to find a note propped up on the table telling him his mum had gone to visit her sister across town, and not to expect her until tea-time. Putting the letter back, he spoke to the empty room. 'We'll work things out, Mum. You wait and see.'

Danny neared his home with an anxious Forest walking beside him. The smell from him was a bit ripe, and he wondered, having brought him home, how his mum would react. He tried to imagine the sort of life he must have, especially with his mum's boyfriends being in one room and him being in the other on his mattress. 'That's my house, Forest, near the end of the street.' Danny pointed towards a terraced building. 'The one with the dark-blue door. Mum should be home, and dad is probably asleep. He's on nights at the moment. Dad's a warden: he's part of the home defence team.'

Forest listened and felt more nervous than ever as he neared Danny's home. 'Your dad won't be up, then?'

'Doubt it, but mum's in charge indoors. What she say's goes. Is your mum like that?'

Not answering, Forest couldn't remember his mum speaking to him lately, other than the words, 'Wait for me outside the pub', which depended on what public house she was drinking in and who her companion was.

Danny surveyed Forest once more and questioned his decision in bringing him home, while hoping his dad wouldn't frighten him off when he did get up. 'This is it. Wait here and let me tell mum you're outside. Don't go running off or anything.'

Forest shook his head and gripped his hands behind his back. 'I won't.'

Having told his mum almost everything he knew about Forest, she returned with him and scrutinised the scraggy, undernourished lad on her doorstep. Taking charge, she gripped Forest's wrist and led him through the passageway to the outside yard and pulled the tin bath off the wall. With pots full of water heating on the stove, Danny's mum examined the dirty figure that stood in her yard and shuddered with her thoughts. When the water was hot enough, she filled the bath, making sure the water was heated sufficiently, and told Forest to get his clothes off and get in, while passing Danny a bar of carbolic soap. He stood there, not knowing what to do, as she went back inside the house and closed the door.

'It's all right, Forest, our mum's like that. She does it to me sometimes. Get those clothes off and jump in; mum won't come out. She's going to make us something to eat. Here, take the soap and have a good wash.'

Forest looked around him, not believing everything that was happening; but he realised food would be waiting for him and so he started removing his clothes, and Danny realised just how thin he was without them.

'This is all a bit strange, me having to do this.'

'The thing is, you chuck up a bit. Mum said you needed a good scrub; you'll feel a lot better for it.'

'Your mum won't come out, will she?' Forest squatted into the bathwater. 'Is your dad still asleep?'

'He's still a kip; don't go worrying about him.' Danny heard his name called and went into the kitchen, where his mum handed him a rough old towel, telling him to make sure Forest gets some of that dirt off him before he uses it.

Forest turned in the tub. 'I thought your mum was coming out.'

'Blimey, Forest, look at the colour of that water; that'll leave a nice tide-mark.'

Soaping himself, he checked around the water and observed Danny take his clothes away. 'What you doing? I need them. I ain't got no more.'

'Mum guessed as much, so did I. She's getting you some of my old clothes; they should fit you, but they might be a bit big around the waist.'

Forest beamed with delight, knowing he was getting some other clothes. 'Are you sure?'

'Mum is, and, as I said, what mum says happens in this house.' Suddenly, the kitchen door opened, and Danny ended up receiving more hot water from his mum and tipped it over Forest's head. 'Mum said to put some of this washing-up liquid in your hair. It looks like it's all tangled together. I bet it will take a bit to unravel that lot.'

'Guess it will. I don't have a comb.'

'You want me to do it? I'll have a go at it if you want.'

'I've never had anyone wash my hair before.'

Sat in the filthy water, Forest was astounded about what was happening to him.

'Your mop is like wire wool. Keep still, I don't want any of that water on me! I've already washed, and I don't want another one just yet.' Danny poured almost the whole bottle onto Forest's head as he tried to separate strands of his hair. 'When did you last wet this lot – last Christmas?'

'Not that long; probably when I went fishing a couple of weeks ago.'

Danny thought, 'Well, that wasn't washing', but said nothing other than, 'Crikey, I bet that was cold.' It took some effort on Danny's part in untangling Forest's long curly hair, but eventually the liquid penetrated the mess, and some shine emerged. Bringing yet another pot of water out, Danny told him to stand up and tipped the warm water over him, rinsing the scum from his body. 'You know what, Forest, I can see who you are now.'

The laughter erupted between them as Danny handed over the towel. 'Don't dry yet; I think you need another pot. There's still some suds on your back. Bringing out more clean water, Danny told Forest to stand on the paving stones and tipped the lukewarm liquid over him. 'Sorry, that one wasn't as hot as the others. Now you can dry yourself. You look like another person. Here are some pants, shorts and an old shirt of mine. Mum says you can have this belt should you need it. These are an old pair of plimsolls mum had kept for someone else, but she said you were a more worthy cause.'

As Forest climbed into fresh clothes and pulled on the slightly bigger-sized plimsolls, Danny could see that he regarded him with some affection.

'No one has ever done anything like this for me before; black kids usually have to fend for themselves. Thanks, Danny.'

Chapter Six

Eddie listened to his mum, telling him again how lucky he was to have a proper meal, and all because of her chickens. But what she didn't know was that while cleaning them out that morning, he put the eggs on the grass instead of bringing them straight indoors, and kicked one accidentally, breaking it. It had taken a while to get rid of the evidence, but he was sure no traces remained. If his mum ever fathomed out what he'd done, he knew she would be agony to live with for days. His mum loved her chickens as much as somebody would love a dog or a cat. She always ensured they were safe in a bombing raid by putting them under the stairs and covering them with her winter coat, even though they pecked into it. Eddie was surprised they could still lay an egg with the explosions and loud noises that went on.

'Me and the boys are going larking, Mum. I might get some decent coins, seeing a couple of ships are in for repair. The sailors like to chuck us a penny or two, depending on what a good time they had ashore.' Straight away, he knew the last sentence should have stayed inside him. 'Sorry, Mum, I meant in the pubs.' Her face coming back told him she knew what he was talking about.

Tipping the bathwater out onto the back yard, Danny broomed the scummy waters down the drain and wiped around the tin bath. Forest, fingering his clothes, felt like he had won the pools when he spotted Danny's go-cart standing beside the privy.

'Did you make that, Danny?' He pointed towards the cart while rubbing his hair dry. 'I bet that moves.'

'It does.' Danny remembered when he and Eddie made it, and they used it out on Southsea Common. 'I think it might have had its day now. You need some decent slopes to make it run properly, and there aren't any around here.'

As they walked into the kitchen together, Danny's mum nodded her approval, before seeing the state of Forest's fingernails. Finding a metal nail file, she told him he needed to get the dirt out from under his nails, and his toenails if they were in the same state.

Sat down at the kitchen table with sandwiches in front of them, Forest reached out towards the food when Danny's dad walked into the room. Seeing the large man standing there looking his way, he froze, anxious about sitting there, and he put his hands under the table. Danny's dad gave Forest the once over and picked up the newspaper, ignoring both boys.

Looking at the raised newspaper, Forest felt Danny give him a dig. 'Come on, tuck in.'

Hesitantly picking up his food, his hunger got the

better of him, and he dived into eating the filled sandwiches in wonderful fresh bread. With Danny's mum putting a mug of tea in front of her husband, she asked Forest if he wanted one. With a mouthful of food, he nodded his head and swallowed a mostly unchewed portion of food, giving her rise to wonder if he would choke. Removing his newspaper and picking up his drink, his dad noticed Forest looking his way and gave the lad a nod; he returned to his paper, completely unaffected that a stranger was at his table. Having eaten their fill, or at least Danny had, Forest followed him upstairs to his bedroom, where he gave him an old pair of shorts.

'I was ready to throw these out, but I think they would come in handy for you when we go larking. Take those pants and shorts off mum gave you and put these on. You will need something old clambering about in the mud. Keep these clothes for afterwards; you don't want to ruin them.'

Danny changed into another pair of shorts as Forest did the same while looking around the bedroom, wishing he had something like this. Danny decided to ask a question that he'd been thinking about. 'Forest, that's a strange name. I don't think I've ever heard of it as someone's name before. How come your mum gave you that?'

Forest wasn't sure whether to tell Danny.

'You going to tell me?'

Deciding he might as well, Forest said, 'Mum told

me she was in Epping Forest, that's north of London, with her boyfriend when I came about.'

'What, conceived, you mean?'

'Yeah, he was in the Services visiting when he met mum. She told me he took her out for the day, and when she came back, I was inside her.'

Surprised at how Forest came out with the information, Danny pushed his fingers through his hair. 'Blimey, never heard of anything like that before.'

'I know mum wished she never had me.'

'She told you that?'

'Lots of times. She said I ruined her life coming along and being black.'

Danny couldn't believe what his mum had told him. 'You're not that black, and I don't care what colour you are; me and the others like you.'

Listening to Danny, Forest studied him, knowing he meant it.

'You can muck in with us while you live around here. You fancy that?'

'I'd like that a lot.'

'Come on, let's get in the mud.'

They both giggled and hurried back downstairs. Danny's mum called them into the kitchen, telling Danny to sit on the chair. Then she produced a pair of scissors. Five minutes later, Danny stood with his hair trimmed.

'Mum, you want to have a go at Forest's mop; that needs something doing to it.'

After some convincing, Forest sat there watching his fuzzy locks fall to the floor as Danny's mum pulled out various lengths, slicing them off and trying to tug a comb through the remaining curls. Eventually, having been told that was all she could do, he emerged, looking like a different boy. With his new clothes in a paper bag, they left the house ready for what the afternoon had in store for them.

'I like your mum, Danny, but your dad don't say much.'

'My dad's like that. Come on; we'll be late if we hang around any longer. The tide is probably out now, and Eddie and Johnny will be waiting for us.'

Unfolding his paper bag, Forest looked into it and discovered more clothing inside. 'What else is in here?'

'Mum told me to put in another pair of pants, shorts, and a shirt in case you mess those up, and there's a couple of pairs of darned socks; and don't lose that nail file mum gave you; she'll want that back. Your toenails need a good clean, but the mud in the harbour will help loosen some of that muck grimed in there.'

As they walked on, Forest rummaged inside the bag, feeling the clothing, and a smile swept across his face. 'That's nice clobber, Danny. Were they yours?'

'They were, but now they belong to you, so look after them.'

Reaching the harbour, they found people were busy crossing the bridge walkway, ready to catch the ferry across to Gosport on the other side of the water. The dockyard gate nearby was just as hectic, with sailors entering as they waited to cross the road with the sun out. The old sergeant on duty stood at the entrance, watching the boys as he squinted through his glasses in the bright sunshine. Forest saluted him with a cheeky smile before the sergeant returned his attention to someone entering the gate.

'Don't get on the wrong side of him, Forest: he could chuck us off the mud if he wanted.'
Knowing the gatekeeper still had an eye on him, Forest gave him another salute. 'He's told me to sod off several times when I've tried to get in and have a nose around.'

'You're lucky that's all he did. Quick, we can get across the road now.'

Chapter Seven

Eddie met up with Johnny, and together they hiked towards the harbour, discussing when they would flatten some of the bombed-out houses. 'That house, Johnny, a week ago it had inside walls standing; now they've all caved in! What a mess everything is.'

'The Browns lived there; they were lucky they were in the Birkinshaw's shelter: they just lost bits off their roof.'

'When's all this going to end?' Eddie thought of what Johnny had told them about his dad going off the way he did and his dad in the engine room on a Navy ship with U-boats attacking them. The news on the radio was terrible when they reported losses almost every day. 'We'd better get a move on. Danny and that other kid should be there by now.'

'Do you think he'll turn up?'

'If Danny's mum has fed him, he will. That's if she didn't throw him out, smelling the way he did.'

Eddie and Johnny crossed roads, running through the ravaged streets, dodging rubble and other debris, before arriving at the shore.

'We must be first; I can't see Danny anywhere. Let's get ready in case they don't make it.'

'Make sure you put your stuff out of sight under the bridge, Johnny. One of the Macey kids had his clothes pinched last week; they think it was someone from the other side of the harbour.'

Seeing Danny run across the road, Johnny nudged Eddie. 'Take a butcher's at the skinny kid. Danny's mum must have had a go at him; he looks so different.'

'Crikey, don't he.'

Johnny removed his shoes. 'You wouldn't think it was the same person. His mum must have taken a liking to him. Danny's seen us: give him a wave.'

The four boys got together with everyone knowing Forest was wearing Danny's old clothes, but no one let on about it.

'You scrub up well, Forest. Have you done any of this mudlarking before?'

Forest shook his head in answer to Eddie's question.

Johnny put his hand on his shoulder and eyeballed him. 'Now look here, you need to speak to us if you are going to be friends with us; no more of this head-shaking.'

Eddie chipped in. 'He's right. You can be one of us if you want to. I know you are smaller than us, but that can be useful sometimes; ask Danny.'

Forest stood there, feeling uneasy still. 'Can I be friends with all of you?'

Danny took hold of his arm. 'I said you could. Now let's earn some money; you follow our lead when we get out there in the mud and don't go too far out, or you'll get sucked under. Understand?'

'Sure, Danny.'

Forest watched him remove his shoes and top, ready to go. Standing there in his new clobber, he touched the shirt Danny's mum had given him, not wanting to part with it.

'Give me that bag of clothes and get those plimmies and shirt off, or you'll mess them up. Any mud you get on those old shorts, we'll wash off over there by that inlet; that's clean water. Seeing it's a warm day, you won't take long to dry off. If Eddie's mum ever found him covered in mud, she wouldn't be very pleased with him. Would she Eddie?'

'No, Danny.' And a rude gesture came back at him.

Danny put his finger up in return. 'These old shorts are a lot easier for us down there in the mud. Just make sure you keep them for larking.'

Forest watched his bag of clothing, along with Danny's, disappear under the bridge with the others.

'Are they safe under there, Danny?'

'They will be, I promise.'

Anxious as he was, Forest felt good in himself, as nothing like this had ever happened to him before.

Johnny smiled and slapped him playfully. 'That's the most I've heard you say. Keep it up.'

The others could see Forest was in high spirits. Gone were the anxious looks and worries as he made his way down into the mud.

'Follow me in and do as I do, and make sure of your balance once you're out in the mud. Fall over, and it can be a bugger to get up. And keep your pants on. Them up there don't want a view of what's down there.'

Forest giggled at Danny's remark.

'Right, you ready to earn some pennies?'

'I'm game for a lark, Danny.'

Hearing the statement, all the boys laughed as they waded into the smelly, sticky brown sludge, with people peering down at them as they edged further out into the mud, with it clinging to their limbs, throwing out a reeking pong. Forest put his hand out and dipped it into a depression, retrieving a coin.

'I've found a penny.' Holding it up, he showed it to the others. 'I saw it in the mud.'

Danny told him to wash it off in any water he found and put it in his pocket, or he'd lose it.

Doing it, he quickly caught up with the others and stood alongside Eddie.

'Johnny and Danny are ready. Now you watch them earn some coins.'

Forest listened and took in all the talk as the boys called up to the people crossing the bridge. 'Come on, governor, chuck us a penny' and 'Give us a penny, mister, and you, missus, a halfpenny will do. Make it a good one.'

'Why did Danny say, "make it a good one"?'

'Because some of the buggers toss foreign coins in, and they ain't no good to us.'

Forest thought about those words, knowing differently.

'You ready to join the others?'

'Am I!'

Within moments, Forest made his way with Eddie and joined in. He stood there watching people look down at him and the other boys calling out; Forest tried his luck. 'Hey, Mister, chuck down a coin. I got to eat tonight, and yours will help feed me.' A coin tossed over the rail landed next to him; seeing it land, he dipped his fingers into the brown sludge and retrieved it. 'Wow, a threepence; ain't never had a threepenny bit before. Thanks, Mister, God bless yah.' Another coin fell beside him, and reaching for it, looking up, he saw a lady pointing a little further out to where he was searching. Moving his hand around, he soon discovered another threepenny piece. Finding it, he lifted it aloft and showed the lady he'd found it. 'Bless yah, Lady, bless yah.' More coins came down around him, and the mud began to creep up Forest's arms and torso as he explored the shore around him. He found a puddle of seawater, and with a hand full of coins, rinsed them before putting them deep into his pocket, and he began again.

Eddie, seeing Forest gather the coins, spoke to Danny. 'He soon picked up on what to do; he's only been here five minutes. I bet he's earned a shilling already. For someone who doesn't talk very much, he's sure learning quick! Listen to him.'

'Hey, Sailor, how about treating a coloured kid to a meal? You can see how skinny I am. Come on, toss a coin over.'

A matelot looked over the railing, about to say something, when a gust of wind took his hat. Watching it sail through the air, Forest – being nearest – quickly headed towards it, and as it was about to land, he dived across the mud and caught the hat right on top of his head. The cheer that went up was unbelievable as the other matelots removed their hats, waving them about, and coins rained down among the boys. The sailor whose hat blew off pointed towards the shore, telling Forest he would meet him there. Clambering towards the waiting matelot, with the other boys watching him, the sailor pulled a coin out of his pocket, and as Forest neared him, the sailor removed his hat from him and placed a shilling in his hand, while thanking him for being so ingenious.

Chapter Eight

Danny, Eddie, and Johnny watched as Forest made his way back into the mud, with people calling him to do another trick. More pennies rained down as he made his way towards the others. Twice, someone waved their hat over the railing, but neither time did that person let go of it. Reaching the astonished threesome, he opened his hand, showing the shilling the sailor gave him.

'Are you messing with us? I think you've done this before.'

'Never, Eddie, I've never been in the mud before, honest.'

Danny put his stinky brown hand on Forest's already mud-covered body. 'I think you are going to out-earn us today. They sure like you up there, but you nearly lost those shorts doing that dive. Tuck your waistband inside and be careful if you do that again.'

Forest giggled, and Johnny threw a bit of mud at him.

'He's done this before. I know he has.'

'Never have, Johnny. I haven't.'

Seeing Forest inspect the silver coin, Danny called out, 'He can stay with us as long as he wants. What do you lot say?'

Forest watched as another coin landed next to him and he searched for it. 'Look, another threepenny-bit.' Looking up, he called out a noisy thank you to whoever threw it over.

The afternoon edged by, and the harbour water eventually called for the boys to vacate the mud as it crept towards them and swallowed one or two coins they might have missed. Once ashore, they cleaned off their bodies and shorts in a water hole and rinsed their collected money. Danny, Eddie, and Johnny counted the money they had gathered, which came to one shilling and nine pence between them. With Forest still washing the mud from his shorts, they waited for him to arrive. Wiping at a stubborn piece of grime, he saw the others waiting, and with his shorts more or less clean, joined them and held out the money he had collected.

Seeing Forest ogle the coins in his hand, Danny came up to him. 'Forest, that was a good afternoon's work: you'll have to come down here with us more often. I told you we share out all the money we collect. You still happy with that?'

Forest saw the others looking at him and knew he had to give the money over. 'Yeah.' He passed his earnings across to Eddie, who held all the coins.

By the look on his face, Danny gathered that Forest was a bit disappointed in doing it.

'Blimey, Forest, you collected all this.' Eddie checked out the coins he had given him. 'I think you earnt that shilling piece from that sailor.'

'How much has he got?'

'A lot more than us, Johnny. Let me count it properly.'

Danny also checked it and couldn't believe what he had made.

'There's three shillings and four pence here.'

Johnny moved nearer and touched the coins, before looking back at Forest. 'You sure you've never mud-larked before?'

'Never.'

Danny told Eddie to put the coins into his pocket until they dressed. Forest made sure his clothing bag was intact before moving off the shore and crossing the road. Once they were away from the harbour in a quiet spot, Eddie began dividing the takings and placing the coins into four piles.

'There's five shillings and a penny here. That's one shilling and threepence each.' Passing Forest the odd penny, Eddie added, 'Here, you found that before we began. I can't split that coin; we got no farthings this time.' Handing out the money, Eddie placed Forest's share into his hand. 'We always share what we earn. I know you collected the most today, but another time it could be one of us.' He could see Forest was watching the others put the money into their pockets. 'You still want to stay with us?' A nod came back. 'I take it that was a yes?'

Danny put his arm around Forest's neck. 'You did great in there, performing as you did. The one thing you have to remember is that other kids from the area use the mud like we did today, and you have to make sure you keep the coins you collect safe: otherwise, it will make its way into someone else's pocket.'

Johnny, re-counting the coins given him, joined in. 'We've never collected this much in ages. You must be our lucky mascot. Don't ever come down here without me.'

The boys made their way home, with Forest first to leave, telling them he would see them tomorrow, and he legged it across a bombed-out piece of ground with one hand in his pocket, ensuring he wouldn't lose a coin. Jumping over rubble towards the two rooms he called home, he hoped that the place would be empty when he got there, and his mum was out doing what she usually did about this time, meeting up with one of her customers.

Coming around a wall, Forest saw the curtains drawn together and knew there was no way he could go into the house. On several occasions when he had tried, he needed to run for it, as one of his mum's drunken boyfriends tried to pick on him.

Suddenly, it started; the sirens sounded, and the few people around that still lived there came running out of their houses, heading for the nearest shelter as German bombers made their way across the skies. Cowering in the shadows of the derelict building he was squatting in, Forest saw the front door open, and two matelots came out with his mum, staggering, making their drunken way along the pavement. Knowing this was his chance, he waited until they disappeared from view and hurried across the open space and put his shoulder against the jammed front door. Once inside, he climbed the stairs, hoping no one else was there. Edging his way in, he found the place empty. In the kitchen, his mattress stood on its end where he'd left it, jammed between the cracked sink and the cupboard.

Removing his damp shorts, he opened the bag Danny's mum had given him, ready to dress into decent clobber. He used the nail file and was surprised at how the black came out of his fingernails and toes. He couldn't ever remember wearing underpants or socks as he climbed into them. Smiling to himself, he put the rest on, before slipping the belt around, making sure his new shorts stayed up. He hid his mudlarking ones behind the mattress to dry out properly, after removing his well-earned money. On the landing, he found an open section in the wall that had gotten bigger, and the remaining few garments left in the paper bag he placed inside the crack, seeing it was dry and full of cobwebs – somewhere his mum wouldn't put her hand, seeing spiders wasn't her thing. He knew she would sell the clothes if she knew about them, even though she wouldn't get much for them; but it would buy a bottle of something for her. Slipping his plimsolls back on, he left the flat as the all-clear sounded. Wherever the bombers were heading, they decided to give the city a miss this time. Feeling the coins in his pocket, he knew he would have a proper meal tonight; no bread and dripping or searching in bins. Fish and chips flashed before his eyes, covered in salt and vinegar, a chip-butty, and a bottle of pop. Licking his lips at the thought, a tear came down his face thinking about it.

Chapter Nine

Forest found the chippy crowded, seeing the bombing never happened, and he waited in turn outside the shop. Eventually, getting inside, the smell of the cooking sent waves of delight into his body as his stomach anticipated a forthcoming feast. He looked up at the man who stood behind the fryers with his hands on his hips, which were more than ample for a bloke his size, and then he spoke to him.

'I hope you're not in here to thieve anything, young man. I've enough trouble with the Luftwaffe trying to bomb me out of existence.'

Most people in front of Forest turned to see who the chippy was addressing. After seeing him put his head down, they all returned to whatever they were doing. The battered fish lined up inside the hot cabinet above the fryers took his attention as his mouth watered while listening to his stomach. The old bloke in front of him stopped reading his newspaper and peered at him.

'Sorry, mister, guess I'm a little hungry. Can't help it!'

Turning back to his newspaper, the man shuffled forward as the queue shortened, while noises continued to tune their way out of his belly. The man in front collected his change, then the chippy behind the counter leaned over, regarding the skinny individual stood there.

'So, what do you want? Scraps?'

'Can I have a nice piece of fish and some chips, please, and two slices of bread and marge?'

'You can want, son, but it doesn't mean you're going to get it.'

Pulling the money from his pocket, he held it up. 'See, I've got enough.'

'I hope you didn't pinch any of that, matey; there are people around here who need everything they can get hold of without little urchins like you interfering.'

'I went larking with my mates today – mudlarking, that is – down in the harbour.' Grinning and telling the bumptious man he had friends. 'We all earnt over a shilling each.'

The chippy put his hand out. 'Let me see that lot, just to make sure you got no dodgy coins in amongst them.'

Forest handed the money over anxiously as the man checked them, and he hoped he wouldn't diddle him.

'What fish do you want?'

Forest grinned magnificently towards the huge man. 'Have you got any haddock or cod? I've never had them before.'

'I have a nice size haddock in there; will that do?'

'Yes, please, mister.' Forest's stomach growled even louder at the thought of tucking into the battered fish. And if you've got any spare scraps, can you put them in as well, please.'

The chippy could see that Forest came over as a polite lad and somehow felt sorry for him and decided not to charge him full price. 'Do you want a lemonade to go with this lot?'

Hoping his luck would last, he nodded. 'Have I got enough money with the bread and marge?' Forest watched as his dinner, a large piece of haddock, exited from the cabinet and he heard the scoops of chips settling into the newspaper.

'You have enough. I've taken one shilling and a penny. Keep the threepenny bit; you might want it later. You want salt and vinegar on this?'

'Please.' Forest's feet couldn't keep still as he moved them about like they were dancing on their own.

Handing Forest's meal over wrapped in the newspaper, the man spoke again. 'You can get a penny back on the bottle from most places around here once you return it. So don't break it.'

'Thanks, mister.' Forest pocketed his change and hurried from the shop.

Sat at the back of the chippy on a derelict site, he found an uncluttered piece of ground and made himself comfortable. Unwrapping the newspaper, he used it as a tablecloth, laying it out on a flat piece of concrete. He looked at the meal, not believing his eyes: the golden batter and hot chips all coated in salt and vinegar – the bread and marge, fresh, not stale like he usually ate. Unable to hold back any longer, he dived into the food, and once started, he scoffed it down without hesitation. The chip-butty he made slid down his throat, sending him into raptures as his stomach swelled. Emptying his lemonade bottle, he carefully put it to one side and stretched out on the ground, looking up at the darkening sky.

Forest thought of Danny and his family and what his mum had got him to do before sitting at their table, and his dad studying him the way he did. He usually got told to hop it with curses and names thrown at him. Without warning, his stomach began to ache something awful, and he rolled over on his side as pains shot across his body. He knew he was going to be sick, and the thought of losing his dinner scared the hell out of him as he tried to hold it in. Kneeling beside the lemonade bottle, he puked all over it. Bits of haddock, chips, batter, and bread stormed out of him. On his knees, even the sandwich contents Danny's mum had given him appeared as the gripes tore into him, and he guessed he'd eaten it too quickly, especially not having eaten a meal like that as far back as he could remember. He cursed and cursed as he cried from the severe ache that continued to wrack his body. It must have been another hour or so when the pain passed and his body eased, and all he could think about was how bloody hungry he was and the money he had spent. The mess on the floor was swarming with insects, obviously enjoying what he'd given them. Hopefully, the threepenny bit in his pocket would be enough to buy something tomorrow, and then the pains returned once more.

The next morning, he left the kitchen quietly after hearing a deep voice in his mum's bedroom and knew she wouldn't want him around, so he decided to try and get some breakfast before going to school. A couple of roads away, a grocery shop still stood that sold all sorts, and they made some lovely sticky lardy cakes. Checking his money, he wondered if he had enough to buy any. Finding the shop open and noticing a tray of them inside the window, he felt his stomach growl just looking at them. Opening the door, ringing its bell, he noticed how much they were and was a penny short of buying two. Seeing the lemonade bottles behind the counter, he knew another penny would buy the cakes. He asked the lady if she could keep two back while he went home and got an empty bottle, enabling him to purchase two.

'Well, don't be too long. I have other customers who like them; they go quickly.'

Leaving the shop, he ran to the open ground behind the chippy. The lemonade bottle was still there, covered in yesterday's dinner. Picking it up, he peed over the messy bits, getting the worst off, and found a puddle of water not far away and rinsed it before drying it in a piece of material he'd seen. Sniffing it, making sure it was clean, he hurried back to the shop. This time he took his time eating his breakfast; he wasn't going to lose that as well.

Chapter Ten

A couple of days later, Danny walked into the kitchen, and his mum asked him about Forest. Beginning his storytelling, he told her how he thought Forest lived on his wits most of the time. By the time Danny had finished, his mum had expressed that if he ever looked hungry and needed something, Danny was to bring him back to the house, and she would do her best to help. But he should not encourage him, seeing she had enough family to feed, what with helping out her three sisters and the old lady next door. Danny knew his mum was a good sort deep down. She would never let anybody go hungry if she could avoid it, and dad seemed to go along with her most of the time.

The city had taken more hits after Hitler's boys dropped more bombs after returning from a raid up-country, and Danny's school had been one of the places to collect a direct hit. Seeing there was no schooling for the immediate future, Danny's dad asked him to help out with some work that needed doing, shifting sandbags, while he and some other men shored up a couple of walls.

Later, Danny walked around to Eddie's place and found Johnny already there, seeing school was out.

They all waited should Forest turn up, seeing his school had caught fire, but he didn't show. The boys made their way towards the topsy-turvy building where he lived and called out for him, while not wanting to get too close to the house should he not be there, and his mum was entertaining. Three times they called him, and as they were about to walk away, a head appeared up at the window.

Seeing Forest, Danny shouted up, 'Forest, you coming out?'

A shaking of the head seemed to tell them he wasn't. Danny, inquisitive, walked nearer and saw the shiner on Forest's face. 'You got a black eye? Who did that?'

Johnny peered up at the window. 'How can you tell if he's got one?'

'Don't be stupid; you can see someone's had a go at him.'

The boys kept telling him to come down, and then he disappeared back inside. Guessing he was staying indoors, they walked off, climbing over a bomb-site discussing Forest's damaged face, when he emerged from the building, running after them. Hearing him, the group turned around and saw the state of his face.

Danny held him still. 'Christ, Forest, who gave you that?'

Not answering, he carried on past them.

Johnny, now eager to find out, caught up. 'What happened? Did some kids pick on you or something?'

Forest turned towards all of them and realised he had to tell. 'It was one of mum's friends; he thought I was a cheeky bugger. He's up there now with her. He said to me if he had his way, he would throw me out of the bedroom window.'

Danny put his hand on Forest's shoulder in some kind of sympathy. 'You're not going back, not with him in there, are you?'

Ignoring the question, Forest shuffled his feet and passed Danny his mum's nail file. 'Give this back to your mum and thank her.' Seeing the others looking at him like he was a stranger, he added, 'Ain't you seen a black eye before?'

Johnny piped up. 'Not one like that, I haven't.'

'Well, now you have. Can we do some more mudlarking, Danny?'

'Not today. A bomb landed on the harbour station again. There's some heavy equipment moving about down there. I think it will be a no-go area for a while.'

All of the boys saw the disappointment in Forest's bruised face. Johnny suggested they make their way out to the seafront, as there was bound to be something going on, but Danny told them his dad said it was all closed off along the beach as the military was conducting something or other out there. Eddie, still looking at Forest's face, asked the question.

'So where can we go with him looking like that?'

Forest began one of his grins as he thought of something, and with the shape of his face, he looked more like some baddie from out of a comic strip.

'Tell us what you're thinking.' Johnny could see a smile trying to emerge.

'Let's go to the flicks. There's a film on at the Pally that I fancy seeing.'

'You've got no money, and neither have I to go to a picture show. I had to give mum all the money I collected the other day.'

'You don't need money to get in there, Johnny. I can get you in.'

'How do you do that?'

'A lot of sailor boys use that place for a bit of you-know-what with their lady friends. I know the old lady at the pay desk. I think she has taken a liking to me.'

Pointing at Forest's eye, Eddie blurted out, 'Not if she sees you looking like that, she won't.'

'This face will give her more reason to let me in; she knows where I live and feels a bit sorry for me – I think.'

'Not all of us, she won't.'

'Course she ain't going to let us all in. I'll do that at the back doors.'

The more Danny thought about it, the more he fancied it. 'What's on, Forest, do you know?'

'They're showing *The Thief of Bagdad* and some other film, but if that's a bit rude , she'll tell me to come out after I've seen the main showing.'

Eddie spoke to the others. 'My dad was going to take me to see that when he came home.'

Johnny sarcastically spoke up. 'You're lucky to have a dad to take you.'

All the boys saw the hurt in Johnny's features, and Danny stepped forward. 'Come on, Johnny, Eddie didn't mean anything by it.'

They all waited for Johnny to settle, when Forest spoke to him. 'At least you've had a dad; more than I've ever had. It's not so bad after a while; you'll get used to it.'

The boys witnessed the tears gather inside Johnny's glasses as he moved away. Forest put his arm around him, but no one heard what was said. Making their way to the picture house, they studied the poster advertising the film, while avoiding the woman sitting at the pay desk.

Forest put his finger to his lips as not to speak. 'The next showing is at two o'clock; we've got half an hour to wait. I don't want to go in while that other film is showing.'

Danny whispered, suggesting Forest go and see if he would be allowed in, and they would meet him further up the road. Forest's unruly face grinned as he came back, telling them she would let him in just as the film was starting, when the lights went out. He told them the other picture, *Algiers*, was some romantic film.

They all walked away, with Eddie saying he would buy some sweets and tiger nuts for them all to share.

Forest grinned at the thought. 'Good on you. You're a champion.'

Chapter Eleven

Reaching the sweet shop, the boys followed Eddie into the store, with Forest studying the different jars of sweets stacked on the shelves. Eddie came out dipping into his paper bag full of tiger nuts, with Johnny and Danny having their fill, while he waited for Forest to take some.

'You want some of these nuts before they all go?'

Forest stood back, shaking his head from side to side.

'You like them; that's why I bought extra.'

Johnny saw it first as he approached Forest. 'You've got something in your mouth. Did you pinch some sweeties from in there?'

Danny could see there was something sticky in his mouth with the way he was chewing, and with the battered face from the bloke who had hit him it must have hurt his jaw as he tried to finish the sweet.

Eddie closed his bag and stuffed it into his pocket. 'Forest, did you take something off the counter in that shop?'

Forest knew he'd been caught red-handed by the others.

'If you get caught!'

Danny smiled at Eddie, getting serious about the

situation. He obviously never gave much thought to when the three of them borrowed the odd this and that from one of the scrapyards around the area, especially when they made a couple of shillings out of it, reselling it back to another scrapyard. They all watched whatever was in Forest's mouth disappear.

'It was only a toffee! I've got some more in my pocket if you want one, and a couple of humbugs.'

Eddie was taken aback by Forest's disclosure. 'No, thank you; you'd be for the high jump if the owner had caught you. That's stealing.'

Danny decided to calm the situation down. 'We nick bits and bobs from the yards. You can't say too much.'

Eddie became a little annoyed. 'But that's different.'

'If you say so.'

Johnny came up behind Forest. 'If you got a spare toffee, I'll have one.'

'Liquorice or plain? I've got both.'

Danny and Johnny burst out laughing as Eddie realised he was making a fool of himself.

'The plain one. I'll let you have the black ones, seeing they go with that face of yours. You watch your teeth don't fall out where that bloke hit you; he may have loosened some.'

Forest pulled out his pilfered toffees and offered them around. 'You're not going to tell on me, are you, Eddie?'

Eddie grinned at the face-pulling as Forest slid another chewy one around his mouth. 'I wouldn't do that, but the next time you stay outside.'

Danny knew the time was getting on. 'That film should be starting soon; we had better make a move, or we'll miss the beginning.'

Forest got them in through the back door of the picture house just as the film was starting. The four of them crept into the darkness and crouched low in the seats to one side, should they need to get out quick. There they entered a world of magic and wonder, without too many distractions from the couples sitting further away that made them giggle.

Afterwards, they talked about the Arabian adventure, with Johnny taking another of Forest's sweets. 'That was a brilliant film. I'd love to have one of those flying carpets.'

Eddie watched another toffee go into Forest's mouth. 'How many of those sweets did you nick? I saw you chewing them in the Pally.'

Forest grinned, not answering, trying to pull his teeth out of a sticky centre.

Danny chipped in. 'I think Mr Churchill's boys could do with a few of those carpets. Imagine the fun they'd have with one of those under their bums.'

Eddie, having put aside Forest's antics, joined in. 'My dad and all his crewmates could sure use one.'

They all nodded at that, and Johnny told Eddie he was sorry he went off on one earlier. Walking back home, they made their way through ruined streets, when Johnny started sniggering and called out, 'You still chewing on those toffees?'

Forest turned around with his jaw in full chewing mode as his teeth parted with toffee stuck all around them. The other three cracked up as Forest stuck his finger into his mouth, trying to free his teeth from the sticky mass.

Eddie walked up to him. 'You eat too many, and those gnashers you've got will fall out.'

Johnny checked inside Forest's mouth. 'Blimey, how many you got in there?'

Unable to answer, Forest grinned the best he could and put up three fingers as his facial antics wrenched this way and that, and all the time his eye was closing from whatever had happened earlier.

The talk became more serious when Eddie shifted the conversation as they got closer to home. 'Do you think Hitler will send any more of his bombers over?'

'He's bound to. My dad said the city is a prime target. Just make sure you keep your head down when he does, and that goes for all of us.'

Johnny nodded in agreement, and Eddie spoke up loudly. 'If those Germans touch mum's chickens, God help them. She'll join up, and if she gets out there, her nagging will convince Hitler to chuck it all in.'

Once again, they all began laughing, as Eddie tried to imitate his mum by wagging his finger at the others, and Johnny ran around, waving his arms about, acting and sounding like a frightened chicken. Forest nearly choked on the remains of his sweet and just managed to swallow a lump, with Danny thumping him on the back as his good eye watered. Turning at the end of the street, Danny recognised his dad with some other men trying to clear rubble where a wall had collapsed across the road, and the boys pitched in, getting a thumbs-up from the men whenever they helped out.

Three days later was another sunny day, and they all met up down at the harbour, seeing there wasn't so much going on. Walking onto the shore, they peeled off their clobber and walked into the mud, with Forest doing his act of charming the punters the way he did. It amazed everyone how someone whose face, still battered the way it was, could sway the crowds. Maybe it was because he was different, especially with that lopsided smile thanks to one of his mum's boyfriends. The pennies fell around Forest as his saucy capers tickled the ladies crossing the bridge as he called up to them, and that's when a threepenny-bit or a tanner came down, but not that often.

The days turned into prosperous ones for the boys, with school still out and Johnny accepting Forest more and more with his mud skills that earned him money for his mum. Forest revelled in the fact that, having a good day in the mud, fish and chips was going to be his supper, and he never kept quiet about it, although he never said anything about what had happened to his first meal at the back of the chippy. The boys knew he had to look out for himself and played along with his eagerness for his forthcoming feast.

Chapter Twelve

Waking up to a noise in his room, Forest squinted before opening his eyes wide enough to see the man who had hit him a few days before, leaning against the door frame, drinking from a small bottle of gin. Getting off his mattress onto the bare floorboards, he reached for his harbour shorts and vest as the man viewed him with hostility. Slipping his plimsolls on, seeing the man continue to stand there, he could see he had had a few drinks by the way he was leaning, and decided to speak to him.

'What do you want, Mister? There's no booze in here.'

The man threw his empty bottle at Forest, having drained it, hitting his shoulder, and listened to him squeal from the force of it. 'Don't speak to me, you dirty little bastard.' Holding onto the wall for support, he moved nearer to Forest. 'How that woman in there can allow something like you to escape from her loins, I'll never know. Seeing you here makes me feel unclean, knowing what she did. If it weren't for the essential requirement of a man, I'd cut her throat.'

Forest grabbed the windowsill, noticing it was getting dark outside, and edged nearer the wall, away from the threat coming his way.

'You're coming with me, you piece of shit.' And he ripped the vest from Forest's body.

Trying to escape, Forest ducked past the man, hoping to get out of the room, when a hand caught his throat and tightened on it.

'You want to get out of here; well, come with me.' The man, keeping a grip on his captive, edged him down the stairs and out of the house. 'Over there to those bombed-out houses. I've got a little surprise waiting for you.'

Trying to get free and unable to cry out, Forest tripped and staggered towards whatever awaited him in the derelict houses. With no one around and the vice-like grip almost choking him, the two of them stumbled across rubble and shattered tiles. Once at the abandoned premises, the man forced him inside. Pulling his captive around, he struck him in the face, with Forest temporarily blacking out. The man picked up a piece of cord, placing it around Forest's neck, securing him to a heavy joist supporting an adjoining wall. Coming to his senses, Forest felt the vibration as the beam shuddered with each impact as the man smashed into the bracing support with another piece of timber.

With a piece of rag almost gagging his speech, Forest tried to talk into the muffled material. 'What are you doing? You'll bring that wall down if this piece of wood moves.'

The smile that came back at him as the moon came

out of the clouds made him aware that was this man's intention. Another bottle of gin came out of the man's trouser pocket, and he flipped the top off, taking another hearty swig while grinning all the while.

'Please, Mister, you can't do this.'

'I told you not to speak to me.' Standing his piece of four-by-two to one side, the man edged towards Forest and slapped him hard enough for him to slip down the joist, still tied to it. 'Now, where was I?'

Forest, realising his situation, felt the cord loosen and went about trying to unpick the knot as the shuddering length of timber continued to dislodge itself. With his fingers attacking the twine, he could hear the movements as the wall groaned with each impact. Pulling desperately at the tight knot around his neck to get free, he saw a ten-shilling note wedged in the rubble beside him. 'Mister, look, there's money under the brickwork.' Pointing with one hand, he continued to unpick the twine with the other. 'If that wall comes down, you'll never know how much is under there.' Straight away, he knew the talk of money found its way into the man's foggy brain.

'If you're trying to…'

'Look, there may be more underneath.'

Dropping his wood piece, the man crossed to Forest, checking out the wall, ensuring it was safe, and took the money from the rubble.

'You see any more?'

'That looks like some by that pipe.'

Seeing another note, this time with a pound sign on it, the man dropped to his knees and began pulling bricks and slate away, probing for what might be underneath. Freeing himself, Forest saw his chance; he removed his gag and gripped a house brick, smashing it against the man's head. Finding the timber the man was using, he picked it up and used all his strength to slam it against the joist. On the second hit, the holding beam moved, and with a third, it fell away, with the wall groans increasing. With the man still groggy, he looked up as the wall collapsed, burying him under a vast amount of brickwork. The noise caused by the wall collapsing went unnoticed, disregarded by anyone who might have heard it, as many a time the cave-in of a derelict building was always happening. Forest waited until he was sure nothing else would fall and made his way towards a hand protruding from the rubble. He leaned over, took the ten-shilling note and placed loose debris over the hand, ensuring it wouldn't be noticed if anyone came in.

'You wanted to come here, you bastard. Now you can stay here with the rats.'

Walking into the house, Forest checked his mum wasn't about, before climbing the stairs. Reaching the top, he saw the bedroom door was closed and crept back into his room. A partial reflection in the window as moonlight came through portrayed the injuries to his face. The ache there convinced him he'd have more marks showing, although his mum probably wouldn't notice. His vest was no more than a rag after what had happened. He kicked it against the wall while still feeling the man's grip around his neck. Dropping onto his mattress, he leaned back against the wall, listening to whoever was in the other room as they loudly expressed something in their Scottish accent, and that's when the tears came.

Bringing his knees up under his chin, he thought of Danny and his way of life, knowing it would never be for him all the time he lived at home. Searching the room, he considered that word: nothing in the place was a home, just a business for his mum. Sat there looking out of his bare window, thoughts came back as the wall collapsed onto the man, burying him, and Forest knew it could have easily been him. Unable to sleep, he changed his clothes and went downstairs and out into the oncoming night, not wanting to stay in the house.

With his hands deep in his pockets, he strolled across the debris-strewn waste ground in front of his house, angry and confused. Glancing across at the derelict building where a body lay buried, he thought back to London, where another murder had happened, and remembered his mum telling him it was him that had killed the man, and now he had murdered another.

Chapter Thirteen

Forest, nearing Danny's home, walked down on the other side of the street and peered at the house with the curtains pulled for the evening, keeping the family inside warm and safe, as long as the Germans didn't drop a bomb on them. He liked Danny and his parents, especially when his mum gave him food. Johnny was all right, but Eddie was a bit strange with some of his remarks. Reaching the end of the street, he turned, making his way towards the harbour, and eventually he sat on the railings, looking out across the dark waters. The harbour ferry was still operating, with people hurrying to and from it, anxious to return to their ships or wherever they were from.

'You alone, son?'

The words brought him back from his thoughts, and turning, Forest stared into a weather-worn bearded face. 'Just getting some fresh air, Mister.'

'Shouldn't you be in bed at this time of night? Some of these revellers with a few drinks inside of them might take advantage of a youngster out by himself.'

He stared at the man warily. 'What you saying?'

'Just that you should be indoors.'

'I'll go soon. I want to sit here a while.'

'I live not too far from here. You can walk with me if you want.'

Straight away, he went on guard with the statement. 'No, thanks.'

'I'll buy you some supper if you want; I can see you look hungry. Why don't you think about it?'

The times someone had approached him when he had sat outside the pub waiting for his mum, trying to entice him with money or food. He knew what was behind the chat-up line. 'My mum will be along any moment; sorry, Mister.' Forest ensured he was capable of fleeing should he need to as the man closed on him and stretched out his arm.

Jumping off the railing on the other side, he moved away from the man, knowing what he wanted. Seeing a woman coming from the ferry, he called out, 'Mum. I'm over here.'

The man quickly turned away as a crowd of people came from the ferry and disappeared down a side road. Seeing him vanish, Forest watched as the woman with her man-friend came nearer and stopped.

'Were you speaking to me?'

Forest smiled and shook his head. 'Thought you were someone else, sorry.' He listened as the man with her said something about him as they passed. Probably the state of his face. Even this time at night, it must have stood out. Making his way back to the house, he watched as a sailor left, and another entered. 'Christ, Mum, come on, I'm tired.' Seeing the light go on through a crack in the upstairs curtains, he left and managed to buy a pie and chips from the chippy that was still open, before returning, and now needing to get inside as a drizzle came down. Quietly, he entered the living room and sat in the worn armchair they inherited. The mantelpiece's cracked-glass clock showed eleven o'clock, when another knock came on the front door. Hearing different voices outside, he recoiled into the chair, wondering if it was customers for his mum, or had someone seen him enter the derelict building and come out by himself? Fear gripped him as more knocks beat against the door, with rowdy comments shouted up to the first floor. Hearing footsteps coming down the stairs, he hid behind the chair and peeked at the almost undressed man as he answered the door.

'Will you lot keep it down. You brought any beers with you?'

'A crate should see us through and a gin for her. You started without us?'

Forest closed his eyes, knowing he wouldn't be sleeping on his mattress any time soon. As the last man disappeared up the stairs, he sat back in the chair, listening to the drunken gathering as they streamed strong vulgar language at one another. Putting his head into his hands, he winced at the bruises he knew were beginning to show.

Johnny met Danny the next day, and together they knocked on Forest's door, when suddenly the front room curtain parted, and a face appeared.

Seeing the two boys, Forest made his way cautiously to the bottom of the stairs and opened the front door.

'You look like you've been in a brawl again, Forest; what happened this time?'

'I went down the harbour last night, and I slipped on some seaweed. Honestly, Danny, that's all.'

'You sure about that? One of your mum's customers didn't take another poke at you again, did they?'

'Not this time, Johnny. As I said, I slipped.'

Danny studied Forest's face, not believing a word. 'Are you coming out for a bit of larking? Me and Johnny have changed.'

Forest thought of the men he witnessed going upstairs. 'Give me a moment; mum's got company.'

The boys watched as the door closed on them, and they whispered to one another as to why Forest's face was so bruised.

He climbed the stairs and saw one of the men in bed with his mum, sound asleep. Pushing open his bedroom door, he discovered the other two asleep on his mattress in their underwear, with beer bottles lying alongside them, again sound asleep. Tiptoeing into the kitchen, he noticed they had used the sink for a toilet and began changing as quickly and as quietly as possible, praying that neither would wake. Twice, one of them moved and turned over, disturbing the other one. Standing there near-naked, he froze when he heard a noise from his mum's bedroom and listened to the deep-throated voice. He knew the man in there was awake and quickly pulled his shorts and plimsolls on, before hiding his other clothes in the opened section of the wall that was still increasing in size. He listened to the man get out of bed and picked up on the swearing as he knocked into something, before peeing into a chamber pot, farting and coughing simultaneously. Peering around the corner, he noticed the man had his back to him and hastened down the stairs. Opening the front door, he put his finger to his lips, telling the others to keep quiet, and pulled the door shut as best he could.

Danny and Johnny realised the situation and said nothing, knowing what he was doing, and they raised their eyes at one another. Looking back at the house, Forest knew breakfast would have to wait until he had earned some pennies in the mud, seeing he had left his money in his other trouser pocket, while praying his mum wouldn't find it.

Chapter Fourteen

The months passed, with air raids taking their toll on Portsmouth. Many more houses and streets perished, but people persisted in living in their homes no matter the outcome. Some children who had to evacuate became homesick, and, in some cases, returned to their parents as air raids continued, with the Navy being on their doorstep. Regardless, people knuckled down, determined to fight it out as the Luftwaffe increased their visits. The crack in Johnny's kitchen wall survived the onslaught, as, thankfully, whatever his dad did, he had done an excellent job of shoring it up. As Johnny's mum told him, it was about the only decent thing he had done.

Forest's house had a direct hit, but, fortunately, he was out sitting in some doorway waiting for his mum, who was with her boyfriend in a boozer and never left as bombs rained down far and near. Forest told the other boys if he had been one of the unlucky ones, so be it. There wasn't a lot else going for him. He also said his mum was unbothered by the air raid as she and her boyfriend remained to top up their drinks while everybody else headed for the shelters. However, it did scare the pants off him. Luckily, his mum managed to get another house a road away from Danny's, thanks to one of her acquaintances, and he was thrilled seeing he had got a proper bedroom to himself, even though he had lost his money and most of his clothes, like his mum had. Unfortunately, the water supply had a direct hit, and the only way to collect any was from the standpipes in the street. Danny and Eddie were none too pleased with the Germans, seeing they had to fetch it if their mums wanted any, but it was almost outside their front door for Johnny, so it never bothered him.

Eddie, along with his mum's chickens, had to move to his uncle's house in the country just outside of the city, seeing his mum had to go into hospital for an operation in April. When Eddie came back a couple of weeks later, he was full of something he'd seen on the hill slopes north of Portsmouth. He told everyone they had to collect some linoleum from some of the bombed-out places and get an old candle, and he would tell them more later. Forest, forever the curious one, made sure they all had what Eddie wanted and waited for him to announce his plans.

With Saturday being a sunny and warm day, the three boys waited outside Eddie's house, itching to find out what would happen. All three of them called for Eddie to hurry up as they stood around, then Eddie pulled his front door to, with them all asking the same question.

'Are you going to let on about this lino business?'

'It will be great fun, you wait.' Eddie put his arm

around Johnny's neck. 'You got some lino yet?'

Forest answered, 'I got it all ready. What do you want a candle for?'

'Not to light a fire, I assure you.'

Away from the house, the other three boys listened to Eddie. 'I'm taking us on a bus ride tomorrow; we can grab a drink with something to eat, and we can spend the day on the hill.'

'What hill's that?'

'The big one north of the city; surely you've seen it before.'

'What, that's it?'

'No, Forest, we can take our old go-cart with us as well.'

Danny quizzed him. 'What are you on about – lino, candles and the cart? You want to take us up the hill to ride down it? What's the lino and candles for?'

'I'll tell you tomorrow. Can you all make it?'

Danny looked skywards. 'So long as Hitler don't bugger it up. My dad said he wouldn't want me as long as nothing happened.'

Sunday arrived, and all four boys headed for the bus stop, dragging their old go-cart behind them. The bus conductor made them put their cart under the stairs and inquired about the sheets of lino. Eddie told him they were going to make something, so he said to them not to make a mess up top as he would come up and check from time to time. The boys got some funny looks as they chatted away in the front seats, but the conductor was an all right gent as he took their fares.

'Come on, Eddie, give us a clue; you've told us nothing yet.'

'I'll tell you when we get there, Johnny.'

Danny pointed out various places to Forest that they passed, telling him how the city was changing since the war began. Getting off the bus at the end of the journey, they headed towards the hill, towing the go-cart. Once they reached the top of the hill road, Eddie walked along the grassy verge towards a big chalkpit.

Forest stopped and beheld the view. 'You can see right across the city.'

Johnny piped up, 'Yeah, and all the bombed-out places to go with it.'

Eddie hurried them along towards some grassy knolls. 'Nearly there; we just need to get to those bumpy bits of grass, and I'll explain.'

'I hope this is worth it, coming all this way.'

'You'll love it, Danny. You all will. Shall we eat our grub before we start?'

Forest knew he never had any and said nothing.

'Forest, mum has done you some sandwiches, so don't worry.' Danny passed over the package and saw the smile come back.

'Thank her for me, won't you. Wow, is this spam?'

'Think so; you'll know once you sink those gnashers into it.'

After everyone had eaten, Eddie edged his way towards a particular slope, with the others following with their lino pieces and Johnny pulling the go-cart. Telling the others to hide the cart in a nearby bush, he sat on the grass, rubbing the candle wax onto the lino's shiny side. Eddie placed his waxed side on the grass and sat on it, with the rest doing the same.

'These are our slides. I'll go first, so you stay here and watch me. Keep your feet up and grip the sides hard or you'll come off, and watch out for bush stumps growing. Otherwise, you will lose the skin on your fingers.'

Danny looked at the squares of lino. 'How do we stop? Do we let go?'

'See those bushes at the bottom of the hill; that's the brakes. Let go of the lino and protect your face, because we go right into them to stop. You might get a few scratches, but it will be worth it.'

Forest, having waxed his piece, sat next to Eddie. 'I'm coming with you. I'm ready.'

Danny and Johnny waited to see them go – and did they move! Halfway down, they heard Forest yelp when he hit a stump, and with legs in the air, Eddie and Forest flew into the bushes, disappearing at the bottom.

'Blimey, Johnny, I've never seen Eddie like that before; but if he can do it, so can I.'

'Come on, I'll beat you down. Watch your fingers, though. I bet Forest has lost some skin the way he shouted.'

Hurtling down the slopes, Danny spotted some other children watching them at a distance. Seeing that they appeared interested in what they were doing, he nudged the others as they climbed back up. 'Those kids over there, it looks like they've got lino, too.'

Eddie noticed two girls in amongst them and called out, 'Hey, Forest, looks like you've got a friend.' Eddie nudged Johnny and giggled as the three boys and two girls came over.

Forest immediately saw what Eddie was on about, as one of the girls was dark-skinned like him. Ignoring the jibe, he walked up to the girl near his age and spoke to her. 'What's your name?'

The girl, in a worn dress, smiled as he sat on his piece of lino. 'Lisa, although they call me Sas. I wish they wouldn't.'

'Why do they call you that?'

'Because I'm sassy at times, I suppose.'

He could see she was friendly. 'Do you do this?' He pointed to the square of lino.

'Sometimes, but we usually watch the boys. I tried it once and got cut in those bushes. Mum's told me not to do it because I could lose an eye.'

Listening to the way she spoke, Forest thought she seemed too nice to be in such a shabby dress, and although she was younger, he could see how lovely she was. 'I got to go. You staying around?'

'Might.'

Returning her smile, he shot off down the steep embankment, picking up speed. Climbing back, he rubbed his face where a thorn had cut him below his ear.

Reaching the others, he saw Lisa talking to the other girl, and gathered they were talking about him. As he put more candle grease on his square, Lisa came over to him with her little handkerchief in her hand.

'You're bleeding, did you know?'

Forest rubbed his ear and looked at his finger. 'It's not too bad.'

'Let me wipe it. You might have a thorn or something in it.'

He sat there, watching her spit on her hanky; she wiped the blood away and laughed at him.

'Just a scratch; you'll live.'

Seeing the handkerchief was all bloody, he smiled. 'Thanks for doing that.'

'Me and my friend are going now; we have to do some errands. I might see you again.'

Watching as she stood, ready to leave, he spoke to her. 'My name's Forest.'

She giggled at that. 'There's a lot of them over the hill.' Then she ran off, looking back, waving at him.

The afternoon passed, with all the boys discovering the safest ways down and avoiding the more dangerous bushes, but they all ended up with cuts and bruises. They climbed the hill so many times, racing one another, laughing and shouting at each other's calamities, and the bad luck when one of them came off on the way down the hill. With the pieces of linoleum wearing out, they collected the go-cart and, with two of them at a time, they sped down the steep grassy slopes, hollering and screeching into each other's ears, before they plummeted into a bush and out the other side, where they tumbled out onto a hard earthen surface. After several trips down, the go-cart began to wobble uncontrollably as the wheels shook and eventually parted, tipping the boys out, with the cart breaking apart around them.

Saying cheerio to the other boys, the four decided they had reached the end of their afternoon fun and buried the remains of their cart in some distant bushes, before heading for the nearest shop to buy a drink with what little money they had. Walking home afterwards, covered in grass stains, cuts, and the odd piece of torn clothing, they confessed it was a fantastic day out, and they must do it again.

Chapter Fifteen

The boys still collected some decent coins in the mud as the summer came to an end. They had the occasional problem when other kids joined them in the harbour, where they disputed who had earned a particular coin; but otherwise, they got on. No one seemed to mind joining together, seeing they were all in the same situation and tried to make it as fair as possible. As October approached, a couple of girls followed them, and Forest became more curious about the giggles and remarks coming from the older girl.

Johnny snickered. 'She's much too big for you, Forest; she'd eat you alive.'

Eddie and Johnny slapped him on the back, telling him he needed to grow a lot more before he tried anything with her, along with other remarks that made Forest smile.

'I might be smaller than you lot, but I know a thing or two.'

Eddie listened to the remark and opened his eyes wider. 'You dirty bugger, what are you telling us?'

'I'll tell you when I get back.' Forest ran across the road, letting the girl know he was interested. Straight away, the big girl ignored her petite friend.

Johnny, seeing the shocked look on Eddie's face, began laughing. 'What's the betting he chats her up? What do you think, Danny?'

'Looking at him, I think he does know a thing or two. See where his hands are. She don't seem too bothered. The dirty sod!'

Johnny laughed. 'Knowing what his mum gets up to, I imagine he knows all about that side of things. Look at him; he's grinning like the Cheshire Cat. She's a bit big for him.'

Danny joined in with Johnny's laughter. 'He seems happy enough.'

Johnny called out that Forest should behave himself, while Eddie stood open-mouthed, not believing what Forest was doing. 'Look, that other girl is moving off. I wonder what's happening. He's touching her bum! I hope that's all he's going to do on the pavement. If someone sees him, he'll be in for a good hiding.'

They stood there watching as he began to say something into her ear as she giggled while Forest rubbed her bottom.

Johnny called out once more to behave himself, but it fell on deaf ears as he continued his affections, and Eddie continued to look on in amazement. They waited for him to return to tell them what he spoke to her about, and the other girl returned to her friend as soon as he did.

'What you up to? I hope you don't have ideas about that big girl.'

'She's all right, Danny. I'm going to see her later.'

Johnny laughed at the way he was grinning as he adjusted himself.

'That's disgusting, Forest.'

'What's up, Eddie? It's natural.'

'Not at your age, it isn't. If her dad finds out, he won't be too happy with you.'

'She likes me; she's going to meet me tomorrow at the back of her privy. She told me it's quiet there, and we can get together a bit more.'

The boys watched the two girls walk off and wave at them, with Forest blowing the big girl a kiss. The occasional look back told all of the boys that he was interested in her.

'She must be about fifteen and a lot bigger than you, Forest.'

'More to get hold of Johnny. Not like her friend, she's a bit skinny.'

'You've only begun putting weight on in this last year. You were more like her friend, skin and bones.'

'There's more of me now, Danny.'

'Yeah, I bet there is.'

'Forest, is she going to… you know?'

'I hope she does, Johnny, I hope she does.'

'Blimey, you would, too, wouldn't you?'

Again, that smile as he put his hands into his pockets and moved them about. 'I told her we're larking this afternoon. I think she'll come down and check us out.'

Eddie chipped in, 'I didn't realise we were going larking. It's not that warm today.'

'Looks like we are now. Forest has just made plans with that one.' Danny pushed Forest, nearly knocking him over. 'I think you're becoming a dirty sod; you've changed one hell of a lot since we met.'

Still with his hands in his pockets, Forest handled his groin. 'You'd be surprised at what I know, Danny. I've seen all sorts of things.'

Eddie's face was a picture, listening to those words.

Laughing, Danny playfully slapped Forest. 'The tide will be coming in a bit earlier today; if we're going larking, we had better make a move and change.' Walking over to Eddie with his mouth still open, he closed it for him. 'Are you finding this all a bit much, Eddie? I bet your dad knows a thing or two about life, being in the Navy. With all the matelots Forest's mum knows, I bet he's as knowledgeable.'

Thanks to Forest's ways, clambering through the mud in the afternoon, the boys were making a profit. Then, about three o'clock, Danny spotted the two girls as they walked nearer to them along the bridge.

'Hey, Forest, your girlfriend is up there. She's looking at you.'

Turning his attention to the walkway, Forest saw and waved at them. With all the boys looking at the two girls, they all saw how big-busted Forest's friend was as she leaned on the rail, peering down.

A quarter to ten the next morning, Danny, Johnny,

and Eddie lay across the roof next to the wholesaler's yard, one of the few shelters left intact. They guessed Forest would make an appearance at any moment, seeing they knew how much he wanted to meet this girl.

'Danny, how did you know when to come?'

'He told me after we got back from larking. Quiet, someone's coming.'

Eddie pointed to the alleyway at the back of the houses. 'Here comes that big girl. Blimey, she's tarted up a bit. She's got lipstick on.'

Johnny nudged the others. 'And here comes Forest.'

'Quiet, they'll hear us,' Danny whispered. 'He's changed his clothes; I hope he's had a good wash-down.'

Within moments, the two of them kissed, and Forest's hands wandered all over her body. A couple of times, the boys dug one another as his hands roamed inside her dress, creeping upwards.

They couldn't believe what they saw as their ringside station gave them a full view.

Eddie's eyes were bulging. 'He's got his hands on her titties, the dirty devil.'

Noticing a movement in the alleyway, the boys saw a figure approaching the two of them.

'I hope that's not...' Before another word left Danny's lips, this tall, tough-looking character emerged and shouted, frightening everybody.

The girl screamed and pushed Forest away from her

as the man came behind him, giving out the biggest clump you ever saw, with his heavy hand connecting with the back of Forest's head, lifting him off the ground.

'You dirty little bastard, put your hands on my girl again, and I'll break your bleedin' neck.'

Another swipe caught him, knocking him to the floor as the girl screamed again and ran off. Forest left, too, with the girl's father swearing at him as he shot up the side of the lav wall like a rat in a fix. As Forest cleared the top of the wall, the girl's father shook his fists at him, again cursing him vehemently. Forest saw his friends lying across the roof higher up and made his way towards them. Landing on a corrugated shelter, making his escape, he shouted as the canopy gave way under him, and he disappeared. More screams erupted as the covering fell onto the butcher's wife, who was doing the same thing with the grocer's boy from next door, and there was Forest in the middle of it. The butcher came out of the back door and intervened with the chaos. The three boys laughed with their hands over their mouths as they watched Forest scamper from the incident, knowing one walloping was enough. As he neared them, they pulled him over and watched him rub his wounds, while Danny pushed him flat.

'I hope she was worth the effort, and I bet the back of your head hurts. Didn't he hit you!'

Forest rubbed the wounded part of his anatomy, and the other boys watched as the uproar continued in the yard below. Hearing a shout in the distance, all the boys looked across as Forest's girlfriend cried with her father shouting at her, before slamming the back door shut.

'Looks like trouble in that house, Forest. If I were you, I'd stick to mudlarking?'

'Danny's right: he could have knocked you out down there if he got hold of you.'

'She was worth it, Johnny. She got some lovely breasts on her. But you're right about him; he nearly took my block off.'

'What did you expect, a handshake?'

All the boys listened to Eddie's words, before Danny interrupted.

'Families around here will have to watch out, seeing you in action, and don't go getting ideas about my sisters.'

'I won't, Danny, promise. I've seen your dad.'

'Too true, he would.'

Chapter Sixteen

Forest touched the back of his head the next morning, still feeling the hand that had struck him. Asking his mum for a few pennies for something to eat, seeing there was no food in the house, he made his way through the streets, looking for what he could buy with the four pennies. After school, and still hungry, he saw the girl he had met the day before and ran after her as she was alone.

'Hey, it's me, Forest.' Not knowing her name, he caught up with her. 'You had better tell me your name; you know mine.'

Recognising him, she turned and smiled as her loose top showed she had nothing under her blouse. 'I'm sorry about yesterday. Did my dad hurt you?'

'A little bit, but I can live with it.'

'Dad told me not to see you again, but I like you a lot.'

That told him he was onto something good with her. 'So, what's your name?'

'It's Nancy.'

'Well, I still fancy you, Nancy.'

She giggled at the remark, and Forest watched as her chest bounced around in front of him.

'Can we see each other again, only this time further away?'

'I can meet you in the park if it's not raining; there are places that you're not supposed to go, but we can sneak into them.'

'That sounds great. When can we do it?'

Nancy suggested they meet on Friday at five o'clock, when it would be quieter. Anxious about waiting almost a week, Forest tried to get her to change her mind.

'Dad said I'm to stay in until then. I'm only out now to meet my mum; otherwise, I wouldn't be allowed out of the house.'

Pushing her into a doorway, Forest kissed her and told her she was lovely, even though she wasn't. Her body heat through her blouse aroused him further, and he tried hard to get her to visit the park earlier. Kissing him back, she pushed him away and moved back into the street.

'See you Friday, at five o'clock. Don't be late.'

Forest met Danny later without saying anything about Nancy, but he could not stop thinking of her, and as each day drew nearer to the weekend, he was unable to keep still. When Friday morning arrived with no school, Danny noticed how on edge Forest was and guessed something was up, as he kept his hands in his pockets, fiddling around.

'What you all jittery about? You got a date or something?'

Trying to sound casual, he took his hands out and tried to change the subject. 'Can we go larking, Danny? I could do with earning some pennies.'

'Johnny and Eddie can't make it today; they had to go out with their mums.'

'That won't stop us, though, will it?'

'I guess not. The tide's going out. Do you want to go now?'

'Let's do it; but it will be cold down there, seeing it rained during the night.'

Standing up to their knees in mud, they did their best, calling out to the crowds as they crossed the bridge above them. By midday, the two boys had collected a pocketful of coins between them.

'Crikey, Forest, this must be one of our best days ever. If Johnny knew how much we collected, he would have joined us and given his mum an excuse not to go out with her. Whatever you do, once we count this lot out, don't tell him how much we earned, or he'll throw a wobbly.'

'Danny, that big woman with the old man, she looks like money and not from around here.' Standing back a bit, he called out to her. 'Hey, lady, that's gorgeous clothes you've got on. They look really nice on you.'

Danny stood there, watching him do his act.

'Is there any chance you could spare a half-penny or something for a poor homeless boy? I've had no breakfast today.' Forest knew that part was real. 'Such a beautiful lady and looking so lovely.'

Danny saw the woman stop with her gentleman friend and speak to him while looking over the rail.

'Looks like you've earnt something. He's got his hand in his pocket.'

The woman, putting her handkerchief to her nose, raised her other hand and dropped a silver coin into the mud beside the bridge structure. Giving a little wave to Forest, she smiled at the older man as they continued their journey. Forest kept his eye on the spot where the coin went in beside the bridge uprights and edged forward. Putting his hand into the mud, Forest searched for the money. Twice he felt something that didn't feel right, and then his fingers touched a sizeable round coin. Making sure he had hold of it, he pulled his hand out and looked at the half-crown. Falling backwards, he sat in the mud with his eyes watering intensely. Danny made his way over and stood there, looking at the big silver piece.

'Bloody hell, she threw that over?'

Forest looked up and smiled through teary eyes. 'I've never held one of these before, let alone had one to myself. Look, Danny, two-and-sixpence all in one coin.'

'Do you want to call it a day now? The tide will be coming in soon?'

Forest wiped his face with his muddy fingers. 'I also found this in the mud.' He showed Danny what he had.

Looking at the shape of it, Danny knelt. 'Is that what I think it is?'

Forest nodded. 'Looks like it.'

Both boys studied the shape of a gun wrapped in an oilcloth.

Chapter Seventeen

Stood together in a quiet spot by a derelict building, the two boys counted out their money while looking at the gun. They had to stop and re-count their hoard three times, as the unusual find kept taking their minds from what they were doing. Eventually, they separated the amount and whistled.

'Seven shillings and eight pence, and that thing.' Danny pointed at the gun. 'Three shillings and ten pence each, and you can have the half-crown piece. I can't believe it.' Again, Danny peered at the other find. 'I don't know what to do about that: there's no way I'm taking it home.'

Forest unwrapped it, and they discovered a revolver, and Forest wished he'd had it the other day when he got beaten. Looking across at the bombed-out houses, he gave a little smile to himself, wondering if anyone had found the man there, but he doubted it. 'I'll get rid of it, Danny. I'll drop it back in the harbour later, once I've had a good look at it.'

'Whatever you do, don't touch that trigger in case the thing is loaded.'

'I know what I'm doing. When I lived in London, my uncle had something like this, and I watched him mess around with it, so I have an idea of how they work. I promise I won't shoot myself.'

Danny raised his eyebrows, listening to Forest and knowing that his dad would go mad if he knew what they'd found. 'Just make sure you throw it back in down by the ferry, where the water's deeper.'

'I wonder who it belonged to. It might have been a spy or a secret agent.'

'Well, whoever it was, get rid of it today.'

Finding his house unoccupied, Forest made his way to his room and, placing the gun down, he kissed the big silver coin, before hiding it away in a tin he kept under the floorboards; the one and four pence left would be enough to suffice his hunger as he listened to his stomach growl. Unwrapping the gun, he thought back, trying to remember how his uncle checked to see if the weapon had bullets. Dithering and touching the revolver, he noticed some marks etched on it and wondered where it had come from. Finding the cylinder latch and pushing the chamber sideways, he found it full of bullets, bar one. 'Wow, nearly a full house.' Clicking it back into position and making sure it locked, he put it back into the cloth and hid it with his tin, placing his old cabinet over everything. Removing his larking shorts, Forest dressed, thinking of food, and made his way out of the house, jingling the coins in his pocket.

Waiting outside the park entrance earlier than told, Forest walked up and down, noticing how wet the grass was, but eager to meet with Nancy. As five o'clock came and went, he began to feel as though she wasn't going to turn up, and he strolled through the park, kicking at nothing in particular as the evening came on. Sitting on a damp bench with a bag of toffees, he cursed his luck after having had a good day, and he was about to stand when Nancy came rushing along the path.

'I didn't think you would have waited; our dad made me do some ironing, seeing mum ain't feeling well. I think she just didn't want to do it.'

Forest stood and put his arms around Nancy, feeling how hot she was and guessing she had run to see him. Straight away, he knew he was onto a good thing with her as she returned his advances with her hands.

'We can't do anything here; follow me, I know where there's a place we can go. I'm wearing an old coat we can lie on, but we mustn't make it dirty with grass stains.'

Thinking she could have done this before, he held her hand as she led him into some bushes, and slipping between them, they came out into an open space ample enough for the two of them to lie down together.

'How come you knew this was here? Have you been here before with someone else?'

Nancy thought quickly and sat down. 'We used to play hide and seek years ago; I guessed it might still be here.'

Not believing what she said, he sat beside her and leaned over to kiss her.

Without warning, Nancy grabbed hold of him and pulled him on top of her. 'Stop talking; we didn't come here to talk. Let those wandering hands of yours do what they tried to do the other day.'

Coming out of the bushes a good half hour or more later, he regarded Nancy in a different light. She had exhausted him with her cravings and demands. Her body was all he had pictured through the week and more as she had held onto him. He stood beside her with his clothes dishevelled as the rain began to come down.

'Tidy yourself; it looks like you've climbed through that bush.' Straightening her dress, Nancy looked around and, seeing no one, she kissed him briefly. 'Next Friday, are you okay to meet me again?'

'I'd like that.'

'For someone smaller than me, you know some things, don't you?'

Again, he nodded.

'Next time, wash under your armpits – they stink a bit – and take your socks off; they could do with a wash, too, or your feet do. Have you got any more of those toffees?'

Unworried about her remarks, he stood there satisfied with his day. He produced the bag of sweets from his trouser pocket and offered them to her. 'Take them: you can have all of them.'

Then, before anything else happened, Nancy pulled her coat together and was gone, the bag of sweets as well.

Grinning to himself, he wandered back to the house, imagining what next Friday would offer. Seeing his home with the curtains drawn back, Forest hurried to get inside with Nancy still on his mind, while hoping his mum and any customer of hers would give the house a miss, at least for a good few hours.

Chapter Eighteen

Saturday evening, sitting against an almost demolished building wall, Forest looked across the debris-strewn space in front of him. As usual, the pulled curtains upstairs told him his mum was still busy, and he thought of his antics with Nancy the day before. It was the first time he had done anything like that and he knew he wasn't Nancy's first boyfriend, the way she pounced on him. Feeling the night begin to chill through him, he huddled his arms around himself and pulled his knees up under his chin. Sitting there for what seemed like an hour, he became bored and walked off into the streets. People hurried past to wherever they were going, giving him no attention as he scuffed along the pavements with his hands in his pockets. Couples held hands or hugged one another as they passed, taking no notice of a forlorn coloured lad. He realised most were sailors on shore leave, having found a girl – then his thoughts returned to Nancy.

As the evening crept on, several wardens told Forest to make his way home and stop his wandering about, as there might be an air raid. After the second telling, sirens sounded, and people left their homes, heading for shelters and, hopefully, safety. Deciding to return to the house, he dodged the crowds and ran home to find his mum and another man running to a shelter. Opening the front door, he climbed the stairs and fell onto his bed, unconcerned about what might happen as aircraft noises sounded overhead. With the sirens blaring and the Luftwaffe trying it on, he knew the house was his as long as nothing happened. With momentarily happy thoughts of Nancy, he lay under his blanket, not hearing the distant gunfire and dogfights as bombs dropped on the other side of the mainland, missing the dockyard completely. Disregarding the air-raid sirens sounding the all-clear, Forest turned over, snuggling up into a foetus position.

'What are you doing here, Forest? Don't tell me you've been here with that lot going over. Have you got some kind of death wish, you bloody idiot?'

'Mum, is that you?'

'Who do you expect, bloody royalty.'

'I was so tired, Mum, I still am. Have you got any visitors coming back?'

'No, those bloody Germans frightened them away. That's more money down the drain. The pubs are still open, so I'm going out for a drink. I might meet up with someone there. Just make sure this door's shut if I come back with someone. I don't want them seeing you lying here; you've caused me enough heartache in this life.'

Forest listened to the words like he always did when his mum was pissed off about losing a customer.

'You want to come with me to the pub? I can just

about afford a lemonade for you if you wait outside, but don't interfere if I find a friend. You hear me?'

'Do I ever, Mum?'

'I'll never forgive that black bugger for putting you inside of me. He ruined my life.'

How many times had he heard those remarks aimed at him, and not only the words *black bugger*? 'I'm staying here, Mum. You go and have a good time.'

'I will as long as those bloody planes stay away. Don't forget, make sure this door's shut and don't come out.'

After she had changed into another dress, Forest watched his mum pass the door and hoped she wouldn't find anybody. Snuggling down again, he tried to sleep, but it took a while, and when the sirens sounded once again, wakening him, he rubbed his eyes and sat up in the darkened room, looking out the window as gunfire and planes came over. Feeling the nearby vibrations as bombs dropped, Forest watched as flames rose in the sky and tracer bullets sped skyward, trying to stop the destruction. Only once did an explosion come near the house, where it landed on the demolished house not too far away, where a man lay under the rubble. 'Guess they definitely won't be finding him now.' Turning away, Forest went to his hiding place and picked up the revolver, wondering if he'll ever use it.

Eddie and Danny helped Danny's dad out the following morning, where more damaged houses and shops lay in ruins. Johnny eventually found them, and Danny told him the shop they were in had no mannequins as it was a sweet shop, so he needn't get paranoid. With his middle finger placed upright, they all laughed and dived into trying to salvage what they could for the owner.

'It's a good job Forest isn't here; these jars of sweets would be walking away with him. I wonder where he is. He usually meets us on a Sunday morning.'

Danny hoped that he wouldn't say anything about the money they made in the harbour if he did turn up. He knew Johnny would go mad knowing what they collected. 'He's probably doing something, Eddie. Just hope it isn't that girl he met.'

'You think he will? Her dad will kill him if he tries that again.'

'Look, that's him over there,' Danny called out. 'Forest, Forest, over here: come and give us a hand.'

'Pocket some of these sweets, you mean.' Eddie needed to get that one in before he arrived. 'Once he steps in here, his fingers won't know where to go first.'

Johnny told Eddie to keep quiet. 'We'll all get something for helping out; you know what Danny's dad said.'

'Forest, you're late today.'

Having heard and ignored Eddie's remark, Forest saw all the jars of sweets. 'I'll have some of them. Are they going free?'

'No, they're not, but some might come our way after helping out, so behave yourself if you're coming in.'

With all of them assisting, Danny eventually got Forest beside him and whispered, 'You won't say a word to Johnny about us larking.'

'No, I won't say anything.'

'You get rid of the gun?'

Forest knew he had to lie on that one. 'Yeah, it's at the bottom of the harbour. Will we get some sweets out of this, Danny?'

'Dad said we would.'

'Over there, there must be jars of smashed toffees lying about, and they're wrapped.'

Eddie jumped into the debate. 'Leave them alone, Forest. If someone sees you taking some, none of us will get anything.'

'What you so touchy for? Did you get out of the wrong side of the bed this morning?'

Johnny and Danny could see friction mounting between the two, so Danny got Forest to move away from the broken jars, seeing he was about to say something. 'Forest, leave it; his mum was in a right old mood this morning, and he copped an earful from her.'

'He's bloody lucky that's all he gets from his mum. He wants mine to live with, then he'll have something to moan about.'

'You boys all right back here?' Danny's dad nodded his head at Forest. 'You come to give us a hand, son?'

With a nod for an answer, he began to help out.

'The owner is giving out some of his stock afterwards, so don't go running off before you get something, and watch out for broken glass: it's all over the place.'

'Okay.'

With much of the stock secured into boxes and debris moved away, the owner thanked the boys for their help. 'Lads, that box over there, you'll find all sorts inside; help yourselves, but don't get greedy.'

Walking away from the ruined shop, all four boys made their way home with various sweets: Danny with humbugs, Eddie and Johnny with barley sugars, and Forest chewing on his toffees.

Chapter Nineteen

Forest's mum began drinking heavily as Christmas neared: any chance of getting more money, she took it, either by selling household items or clothing. But with Forest having his hideaway of coins and clothes, he remained alert as objects around the house dwindled further. One of Forest's mum's customers worried him. Ernest, a big man that worked in the dockyard. Whenever he came to the house, he made sure Forest went out. Otherwise, he quietly threatened him with physical harm and called him names that hurt. With her booze supply, his mum never said anything to him until after Ernest left, and then it was to say he never meant it as it was the drink talking.

Having come back home after seeing a film with Johnny at the Pally, Forest left him outside the front door and went in to get some pennies, seeing the curtains were half-open upstairs. Forest crossed the landing and went into his room, before hearing Ernest's unmistakable voice as he puffed and panted like an old warhorse. Lifting his money from its hiding place, Forest replaced the boards, but then the tin slipped through his hands, spilling coins onto the wooden floor, making a racket. Picking them up, he was about to put them back when a shadow appeared in his doorway. Ernest stood there, evil-eyeing him with his arms crossed over his enlarged stomach.

'What are you doing here?'

The near-naked individual took a swipe at Forest but missed him as his trousers fell around his knees. 'You know you're not supposed to be here when I visit. You spying on me, boy?'

Forest shook his head, knowing he had to get past him. Grabbing his trousers, the man aimed another fist at him, glancing his shoulder, before taking another step forward.

'I only came in for a coin, Mister; my mate is waiting outside for me.' He hoped that the man would let him leave by mentioning somebody else.

'You want to leave, boy, then I suggest you do just that. Open that window or collect another thump. Your choice.'

He did what the man said and looked down at Johnny below, putting the money into his pocket.

'I could hurt myself if I jumped.'

'You'd do a lot worse if I chucked you out.'

Looking down once more, he realised the man meant it as he closed in on him, securing his trousers. Deciding he had no choice, Forest climbed onto the windowsill, feeling the man's presence close in on him.

'Get out of the way, Johnny.'

Looking up at the unexpected sound, Johnny saw Forest edge out of his window and then jump. As Forest landed beside him without falling over, Johnny went to him. 'Are you all right? What did you do that for?'

Forest held onto Johnny as a pain shot through his right leg. 'One of mum's customers – Uncle Ernest – he wanted me out of the house.'

'Uncle?'

'I know he's not a relation or relative. None of them are.'

'Couldn't you have come down the stairs?'

'Didn't have much say in it. This one hates me being in the house when he's there. The fat bastard caught me in the shoulder with his fist.'

'What about your mum? She's in the house, isn't she?'

He gazed at Johnny, not bothering to answer. 'Give me a shoulder; my knee took a pounding when I landed. I'm sure it's not broken, but I need a hand for a moment until it eases.'

'You need to get that leg looked at down the hospital; you could have damaged it.'

'Suppose you're right. You okay to help me get there?'

They both looked back up at the window, but, seeing it shut, they carried on, with Forest holding onto Johnny as he limped his way up the street.

'Thanks, Johnny, I'll be okay now; you go on home. I expect your mum will be wondering what's happened to you.'

'You sure? I don't mind waiting.'

'No. I'll be all right now. See you tomorrow.'

Johnny made his way home, thinking about the incident. He pictured Forest hurtling to the pavement and decided to mention it to Danny when he saw him next.

When a doctor checked his knee, he questioned how the accident happened.

'I don't believe you were jumping out of a first-floor window, son. Are you going to tell me the truth?'

'Okay, I was in a derelict building collecting firewood when a part of a wall fell onto my leg. That's the truth, doctor.'

'More like it. The next time you do anything silly like that, it may be your body arriving here in a canvas bag. A nurse will look after you: I have told her to put a cold compress on it and a bandage, seeing you've bruised it. And no more going into bombed-out houses; you know you are not supposed to do that. Understand what I am saying?'

'Yes, doctor; sorry.'

'You should be.'

Forest came away from the hospital hours later as it was getting dark and decided not to go home that night. Coming out of the hospital's entrance, he saw Johnny waiting for him.

'What are you doing here? I told you to go home.'

'I did. I told mum how you fell over hurting your leg, and she said you could come home with me tonight if you wanted. I never told her anything else about what happened.'

Walking into Johnny's house, Forest met Johnny's mum for the first time: she never said much, just a nod or a quick question. But he did get a sandwich, which he realised she could not really afford to give away. Putting a few coins in Johnny's hand, he told him he had a lucky encounter that morning picking up some money from a bomb-site he passed. It took a while for Johnny to accept it, but eventually he did.

With Danny and Eddie coming around the following day, Johnny secretly explained what happened and told them not to bring the subject up, as Forest might get funny talking about it.

Forest spent a couple of days at Johnny's house, and with the partly re-erected school finished early due to no more bombing raids, he went back to the hospital to have his bandages removed. Seeing a different doctor, a man of colour like himself, Forest wondered if he might get a good job one day and learn to become something more than what he was now – a nobody.

Chapter Twenty

Forest told the other boys that he would be going to his mum's friend's house for Christmas, one that he got on with that lived near the town centre. Eddie and Johnny accepted the lie, but Danny challenged him later on what he'd told them, unconvinced his mum would take him anywhere.

'You never said anything about this before. You sure you're not telling porkies?'

'It's a one-off, but it could all change. I'll have to wait and find out.'

'Mum's putting some decorations up at home today. She told me there'd be a Christmas dinner for you if you wanted one.'

He could imagine what Danny's table would look like if he went, but his mum would miss him if she was in the pub and needed him to take her home. 'Thank your mum for me, but I had better give it a miss.' Saying those words made his stomach cramp. 'Nice of her to offer.'

Heading home with a few pennies in his pocket, he stood opposite his house, seeing the curtains parted, and guessed his mum was out. Getting ready to move, he saw the front door open, and Ernest stood there, kissing his mum, before running off and looking at his watch. Forest hoped that wherever he was going, he'd be late and get into trouble; or better still, he would fall over and break his bloody neck.

His meetings with Nancy were becoming a regular event, as long as the weather wasn't too bad, which usually it was, but he welcomed her advances every time. Her friend, Flo, cornered him one afternoon, telling him she knew what he was doing with Nancy, and said to him she wouldn't say anything if he would meet her in the park, seeing she'd never had a boyfriend before. Looking at the girl, Forest guessed he had no choice but to indulge her.

'When do you want to see me?'

'Tonight, about seven. I can wait for you at the park gate.'

'Okay, at seven o'clock. But it will have to be a quick meet up; I have something on later.'

'Thanks, Forest, I'll be there.'

'Don't you dare say anything about this to Nancy; otherwise, I'll walk away. You understand what I'm saying?'

'I won't. See you at seven.'

'Okay.'

That evening, he met Flo, who was so much taller than Nancy and skinny with it. No meat to get hold of, and her ribs stuck out like a skeleton, and no titties to get hold of at all. Watching her dress and get ready to leave him afterwards, he knew he was skinny once, but nothing like her.

'Bye, Forest, can I see you again?'

Cringing at the thought, he tried to come out with an excuse. 'It will have to be in a couple of weeks. I'll let you know: I'm going to be busy with the boys.'

'Oh, all right, but I would like to see you again.'

Tucking his top in his damp shorts, he told her she had better run off in case someone found them together. Seeing the lanky strides as she ran away in her wet dress, he shook his head, wishing she was like her friend, chunky and spirited.

As the winter months moved into 1942, mudlarking days were few and far between. Eddie did take them to the hill slopes once more in March, but it turned out to be awkward as they found other boys playing there and fights happened, with Eddie getting a black eye and Johnny a broken tooth. Forest held his own, as did Danny, but seeing how many local kids there were, the four of them left. At the bus stop, Eddie had a moan.

'My face feels like it's swelling.'

'Guess this place won't be the same anymore, Eddie. You'll have a lovely shiner there tomorrow; you mark my words, I know!'

'You didn't help, hitting that kid: you could see how big his brother was.'

'He started on me first. I wasn't going to let him get away with what he said.'

'Johnny's got a toothache. His mum, like mine,

won't be too pleased with us going home like this. It's the last time I'm coming here.'

Danny could see Eddie was mad as he kept touching his eye. 'Here comes our bus.'

'Forest can get his own fare home; I'm not paying for him after this.'

'Don't be nasty, Eddie; if those kids come back...'

Johnny rubbed his tooth with a finger and watched as the boys they fought with came into view.

Danny pulled Forest nearer the bus stop. 'I'll pay for you. Let's get on the bus.'

The quiet trip home struck Danny how Forest's joining them had brought tears and laughter with his antics. But he knew how Eddie could be. Once he was upset about something, he guessed it was his mum coming out of him at times like this.

The following weekend happened to be warmer for the time of year, and, after some debate, the boys decided to try their luck in the mud. The water in the puddles was freezing as they clambered about. But pennies and the odd threepence came down. While Danny searched for a coin, he noticed something wedged under a flat piece of timber that had washed up further away.

'Hey, Johnny, looks like something is under that board over there. Shall we have a peek?'

'I'll have a nose. If it's something good, perhaps I can take it back for our mum. She's a little teary today.' Dragging himself through the mud, Johnny pulled his legs in and out of the slime, nearing the object. 'Something big, I think. If I can throw this board off it, I might be able to…' Suddenly, Johnny shouted, making everybody turn and look his way. 'It's a man! I think he's dead!'

Danny made his way over as Johnny hurried back, anxious to get away from the corpse.

'You sure it's not a mannequin?'

'That's no dummy. His eyes are open.'

Listening to the commotion, Forest left off searching for the halfpenny and passed Johnny. 'Have we got a dead body out there?' With no answer, he carried on past and met up with Danny, who was looking at the sailor lying in the mud. The people on the bridge, hearing the racket below, edged towards the railing, trying to see what was happening. Forest and Danny slid the piece of board completely from the sailor, and, sure enough, they could see the man was dead.

'We'd better let people know what we've found.' Turning, Forest cupped his hands and shouted up to the people on the walkway. 'Someone had better call the police. We've got a dead body in the mud.'

Within moments, the Sergeant-Major from the dockyard gate came running over the bridge, telling them to get out of the mud, which was easier said than done with the slimy harbour clinging to them. Eddie and Johnny were almost out of it, but Danny and Forest hung back, pretending they had difficulty moving. Next, two sailors arrived and stripped to their underwear, wading into the sucking slime. Both boys could see they were big men as they struggled towards them.

'They're not going to make it, Danny,' Forest said, and he shouted at them, 'You're too heavy; the mud will take you under.'

A policeman came along the bridge, looking out at the body.

Forest called up. 'You want us to pull him out, Copper?'

'No, leave him. Both of you get out of the mud.'

Of course, neither of them paid any attention to the policeman's order, and Danny shouted to the struggling men. 'Find someone lighter.'

The two sailors, hanging onto their underwear, returned with the Sergeant-Major, now onshore and cursing them for their inadequacy. Three more tried coming out, but the boys could see the same thing happening. The smaller matelot amongst them managed to get closer, and Danny called to him.

'Don't let your legs go too deep into the mud, or you will have trouble getting out. Lay flat if you have a problem, and we'll help you.' Seeing the nod and the other two men returning, Danny encouraged the man until he was alongside him and watched as one of the retreating sailors fell over, cursing aloud while spitting the foul mud from his mouth.

'You two boys all right? Any of you seen a dead person before?'

Danny shook his head, but Forest nodded, telling him he had seen one in London once, but saying no more as the sailor acknowledged his remark.

'We had better try and pull him out before the tide comes in. You, son,' the man spoke to Forest, 'can you try and close his eyes? The poor sod appears to be watching us.'

Being close to the man's head, Forest laid his hand over the eyes, feeling a softness there and trying not to think about what he was doing. Bringing his hand away, he felt worthy, knowing he had done what the sailor asked.

'Good, now let's get him ashore if we can.'

Danny took hold of the dead man's sleeve while Forest gripped his cold, clammy hand, seeing the sleeve was up around his elbow. With the sailor pulling on the other side, they inched the body across the harbour's mud towards the awaiting policemen and ambulance that had arrived.

Out of the mud, the police constable covered him over with a blanket, having checked his pockets, and it was then they all saw the knife in the man's back.

'No wonder he was hard to pull out, Danny, with that thing stuck in him,' whispered Forest.

The Sergeant-Major told the boys to wash off and then find him. Both thought they were in trouble as Eddie and Johnny looked on from a distance, having cleaned themselves. Eventually, they made their way to the dockyard gate.

'I bet this will be the last time we get to use the harbour, Forest.'

Seeing the Sergeant-Major stood there in his finery, the two boys crossed over to him, waiting for a telling-off of some sort.

'You did an excellent job getting that poor bugger out, boys. I appreciate what you did there.' Putting his hand in his pocket, he tossed both boys a sixpence, before returning to his position.

'Where are they taking him, Sergeant-Major?'

The look coming back told them there would be no answer.

'That wasn't so bad, Danny, and we got a tanner for it.'

'Touching his eyes as you did, I bet that was horrible?'

'Yeah, it made me a bit queasy, but as that sailor said, it wouldn't be right to leave his eyes open. If we find another one, I'll let you do it.'

'No way you will!'

Chapter Twenty-One

Finishing washing off the harbour from their shorts, the boys met up, while Johnny watched the ambulance pull away before he began asking questions.

'What was it like, Danny, pulling a dead body across the mud? Was he set upon and murdered? I saw the knife in his back.'

'Guess he could have been.'

'Was he stiff or slimy? He couldn't have been in the water that long with his eyes open. I can't believe Forest closed them. That gave me the creeps watching him do that.'

'Forest did most of the pulling with that matelot. They had his arms and hand; I just held onto his tunic.'

'What was it like, Forest?'

'Will you shut up about it, Johnny? I don't want to know all the gory details. I'm leaving. Are you lot coming?' Eddie walked ahead of the others as they continued to speak about the incident.

'I've seen dead'n's before when there was an accident in London's docks where I helped out. He wasn't that bad; otherwise, I wouldn't have fancied touching him. Me and Danny got sixpence out of it from the Sergeant-Major,' said Forest.

Eddie piped up from a distance. 'You're welcome to it.'

'Was it bad, Forest, the accidents, I mean, in London?'

'For someone who shouts and hollers when they see something like that, you want to know a lot.'

Eddie came back and stood with his hands on his waist. 'I don't want to hear about this stuff. Can we talk about something else, or I'm going home?'

Danny and Johnny pulled a face and stopped talking as Forest called out, 'Are you sharing out the money, Eddie?'

'I'll share it if you lot shut up.'

The boys stood there as Eddie counted the coins, and they all ended up with eleven pence each.

'We could have collected a lot more if that body wasn't there.'

'You pulled that board off of him, Johnny. That's your fault.'

Johnny gave Eddie a dirty look. 'What do you expect? It could have been something interesting.'

Danny grinned. 'Well, I think it was interesting enough, don't you?'

As the talk found its way back to the incident, Eddie called out, saying he was going home and would see them later. Walking on, Forest and Johnny went their own way, leaving Danny by himself. Reaching his house, he was about to go indoors when he saw his dad hurrying towards him.

'What's up, Dad?'

'Let's go indoors; I'll speak to you in your room. I need a word with your mother first.'

Climbing the stairs, he sat on his bed, wondering what his dad was going to say. He could hear him telling his mum something, then listened to the heavy footsteps coming up the stairs. With his heart beating quicker, he waited for his dad to come into the room.

'So, you and your friends are pulling dead bodies out of the mud now, is that right?'

Danny watched his dad's expression and waited for the ticking-off. 'We only offered to help when the first two sailors got stuck in the mud. They were too heavy and got bogged down, so we…'

'Son, I don't mind you mudlarking down there, but that body was in a dangerous place. The mud is treacherous that far out. Bert told me he was watching you do your bravery antics with Forest. Probably half the city did as well.'

Danny put his head down as his dad continued.

'I want you to promise me that will be the last time you do anything like that again, you hear me?'

'Sorry, Dad. I didn't think. I won't do it again.'

'Good. I'm pleased that's settled.' He ruffled Danny's hair, giving a little smile. 'I'm proud of you, son; not many people would do that. How do you feel?'

'Okay, I think.' Although, having thought about what he'd done, he felt his body tremble inside.

'Remember, stick to the bridge in future and earn

pennies like you usually do. I don't want to come home one day and find out something bad has happened. I don't think your mum could handle that as well as this war.'

Hearing his dad stomp down the stairs, he sat there, thinking about what he had said. It was the first time he had ever talked to him like that. He knew his dad was only a war warden because of his clubfoot and knew he had always wanted to enlist with his friends to serve his country. But he was glad he had stayed, even though he did some scary things, and now he had shown he loved him.

Eddie walked into the house to find his mum in another one of her moods. One of her neighbours had complained about her chickens, telling her she should share them with others so everybody could have an egg for breakfast or a nice roast dinner.

'Eddie, if you see anyone coming near those birds, you let me know, and I'll happily damage them with my rolling pin. They take a lot of looking after, and if that woman at number nineteen thinks she is going to…'

'Mum, calm down. She's just jealous, that's all.'

'I'll give her jealous if she tries to hurt one of my hens.'

On the other hand, Johnny found his mum in tears as she looked at the kitchen wall with the crack beginning to open up more and more.

'Bloody wall. Look at it; your dad and his fancy

bit.'

Johnny backed away, trying not to listen any more as his mum continued to rile about his dad's handiwork. He knew that whatever he said would make no difference. But he agreed the crack was getting bigger.

In an empty house, lying on his bed, Forest retrieved the gun he'd found and once more checked it over. Going into the back yard, he found a dead rat that he knew was still decaying and placed it on some bricks. Standing back, he aimed the revolver at the creature and pretended to shoot. Wishing he could do more, he ran into the house and checked out front to see if anybody was there. With the empty street and no neighbours, he came back and picked up the weapon, aimed, and this time fired at the carcase. Missing it by a few inches, he tried again, and blew the creature apart. Hurrying back to his room, he hid the gun and lay on his bed, thinking about what he could achieve if he aimed it at someone.

The following day, the four boys met up, making their way to the harbour, with Eddie ready to walk off should the talk find its way to corpses. Crossing the road towards the harbour railings, they all stopped when a loud whistle pierced the air. Turning, they saw the Sergeant-Major calling them over.

'Blimey, I hope he ain't stopping us from going in.'

Forest nudged Danny on his remark. 'If he tries, I'll sweet talk him.'

Stood alongside the uniformed man, the four studied him. His moustache was thick and generous, coming to a point at either end under his bulbous nose.

'So, the four musketeers are ready to do a bit of larking again, are they?' He glared at all of them. 'Just don't find any dead ones this time. I finish in an hour, and the last thing I want is for you lot to bugger it up for me.'

Forest saluted, right in front of him. 'If that's what you want, Sergeant-Major, leave it to us.'

'You are a cheeky bugger. Forest, they call you, is that right?'

Still saluting, he replied, 'It is that, Sir.'

'Go on, push off and behave yourselves.'

The boys ran off onto the harbour slipway, and as they were about to go further, Forest turned and shouted back, 'What's that over there beside that rowing boat? Is it…? No, no, it's all right, Sergeant-Major, it's just a piece of netting rolled up. Sorry about that.'

The fist that came back made them scarper towards the bridge, laughing as they went.

Eddie gave Forest a shove. 'You'll cop it one day down here; he'll lay in wait for you. You mark my words.'

The others slapped Forest about the body, playfully telling him what a wanker he was. When he asked them if they had been spying on him, the three of them fell about laughing and giggling with one another, although Eddie didn't seem that amused.

Chapter Twenty-Two

The month of March turned wet, cold and a bit snowy. Gone was the odd day of mudlarking. Johnny needed to collect firewood for his mum, and Forest likewise needed some to warm their cold house. Together, they raided some of the more severely damaged buildings, gathering pieces of window frames and broken joists. The boys were stopped twice in their searches by wardens, but they were allowed to continue after explaining what they were doing. Forest, being the more audacious one, reaffirmed to the men that they would never take anything from a house with the owner's possessions inside. With a firm response, the wardens told him he had better not or he would find the law speaking to him. With an axe and a saw, they managed to chop and cut up pieces of wood for their fireplaces, besides making a little profit by selling some bundles. Forest bought some clothes in the market when he had enough money, along with a good sturdy pair of shoes, and days later, he picked up a lovely warm overcoat off one of the carts, and he was sure the seller didn't realise what he had sold him. The warmth from it was unbelievable, knowing how it would keep him warm while waiting outside the pubs for his mum. Those evenings he needed to be alert should someone try and pick on him. Many a time, he had to scarper and hide as a drunken sailor or a malicious individual attempted to have a go at him just for the sake of it. One night, waiting in the cold and rain, a drunken bloke approached him, a Navy man with a funny lisp to his talk. Moving towards him, he asked in a strange voice if he wanted to earn some money, and if he did, not tell anyone. The man put his hand into his trouser pocket and revealed a ten-bob note, saying it could be his. The leering bloke smiled a peculiar smile with his lip broken under his nose, and he waited to see what would happen. Was he in for a shock?

'What do I have to do, mister?' Knowing damn well what.

The sailor beckoned Forest to follow him and turned into an alleyway beside the public house. Staggering, leaning against the brickwork for support, he stopped and took a long swig from the bottle of beer he had with him, before summoning Forest nearer. 'Let me get these pantaloons down; then it's all yours, Blackie.'

Forest cringed at the word and, bringing his foot up, smashed it into the man's groin, doubling him up as the pain shot through his body. The ten-bob note left his hand, fluttering to the ground, and Forest picked it up. 'My name's not Blackie, mister, understand?' Picking up a dustbin lid, he hit him across the head as he fell to the ground, cursing in pain. 'Whatever you're saying, the same to you, you tosser.' Seeing the man try and get up, he legged it up the alleyway, stuffing the note into his trouser pocket. Turning, looking back, he saw the sailor hit his head against the wall and collapse. 'Well worth ten-bob, mate. I just hope I don't see you again.' Sticking his nose into the pub door, Forest watched his mum as she downed a gin, telling the bloke with her to get her another. Leaving with the money in his pocket, he made his way towards the harbour, where he knew he could get pie and chips, along with a hot drink.

It was during the spring when the city took more shelling. On his own, seeing the other boys were having to do errands, Forest was passing the bridge where they mudlarked, when sirens sounded as two of Hitler's boys sneaked out of the clouds and began making a right mess around the city. The harbour railway station got shot up a bit, as did the other buildings along the jetty. The dockyard took a hammering, and suddenly our planes came over, chasing the Messerschmitts. People ran, trying to get away, and Forest huddled under the bridge where they put their clothes, watching the action as best he could. The dogfight above went on for some time as the planes spewed their ammunition. The noise was deafening as bullets tore into buildings. People ran for their lives, with some of them going down and not getting up. Explosions erupted behind the dockyard walls, sending columns of smoke high into the sky. Everything was happening so quickly as shells tore into buildings, and then suddenly it was over. A Spitfire had caught one of the Messerschmitt's as a plume of smoke trailed behind it, as it zig-zagged over the houses. Forest re-emerged from under the bridge and watched the remaining German get caught over the Solent as the fight eased. The Messerschmitt exploded in mid-air as cheers went up all around him. Back on the harbour walkway, Forest picked up a German shell that was intact and put it in his pocket.

Meeting up with the boys the next day, he talked about the battle and how he was under the bridge watching it, then pulled the German shell from his shorts.

Johnny studied it. 'Wow, is that from yesterday?'

Danny felt it in his fingers. 'Blimey, imagine that hitting you. It would pass straight through you. Is there any more about?'

'If there was, they're probably gone. You don't see things like this very often. Not in one piece like this one.'

'There's something on the bottom. It looks German, like an identification mark.'

Forest retrieved the shell from Eddie and put it back into his pocket. 'Whatever it is, it came from one of those downed fighter planes.'

The boys looked across at the smoke behind the dockyard wall.

'I wonder if the Sergeant-Major is okay. He's not standing at the gates like he usually is.'

'He's too keen-eyed to let one of those German planes come near him. I expect he's organising teams of men to what happened inside the dockyard. That's why the gates are closed.'

'I hope so: I'm beginning to like him since he gave us that tanner.'

Johnny saw Eddie's response to Forest's words as his face fumed. 'So, what are we going to do with ourselves? I imagine this place will need tidying up before we can get back.'

'I'll tell you what we can do.'

Eddie was calming down now the talk cleared. 'What's that, Danny?'

'The rowing boat my dad goes out fishing in, that's moored in the creek. If I can get his permission, he might let us go out in it as long as we stay local.'

'Do you think he will?'

'One way to find out. Are you all game for a bit of fun if my dad okays it? I know how to row.'

With everybody agreeing, they followed Danny to where he thought his dad would be. Nearing the harbour railway station, the boys waited as he spoke to one of the security guards who stood there, and saw the man point to just inside the damaged building.

Chapter Twenty-Three

With Danny rowing with one oar and Eddie the other, the four boys made their way into the more or less empty north area of the harbour, keeping away from any naval activity. Hopefully, the cloud-covered sky would thwart another bombing attempt on the city, especially with a Spitfire flying around. The boat's initial finding had been hilarious, with Forest and Eddie climbing into the wrong one and some old bloke shouting at them, telling them to sod off and leave his craft alone. He declared that the Germans hadn't touched it, so he was damned sure he wasn't going to let a bunch of scruffy kids ruin it. Eddie, being Eddie, jumped out of the craft into the water, getting his shoes and trousers wet, and more or less had to hold onto the side, saving himself from going into the water completely. Forest leapt from the back seat and landed more or less on the shore, much to Eddie's annoyance.

Forest checked out Eddie's lower half in Danny's dad's rowboat. 'Your trousers and feet drying out, Eddie?'

Danny stared at him as if to say, 'Leave it.' The last thing he wanted was for Eddie to stop rowing and want to go home. 'You'll soon dry out; it's getting warmer.'

'You don't have to put up with an earful from my mum as I do. The next time Danny points to something, make sure we all know what he's pointing at.'

In the front of the rowing boat, trying to navigate through the waters, Johnny and Forest bent over, trying not to giggle at the picture of Eddie making his escape from the boat with the owner shouting at him. Going around the north shore, Forest decided it was time to get his feet wet. He took his shoes and socks off, dangling his feet over the side and kicking them about in the water.

'Is the water cold?'

'A bit, but once you've got them in, it's all right. Take yours off and try it.'

Danny called out, 'Why don't you two try rowing the boat and let me and Eddie have a paddle?'

'You want to, Eddie? Don't forget to take your shoes off this time!'

'Sod off, Forest.'

'That's not nice. I didn't push you in.' He looked at Johnny while holding his hand over his mouth, trying to contain his emotions. 'Take all your clothes off. You can swim beside the boat, and I'll join you if you want me to.'

Danny stopped rowing and held onto Eddie's arm. 'Eddie, don't go getting silly; Johnny and Forest are only messing about. But you got to admit, it was funny.'

Eddie saw the grin coming at him and relaxed somewhat. 'Suppose it was a bit.'

'Forest, what are you doing? Keep the boat still, or you'll tip us over.'

Johnny shouted out, 'He's undressing, Danny; he's going in.'

'It will be cold in there, Forest; don't say I didn't warn you.'

The three boys watched as Forest, in his underpants, jumped off the rocking boat into the water, splashing them in the process. Johnny, eager to follow, did the same and shouted as he hit the cold water. 'So cold – you never said it would be this cold!'

'You'll get used to it. Danny, come on in, try it.'

'You okay to look after the boat, Eddie?'

Nodding his head, he waited for Danny to join the others. As soon as Danny jumped, Eddie grabbed both oars and began rowing away from the three of them. 'My turn to laugh. If you want a ride, swim after me.' Putting all his strength behind the rowing, he edged away from the others as they swam after him. 'I'm heading for that old castle. Catch me if you can.'

All three boys shouted towards the disappearing rowboat, cursing Eddie as he increased his speed, laughing at them. Forest, the strongest swimmer, managed to keep up with the boat, while threatening Eddie as he continued to call out taunts.

'When we get hold of you, Eddie, you're going in, clothes and all if necessary.'

'Can't see that happening, no way.'

Forest suddenly stopped swimming and waited for

the others, letting them catch up and pointing to where Eddie was heading.

'Those shallows, he's going to take the boat right into them. You two ready for a bit of fun?'

Seeing what Forest was talking about, Danny and Johnny grinned with him.

Unexpectedly, the rowing boat halted, and Eddie looked behind him, realising what had happened. Seeing the others nearing him, he stood up and shouted at them. 'Don't you dare try anything, Forest!' Taking an oar from its sleeve, he pushed the blade end into the mud, trying to free himself from the seafloor.

Forest, nearing the boat, called out, 'Want a hand, Eddie?'

'Come anywhere near me, I'll…'

Danny reached over the side and pulled himself into the craft. 'Why did you leave us, Eddie? We were only having a bit of fun.'

'I was only having a bit of fun as you lot did with me. There's nothing wrong with that. I wasn't going to leave you and Johnny out there.'

Forest caught hold of the side and butted into the conversation. 'If it was just me, you would have.'

'Take his clothes off first; otherwise, his mum will nag him for days.'

'Really, Danny, you'll let him get away with this?'

Johnny eventually pulled himself into the boat. 'Danny's right. His mum can be a pain sometimes.'

'And my mum ain't?'

'That's different.'

'Bloody right it is. I'll exchange places with him any time. He's getting too big for his boots.'

Eddie squealed and fought as the boys undressed him, before throwing him into the water.

With all the boys shoving the boat off the mud, Danny took over the oars. 'Come on, Eddie. Swim.'

As the boat edged nearer to Porchester Castle, Eddie trod the water, holding onto the back of the boat, pleading for Johnny to help him climb in.

'We're nearly at the shore: you can make it. Keep hold of the side and kick those legs.'

'Something's got hold of my foot; pull me aboard, please: it's got my toe. Pull me in, pull me in.' Eddie kicked his feet, trying to get rid of what was there. 'Johnny, Forest, help me, please, hurry.'

Forest put his hand out. 'It's probably a crab thinking your toe was something to eat. Take my hand, you big girl, and stop shouting.'

As Eddie came over the side, the crustacean became visible to them all. Danny stopped rowing and watched as Forest caught hold of the creature and gave it a knock on the top of its body with his knuckle. The sudden interference startled the thing, and it opened its pincers.

'Good job it's not a big one, Eddie, or you would have known all about it. Do you want to throw it back, or shall we take it home? Johnny, you fancy a crab tea tonight?'

'No. It's too small.'

Eddie took hold of Forest's hand and moved it over the side. 'Put it back, and let's get ashore. We all need to dry out before it gets too cold. Sorry about earlier. I would never have left you.'

Forest wondered about that.

The rest of the afternoon quickly passed as the boys investigated the castle's remains and climbed the high tower: looking across the harbour to the hill they played on with the linoleum. The return trip passed without incident as the boys told stories to one another, but it was Forest who put them in stitches with his almost unbelievable tales of the nightlife while waiting for his mum. Once ashore, the man who shouted at them was still there, and they gave him a wide berth, seeing him look their way, with Forest giving him the finger when he wasn't looking.

Chapter Twenty-Four

The summer came, and the war continued; then, one hot, cloudy Saturday, the boys were ready to go mudlarking and waited for Forest to turn up at the harbour. But unbeknown to them, their friend had spent a fitful night in the derelict building opposite his house. Opening his eyes to see the curtains pulled back, Forest knew it was now safe to enter the house. He hurried across the street and opened the front door. Inside, he heard a deep voice laughing in the front room. Standing still, he held the door, ready to flee.

'Forest, come in the front room a minute: there's someone I want you to meet.'

Listening to his mum's words, he moved forward, worried about what he was letting himself in for. Alert, he crossed into the room and saw this big black Army bloke sitting with his mum, drinking beers.

'We've got company, Forest. Come in and meet your father.'

At those words, Forest felt his stomach shift and his legs weaken.

'I met him in the Lord Nelson. He was with some friends. Hurry up, come and say hello.'

The huge man stood up and crossed towards him,

putting his hand out. 'So, you're my boy.'

'He's my special boy, too, Louie, always looking after his mother. Where have you been? Spending time at a friend's house, I suppose.'

Forest turned towards his mum as she uttered those never-heard-before words and laughed inwardly at them. All his life, she had never worried about him, let alone thought about him. Suddenly, the grip taking his hand returned him to the person before him.

'Hi, Forest, so how old are you? Thirteen, Fourteen, I would guess.'

'Spot on, Lou, and he's got your eyes and mouth. He's going to be a looker when he's older, just like his dad was.'

Louie sat back down and picked up his beer. 'You saying I don't look handsome now, woman. You hear that, Forest? Come and sit next to me, son.'

Moving to a chair alongside the Army man, he studied him further. He was darker than him, with hair cropped to almost nothing. He wanted to cry and hold onto him for some reason, but how could he?

'Never knew anything about you until an hour or so ago. You got any mates you play with?'

He explained about his three friends, without saying anything about mudlarking, seeing his mum was there and knowing how his earnings would disappear if she found out.

'Good to have buddies, Forest. Do you have any problems being different? You know what I mean, don't you?'

'One or two, but nothing to worry about.' He would have loved to tell this man about his life and the problems his mum gave him with her customers.

'It can be a cruel old world out there, son. Make sure you look after yourself. Do you do any workouts?'

'What's that?'

'Fitness training, lifting weights and fighting in a ring, strengthening your body.'

'Can't say I do.'

'I would if I were you. You never know when you might need a bit of strength in that body to look after yourself. Look at me; this body has handled many a problem. No one picks on me. You want to pop out for an hour or so while I have a chat with your mum about old times?' Louie put his hand into his pocket and pulled out some coins and notes. 'Here's a pound; you go and have a bit of fun with it, seeing I had a bit of luck, so spend it on whatever you like, and don't lose it. I will see you later. Your mum's letting me stay the night, seeing I have a bit of leave. Then we can have a good talk. Would you like that?'

The tears came to Forest's eyes as his father placed the pound note into his hand.

'You push off now and enjoy that money.'

'Thanks, Dad, I mean Louie, thanks a lot.' He could see his mum's eyes studying the one-pound note in his hand. There was no way he was letting her get her hands on it. 'I'll get my mates an ice cream, and then we can go to the picture house.'

'Good. Now beat it while your mum and me have a few hours together.'

Forest charged up the stairs and hid the pound note in his bedroom under the floorboard. Changing into his old shorts and top, he ran down the stairs and waved at his dad, before legging it down to the harbour.

Wondering why Forest didn't turn up, Danny guessed there was a problem at home, as the others did. Reluctantly, they carried on, knowing they could do nothing about it. No one talked about their friend not arriving as they called out for the odd coin, yet in their faces you could see they were wondering what might have happened.

Seeing the boys in the mud, Forest removed his shoes and top and joined them. Out of breath, he hastened alongside Danny.

'What you looking so happy about?'

'I've just met my real dad; he's at home with my mum, and he's staying the night. He gave me a pound note like it was sixpence and told me I could do what I like with it.'

All three boys stopped what they were doing.

'He gave you all that?'

'He did, Johnny. Any money I get with you today, I'll let you keep it.'

Danny saw for the first time just how happy he was and was thrilled for him. 'I'm pleased for you, Forest.

What's he like?'

'He's a Yank, in the Army on leave. He's with mum at the moment for old times' sake, I suppose.'

Eddie nudged Johnny and whispered to him, 'Another Forest coming, I expect.'

'I heard that, Eddie. If it is, it's sod all to do with you.'

Johnny, feeling awkward, came over to him. 'He didn't mean anything. Is he like you?'

'Blacker, if that's what you mean. And he seems a nice bloke.' Forest saw a penny drop into the mud beside him. 'He never knew about me. He's going to talk to me tonight about things.'

'You're not angry with Eddie, are you?'

'No, I get used to kids taking the piss out of me. Thought he might have got over me being different by now.'

Eddie searched for a coin, trying to get away from the conversation.

'I know your mum gets on at you, Eddie, but I don't know why you're always so stupid at times. Why do you…?'

'Forest.' Danny put his muddy hand around him. 'Leave it. Eddie's in the dog-house again at home. Some of his mum's chickens have stopped laying eggs, and she's having a go at him for not feeding them properly.' Forest went to say something else, but Danny pulled him around, shaking his head. 'Leave him; you know what he's like. He can't help it.'

By late afternoon and having washed themselves off, they made one shilling and five pence each. Having pocketed his coins, Eddie made his farewells to the others, telling them he needed to leave, should his mum want him.

'Johnny, I know Eddie was right about Louie – that's my dad's name – being with mum. But it's the way he says it. You all know what happens to me at home, but I try to look after myself.'

Danny wasn't so sure about that. 'You had better make a move. I expect he's waiting for you; you've got a lot of catching up to do. Where's he from in America?'

'Don't know; I'll have to ask him about that. Here, Johnny, take my money. You need it more than me today.'

Johnny stood there, unsure about taking it.

Danny came over. 'Go on, Johnny, take it. Your mum will be pleased.'

'Thanks, Forest. Thanks a lot.'

Walking into the house, Forest found it extra quiet. Calling out, he searched the rooms upstairs, but there was no one there. With his eyes getting watery, he dropped onto his bed and lay down, when the front door opened, and he heard the distinct voice of his mum call out.

'You in, Forest?'

Wiping his eyes, he hurried downstairs and watched Louie put bottles of beer and lemonade onto the table.

157

'Thought you might like a drink with me later. Your mum's got some fish and chips in the kitchen, lovely big pieces. You like fish?'

'You bet, Louie.'

Chapter Twenty-Five

The evening was one Forest would never forget. Louie began to tell him of his home back in America and how his family had moved from the south of the country, where being coloured was unsafe and sometimes perilous. He told him about his folks who worked on a plantation picking cotton and how they eventually moved north and settled in Chicago, where he was born. Fascinating details came out, like when Louie sang in nightclubs and had a following of women chasing after him. Transfixed with the accounts Louie portrayed, he imagined how that life must have been a great adventure.

'I bet you had a good time, Louie?'

Putting his empty beer bottle on the table, Louie flashed a brilliant smile as Forest replaced it with another.

'It wasn't always enjoyable. I had to watch out for myself, as did others like me. Living in the ghettos in cramped accommodation, with gangs and guns being a way of life, you needed to watch out for certain people, not only white folks. In almost every city in America, there was some kind of segregation or hostility within spitting distance. North as well as the South. I saw things as a kid that I would never want to see again.'

Shocked at his dad's revelation, he changed the subject. 'Are you involved in the war?'

'My whole life has been a war; this one isn't so bad for me.'

'But are you fighting the Germans?'

'Not me. I'm going over there, but I'll be firing the big guns when I get there. That'll be in two days when I ship out.'

Forest watched his dad take a swig from his bottle, not wanting him to leave having discovered him. 'Do you still sing?'

'Sure, I can knock a tune out and pull the ladies.' Louie looked at Forest's mum as she came into the room with a gin bottle and put it on the table, realising how this woman had worn and changed so much since he went with her all those years ago.

'I need to pee, Louie. Stay with Forest; he seems to like you.'

'Louie?'

'What is it, son.'

'Have you got a family in America?'

Louie wondered when Forest might ask that question. 'I have a wife and kids: two boys and a girl. The boys are teenagers doing their own thing, but the girl is only twelve. It's a shame your mum never had any more kids like you.'

At that moment, he wanted to ask if he would take him back home to America with him, but he would be devastated if Louie told him *no*.

The following evening, Louie was gone; and, sitting on his bed, Forest burst into tears, knowing the life he had was going to be the only one he could look forward to. With Danny and the others not coming around, he stayed in his room, imagining the life he might have lived in America. Then the front door opened, and voices came up the stairs. Closing his bedroom door, he sat on his bed and looked out of the window with his mind elsewhere. The cloudy night sky showed hope of a quiet night, except for his mum's room and her overused bed.

The two men came up the stairs with her, laughing and swearing, joining her in her room; and then he heard her door close. Deciding he was safe, he laid down on his bed, trying not to think of his life and picturing having brothers and sisters. He wondered what they would look like: would they have similar features to him, would they be darker or lighter? More tears entered his eyes as he wiped them away with his hand.

He didn't know how long he had slept, but something woke him. Opening his eyes wider, he struggled with reality and saw a dark shape standing in his doorway. Sitting up, still in his clothes, he decided it was time to leave, when a voice entered his ears, one that he had heard before. Realising he was in a dangerous situation, the moonlight showed him exactly who it was. Suddenly, a calloused hand shot out and grabbed his neck, pulling him towards the frightening figure.

'Remember me, boy?'

Forest knew he had to try and get away as the lisped alien voice penetrated his head.

'I've already paid for this service. Now I think it's time to collect.'

The blow across his face knocked Forest backwards across the floorboards until he hit the wall. Gripped and lifted off the floor, he stared into the face of the man he'd met before. The hair-lip snarled at him as another hand smacked him against his ear, where the pain shot through his head.

'You stay where I can see you, you little thief.'

'That's my mum in the other room; she…'

'Screw your mum and screw you. I've paid for it, remember?'

Caught between the window and the man, Forest saw him attempt to drop his trousers while fumbling with his buttons as the drink inside him aggravated his efforts. Then, the man's trousers fell to his ankles. Seeing no way out, Forest looked out of the window.

'No one out there to save you, boy.'

Making another grab for his captive, another round of blows came at him as he attempted to defend himself. Then the sailor slammed his bedroom door shut, and he knew his only chance of getting out of the room had gone. With his hair in the man's fist, he cried out, wanting his mum to come in.

'She won't help; she's too pissed to move off the

bed with my mate on top of her.' Taking another swipe at his prey, the man slapped Forest's face, bringing blood from his nose, and pushed him away. Kicking off his trousers, he stood there aroused, glaring at the little git that had taken his money and attacked him. Grabbing himself, he glared at him. 'You ready for this, boy?'

Panicking, Forest looked out of the two paned windows and, with his arm up for protection, threw himself through one of the panes of glass, feeling the jagged edges tear into him. As he landed in a heap on the pavement, the other pane of glass fell out of its frame and came crashing down on top of him. Sharp fragments and splinters of the window tore into him as he looked up at the angry face glowering down. The relief of escaping took away the agony of glass cutting into his skin.

'You little bleeder, I'll get you yet, now I know where you live; you wait and see if I don't.'

Finding his feet, Forest saw the blood staining his clothes and felt the cuts to his body as he awkwardly stood up, swearing all the words he knew at the sailor above him. With every move he made, he felt his skin tear, allowing more blood to soak over him. Some people in the distance looked across at the disturbance; but, seeing him stand, guessed that whatever was happening, they didn't want to get involved. He walked the best he could towards the hospital, some distance away, in his red-stained clothes. It took him a while as he dodged people should they want to try and help or get an ambulance, but he knew he would end up in a worse state if his mum became involved and the sailor was still there. After some uncomfortable walking, he saw the hospital entrance and walked into the emergency door covered in blood.

Chapter Twenty-Six

Seeing Forest walk into the hospital, three nurses came rushing towards him, concerned about his state. An elderly, hard-talking nurse took hold of him, and he screamed as the glass splinters cut deeper into him. Seeing he was in trouble and noticing the jagged fragments, she told another nurse to look after him as more patients came through the door.

'What on earth have you done to yourself? There's glass all over you. I will have to undress you and see what you have done. What happened?'

He decided he had to lie about everything and began his story. 'I was collecting firewood when this pane of glass fell on me from high up.'

'It is a wonder you are still alive, the state of you. Anyone would think a butcher had attacked you with one of his knives. What is your name?'

'It's Forest.'

'Can you walk in those plimsolls? I can see the glass in them.'

'Just about, nurse. Sorry about this.'

'My name is Margaret. Let me clean you up. What a mess you are. Look at your poor face. Have you been in a fight? Because it looks as though you have.'

'No, but it does feel like it.'

Margaret took him into a small room and began to take his clothes off. She needed to stop often as a piece of glass got snagged in his clothing, ripping his skin, making him bleed more. Although in agony as she removed fragments from his body, he knew she was trying hard not to hurt him too much. With his plimsolls, shirt and shorts off, Forest stood there in his underpants as she removed slither after slither of glass. Her uniform changed from white to red as his blood stained her clothing.

'Where do you live?'

'I live with my mum in town, but she's away at the moment. I was on my own when this happened.'

'When is she coming back?'

'Tomorrow afternoon.' Forest crossed his fingers behind his back. 'She'll go mad when she sees me.'

'You are one lucky boy: do you know that? This could have killed you.'

He knew how lucky he was, getting away from lispy. The thought of what could have happened terrified him more. 'Margaret, I mean nurse…'

'Yes.'

'Thank you for helping me, and I'm sorry about your uniform.' The slight smile that came back assured him what a lovely person she was. 'Have you got another one?'

'I have, and I will change once I have sorted you out, young man.'

The time ticked by, and with her magnifying glass she kept finding little pieces penetrating his skin. 'Forest, I need you to remove those underpants you are wearing I can see there are some blood stains on them. Take them off for me, please.'

He knew what would happen if he did. All the time she had been laying her hands on him, he had to control himself. If he took his underwear off… 'Do I have to?'

'There is nothing there I have not seen before. I cannot leave without checking you down there. If a piece of glass stays embedded in you, it would only cause you problems later.'

Turning his back to her, he stepped out of his pants and held onto his private parts.

'See, here is a piece in your bottom. Sit on that, and you would know all about it.'

Forest felt her fingers going around his buttocks and tried hard not to think about what she was doing.

'Another piece! Are you sure you told me the truth about a pane of glass falling on you?'

'Yes.' He dared not say anything else as he gripped himself tighter.

'I think that is all. Turn around for me, please.'

Forest stood there, unable to move.

'Turn around, Forest, I have to do this.'

'I can't. Is there anyone else that could…?'

'I'll see if the doctor is available; stay there and don't move. I don't want you slipping on all this blood on the floor.'

Within a few minutes, the older nurse came in and, seeing him standing there holding himself, she pulled his hand away and took hold of him. 'Men and boys, you are all the same. Now let me see what you wouldn't let the nurse look at, although I've seen too many to worry about those horrible things.' Suddenly, he yelped as the matron gripped a splinter of glass from the side of his now shrivelling member. 'That could hurt if you started playing with it. I can see another in your scrotum. Two more pieces. Hold still a moment.'

Forest forgot all about his modesty as the abrupt matron pulled and pushed him around.

'I will let the nurse come back and tidy you up now you've settled that thing. Don't let it happen again.'

Holding himself once more, Forest waited for the nurse to arrive when a voice called out.

'Are you decent, Forest? Is it all right for me to come in?'

'Yes. Sorry, nurse.'

'Next time, matron will take over completely. I will check you over once more, so let me know if you feel anything.'

Her hands started to wander all over his body as his eyes went up into his head, trying hard not to let his thoughts wander.

'I think I have got all the pieces out. I am going to dress those wounds, and you are going to have to stay in the hospital tonight. Is there somebody I can telephone, or can I send for your mother?'

'No, she will only worry. Can you leave it until tomorrow?' Forest gave a story about his mum being with a sick relative, hoping the nurse would believe him. With several stitches, bandages and numerous plasters stuck all over him, he stood there otherwise naked.

'I don't know if I believe you or not. Let me put this gown on you, then you can sit in that wheelchair for a moment, and I will take you to your bed. Don't fidget too much, should there be any more pieces of glass in that body. If you do, those stitches could open.'

Every time the nurse passed him, he caught her fragrance and inhaled it, sending warmth into his not very warm body. With a hot drink and a couple of tablets inside him, and a couple of digestive biscuits, he slept in the high bed, fingering the crisp-white sheets while dreaming of Margaret looking after him. Wide awake the next morning, he saw a doctor with the matron at his side and responded to the doctor's questioning.

'They say a pane of glass fell on you, is that correct?'

Yes, it was an accident.'

'Some accident, young man. With all those cuts over your body, I would have said you jumped through a skylight or a window. You may still have one or two pieces of glass embedded in that body, but they will make their way out by themselves. If you start bleeding, you must come back, and we will look again. Today you will stay in that bed. Those cuts need time to close over, so no getting out of bed and no fidgeting. If you need to go to the toilet, let the nurse know, and she will bring something for you. Stay there, and I do not want to see you again. Understand me?'

'Yes, Doctor.'

He watched the doctor speak to the matron and shake his head, before turning to the next patient. The day was boring lying there. He tried to talk to other patients, but with them being older men and frowning at him when he did, he gave up and slept whenever he could.

'Forest, are you awake?'

Opening his eyes, he saw Margaret staring back at him with that beautiful smile she had. 'Hello, nurse. I see you've changed.'

'With all that blood covering me, I needed to. I have come to see how your body is recovering. How do you feel today?'

'A little sore, but okay, I suppose.'

With the curtain pulled around the bed, the nurse checked Forest, should any bandages have bled. After checking him over and him behaving himself, the nurse told him he could leave.

'My clothes?'

'I had to throw them away. They were in such a state. I am sorry.'

'I don't have any more.'

Going behind the curtain, the nurse returned with a bundle of clothing. 'I found these; I think they will fit you. I kept your plimsolls; they were not too bad, but you will need to wash them. There is a belt should you need it.'

He looked at the decent clothing, seeing they were of good quality.

'Now, you get dressed. Do you want me to help you?'

'No, I'll be okay. Thanks for giving them to me.'

'Let me know when you are ready, and I will come back.'

Leaving the hospital, Forest made his way home, anxious about what he would find.

Chapter Twenty-Seven

Glass still covered the pavement as Forest walked into his street. His window had a blanket covering it, and he stood there watching it flap about in the wind. The house looked empty, but the last thing he wanted was for the sailor to be there. After many minutes of standing across from the house, he needed to get indoors as the cold began to bite into him. With apprehension, he opened the front door and called out, 'Mum, you in?'

A deadly silence came back as he edged his way towards his bedroom. The room was a mess where the scuffle had occurred, and his bed was tipped over. Hurriedly, he made for the hiding place where his pound note was. Removing the floorboard, he put his hand inside and, with relief, found what he was looking for and placed it further back, keeping it safe. Searching once more, he retrieved the revolver and was determined to use it if he had to.

Not seeing the other boys for the best part of a week, he allowed his cuts and bruises to clear and removed his bandages and facial plasters when he could. Twice, he had heard his name called from the street, but each time he stayed away from the hole-in-the-wall while listening to his friends speaking about his damaged window.

With the summer having left, Forest continued to collect wood with Johnny from the bombed-out buildings during the day, and the evenings began to show the colder months were on the way. Then, in October, Forest's school closed, leaving him without education. Not knowing where he would end up, Danny's mum intervened, and he wound up in Danny's and Johnny's class. Both boys helped him settle in and realised how good he was with his subjects, especially his arithmetic. Eddie, being in another classroom, kept his distance with any help.

During the middle of the month, things got troublesome for Eddie at home when one of his mum's birds disappeared. There were feathers all over the garden when his mum went out one morning. Instantly, she thought some animal had come in and got into the henhouse. Securing the wiring and making sure the lock was strong, she got Eddie to reinforce the wooden doors on it; and then, three days later, the same thing happened again. Wondering if one of her neighbours she had words with had come in during the night, she made herself comfortable in the kitchen and stayed up all night. Two nights later, at four o'clock in the morning, she caught the bugger. He was a rough-looking character about eighteen, skinny as a rake and sickly looking. Coming out of the kitchen with her rolling pin as quietly as she could, she let fly with the wooden club, giving him what for as the thief yelped at his treatment and tried to get away.

'You've had two of my birds, but you won't have another, you thieving swine.' She continued to bring the rolling pin down on the man as he tried to scale the garden fence. 'I'll have the law onto you, you ever try this again, you bugger. I know what you look like now.'

The fence creaked as the burglar managed to get one leg over, and still Eddie's mum threatened him and whacked him until he hit the pavement on the other side, before legging it as fast as he could. 'Don't come back, or you'll get more next time.'

At the shore on Saturday, Eddie told his mates of the incident as the four boys watched the harbour's naval vessels, hoping they would soon move off and let the ferry passengers continue their journey. With few people crossing the bridge, another group of kids came onto the mud, some they hadn't seen before. The boys in the group, seeing Forest, decided to have a bit of fun and picked on him, calling him all sorts of names. Danny and Johnny jumped into their midst and told them they could have trouble if they wanted it. Eddie, too, unexpectedly stood up as he towered over most of them. Used to the insults, Forest ignored most of them, until one of the two girls with them came over and spoke to him.

'We hardly ever see a coloured kid, only the occasional Navy bloke that comes ashore.'

Forest was waiting for her to continue when a

couple of coins fell into the mud beside the bridge. Going for them, she followed him and spoke again, before he turned back towards the others and called out, 'She wants to know if I'm this colour all over.' Then he pulled his shorts down, showing her his backside.

'Forest. Pull them up, or we'll get thrown off the mud.' Danny, amazed at Forest doing it, looked at the others. 'I can't believe he did that.'

The girl, in her middle teens, put her hand on her hips and called out to Danny, 'I don't know why he didn't turn around; ain't nothing I ain't seen before, is there, Charlie?'

'Shut your mouth, Fanny, or I'll shut it for you.'

'Like to see you, Charlie Butkins. It'll be the last time you stand upright in this mud.'

Eventually, the situation calmed down, with crowds crossing the bridge. By late afternoon, having collected enough money, Danny, Johnny and Eddie began to make their way off the mud, and Danny noticed the girl, Fanny, was still with Forest just under the bridge supports, almost out of view. Eddie stopped, seeing Forest look his way, grinning with that full set of teeth of his as the girl had her hand down the front of Forest's shorts.

'Is she doing what I think she's doing?'

Johnny answered, 'Borrow my glasses, Eddie. You'll see much better. I hope those people up there don't realise what's happening under them.'

'If he mucks this up for us, he can find someone

else to go around with.'

Danny, witnessing the spectacle, looked around, hoping no one other than them was watching. Then the girl, with a don't care attitude, walked off to her friends, while Forest adjusted himself and made his way off the mud.

'Forest, I can't believe you did that.'

'She wanted to do it, Eddie. I didn't ask her.'

'It's disgusting. That's what it is.'

Danny pulled Forest to one side. 'He's right this time. If you got caught, we could lose out coming down here.'

'Sorry, Danny, something I couldn't say no to.'

Johnny, washing the mud from his shorts, called out, 'Other things on your mind, Forest, or should I say your dick!'

Danny creased up as Johnny and Forest did, but Eddie turned his back, keeping a straight face, making them laugh a lot more.

The days passed, and the weather worsened, as Johnny and Forest kept up their hunt for firewood. In the evenings, Forest sat outside pubs waiting for his mum to come home unaccompanied and a bit tipsy. One night, while seated in a doorway, Forest kept back in the darkened space and witnessed two men fight one another in the road in front of him. The Navy bloke was massive, and the other one, a Marine, appeared to handle himself as they grappled on the ground in front of him. Both men were bleeding well, and the language hurled at each other ensured the fight would continue. After what seemed like half an hour, they tired of their contest and, with bloody noses and cut faces, they pushed one another, unable to find the stamina to prolong their battle. Seeing their slow movements, Forest glimpsed the purse lying in the gutter that had fallen from one of the men's pockets. With their backs to him as they sat on the road, trying to continue, he eased himself from the shadows, more or less crawling over the pavement in his dark overcoat. Nearing the purse, he picked it up as quick as lightning from its location and returned to the darkened doorway. Feeling the weight in it, he waited for the men to leave, hoping whoever it belonged to wouldn't check for it until he had gone. As soon as they moved away, he ran off, and with the partial moon giving him enough light, he opened the clip and discovered enough money, with what he already had, that would last him well over Christmas and into the coming year.

Chapter Twenty-Eight

The air raids continued as the war did, and Danny, one Saturday afternoon, called on Forest. Stood outside, he tried calling him through the blanket as it flapped about, and he wondered how on earth he could sleep in that room, knowing how long it had been there. Having knocked on the door, he edged away, should one of Forest's mum's customers be inside, and waited across the street. With nothing happening, he walked away, when Forest came along.

'Danny, what are you doing here?'

'I've got a free afternoon. Dad said I could go out if I wanted.'

'Great, what do you fancy doing?'

'How about the Pally, me and you? The others can't make it.'

'*Buck Rogers* is showing at the Shaftesbury. Fancy that?'

The boys made their way to the cinema, but they had to pay this time. After the film, Forest informed Danny that the woman on the desk at the Pally was leaving, or already had, and the new woman was a bit stuck-up, according to her, and probably wouldn't let him in. Making their way home, Danny spoke about

Christmas.

'Forest, it'll be Christmas Day in a couple of weeks. What do you do with yourself? I know you didn't do anything last year.'

'I don't do Christmas, Danny, never have.'

'You mean you and your mum don't have a get-together and give a present to each other?'

'I don't think I've ever seen mum for more than ten minutes on Christmas Day in all the years that I can remember. She does her thing, you know what I mean, and I loaf around the pubs making sure she's all right. Sometimes I might see her for a while, but not often.'

Danny couldn't believe he had never had some kind of celebration. 'You could have come to our house last Christmas; you told me you were going to stay with someone.'

'I know, but it never happened.'

'Don't your mum give you an orange or an apple? Don't she give you anything?'

'No. It don't bother me. Why should it?'

Danny couldn't believe he never had a proper Christmas and felt guilty bringing the subject up. Angry, he realised just how cruel his mum was to him: the home life he had, the set-to with the men she brought home, and not feeding him properly. 'Forest, I'm inviting you to our house on Christmas Day. My mum will give you dinner and expect a present, even if it is an apple or orange.'

'You don't have to do that, Danny. I get by.'

'Well, you're not this year; you're coming to my house, and that's final.'

As the days got nearer to the twenty-fifth of December, Johnny stopped coming to school, so the three boys went around to his house, but it was deserted, or seemed that way. Then, on Sunday, when the boys were all worried about him, he turned up.

'Where have you been, Johnny? Our teacher didn't know what was happening when we asked her. We've been around to your house a few times looking for you.'

Eddie and Forest nudged Danny to say more, seeing Johnny stay quiet.

'What's the matter?'

'My dad's dead.'

'Christ, I'm sorry, when did you find out?'

Johnny's eyes watered, and he spoke so softly, the three boys had a job hearing him. 'He and his lady friend were in a fire engine up in London. I don't know what they were doing up there, but a burning building fell on them. A friend of mum's sent a letter; it happened a while back.'

All the boys told Johnny they were sorry and stood around, unsure what to say.

'Forest, you ain't got a toffee on you? I could fancy one right now.'

Treacle toffees emerged, and Forest handed them out to everyone, although Eddie declined.

'Going upmarket, Forest? These ain't cheap.'

'I didn't nick them, although the way Eddie's looking at me, he thinks I did. One of mum's friends gave her a jar full. Mind you, *he* could have. You want some more?'

Johnny took some, putting them into his trouser pocket. 'Thanks, Forest.'

Danny decided to ask, 'Johnny, how's your mum with the news?'

'She's all right. She was upset when we heard. Her sister, that's where we've been in the country, she told us. Mum sent a letter to the school; I guess they didn't get it.'

'How are you, Johnny?'

'I'm all right, Eddie. Dad left us, and now this happened. Fate, I suppose. Me and mum are going to her sister's for Christmas, so I don't expect I'll see you lot after tomorrow. Is your dad coming home?'

'Don't know; we've not heard from him.'

'What about you, Forest? Danny said you're going to his house on Christmas Day; that right?'

'Think so.'

'He is, so I hope he's got me an apple or something.'

The three boys watched as Johnny walked off, with his mum calling him, and wondered when they would see him again.

'Just the three of us, then.'

Eddie walked into his home to find his mum in an

anxious state, talking to herself and noisily moving things around.

'Mum, what is it?'

'*That*. That's the matter.' She pointed to a letter that stood on the mantelpiece above the fire. 'I'm not opening it. The last thing I want to…'

Eddie listened, as she never ended her sentences. 'Mum, it could be about dad. You've got to open it; it could be anything.'

'You open it, and don't you dare tell me if it's bad news.'

Eddie hurried to the letter and opened the envelope carefully. With the military paper in his hands, he read something he didn't want to. With his mum across the room watching him, he looked at her as tears ran down his face.

'Oh, no. Oh, no, he's not dead. Please tell me he's not dead.'

'He's missing in action, Mum. I know he's a good swimmer. It would take more than a sub or another ship to hurt dad. Mum, I know he's alive.' Running up the stairs, Eddie fell on the bed, pushing his face into his pillow. 'You are alive, dad. I know you are. Please don't die.' With his fingers crossed under his pillow, Eddie listened to his mum downstairs, banging around doing something while talking to herself.

On his bed, Eddie wondered what time it was and reached for his clock as darkness surrounded him. The luminous hands showed eight fifteen, and he put his legs over the single bed, listening for a sound in the quiet house. Going downstairs, Eddie called for his mum, seeing all the lights were off. Going into the kitchen, he found her sitting in a chair, staring at the letter in her lap.

'Mum.'

She looked up at him and smiled, something he didn't usually see. 'Put the letter on the shelf, Eddie; we mustn't take it as… you know what I mean. What do you want for your tea, an omelette? The hens have been good today.'

'You all right, Mum. Don't give up on dad. Please.' He watched her pull the curtains and put the light on, then go about as though nothing had happened, and she never answered the question.

It was four days before Christmas, and Eddie's mum informed him they were going to her brother's house on the other side of Petersfield for the holidays, and they wouldn't be back until the New Year.

'But what about if dad comes home, Mum? Don't you think we should stay here?'

'I will leave a note on the table, should that happen; but I am not staying here. Your cousin Kevin will be there; you like him.'

Eddie looked towards the letter on the shelf. 'Mum, how will dad get in if we go? He won't have a key.'

'He knows where I keep the spare one. Now, no

183

more talk about your father.'

Eddie tried one more time to convince his mum to stay, until she shouted at him, telling him in no uncertain words that they were leaving and her brother would collect them the next day.

'If you want to say goodbye to your friends, do it now; otherwise, it will be too late.'

Making his way to Danny's, he knocked on the door and asked if he was home.

'Eddie, what are you doing here?'

'Mum's just told me we are going to her brother's for Christmas and the New Year. The chickens are coming with us – can you believe it?' Eddie stood there momentarily, before he continued, 'We've had a letter saying dad's missing in action.'

'And your mum's going away?'

'She's all upset and doesn't want to talk about it. I don't want to go.'

Danny could see he was having trouble telling him about his dad as his eyes told him how he felt. 'I'm sorry, I know your dad: he's a strong man. If anybody can come home, it would be him.'

'That's what I told mum, but she won't listen.'

'When are you leaving?'

'Tomorrow afternoon. She said my uncle is collecting us,' Eddie said, shuffling his feet, not wanting to walk away. 'Is Forest still coming to your house for Christmas?'

'I've told him to come. He'd better turn up. Mum's

cooking extra food.'

'See you later, then.'

Danny heard his mum call him. 'I'll tell Forest you've gone. See you next year.'

Chapter Twenty-Nine

Keeping out of his mum's way, Forest counted out his coins, sat in his cold room, and noticed how they were diminishing, after he had bought something for Danny and his family. The gun was still with him, and with nothing else to do, he retrieved it once again and checked it over. Hearing laughter come down the street, he lifted the blanket, feeling the bitter evening. Seeing his mum walking with a familiar face, he knew he needed to leave immediately. Putting the revolver in the back of his trousers like in the few films he had seen, he hurried downstairs as the front door opened. His mum stood there with the lisped sailor that had threatened him, and the look he encountered told him he was in trouble if he didn't try and get away.

'Going out, Forest? Bring me a bottle of gin back from the off-licence.'

'Yes, Forest, bring your mother her gin back.'

Those words frightened the hell out of him as the man brushed past him, digging him in the ribs with his finger.

'Leave it on the table in the front room.'

Another sailor walked through the door and ignored Forest and his mate as he made his way upstairs, gesturing something crude in his Scottish tongue. The lisped matelot held onto Forest, pinning him against the front door with his hand over his mouth until his friend disappeared into the bedroom.

'Now, let's get your mum's gin.'

The man dragged Forest out of the front door with his hand preventing him from calling out. With the street deserted, he hauled him into a recently bombed-out house, not far from his encounter with another of his mum's customers. Once inside the ruined premises, Forest received a backhand across his face and another to his head. 'You will not be jumping out a window this time, boy.' A punch caught Forest in the stomach, and he fell onto broken rubble, where wooden splinters penetrated his skin. Blood seeped into his clothing as the man pulled him upright and continued to hit him until he fell to the ground, bleeding profusely. Unable to get up, he tried to plead with the man to leave him alone, only to receive more punches to his already weakened body. As Forest lay there, the man ripped his clothing from him, leaving him naked, bloodied and bruised. 'Now, I will have what I paid for.'

Forest could feel one eye closing and blood coming down his nose. Suddenly, he felt himself being lifted and thrown face-down onto the ground. Then, Forest saw the gun beside him, nestled against a piece of timber. As he put his hand over the revolver, the man fell onto him, and another slap caught him around the back of his head. Fighting to prevent what he knew was coming, he gripped the weapon as his attacker lifted from him momentarily, and then he fired, just missing the man. The sailor, stunned at the sudden turn of events, looked at Forest and watched him turn over, pointing the gun at him. This time the bullet hit the sailor in the face. The whiplash of the impact threw the man backwards as he lay quiet, unmoving, alongside Forest's torn and discarded clothes.

Running feet came along the pavement as he lay bleeding and in agony. Someone spoke to him as they tried to lift him - then he passed out with the pain.

Opening an eye, Forest looked at the bright lights and squinted as it brought an ache to his head. Lifting his hand, he wondered why his other eye never opened, and he felt the enlarged bandage wrapped around his head covering it. His whole body ached as he tried to move, and then a soft voice spoke to him.

'Forest, is that you under all those bandages?'

Knowing he had heard the voice before, he saw the shadow fall between him and the brightness. 'Hello, nurse.'

'It is you. You poor boy. Tell me, how are you feeling this morning?'

Forest tried to smile. 'I'm sore all over.'

'I'm not surprised after what happened.'

With doctors and nurses attending him and the police asking him questions, he explained how the man pulled him into the bombed-out building and tried to assault him. They asked about the gun, and he said he thought it belonged to the sailor when he saw it on the floor. He didn't mean to fire it, but it happened.

After being questioned several times by different people speaking to him about the incident, it became clear that Forest was the victim and was lucky to be alive. His mum came after being found and visited him, showing how loving she could be, and by the evening of the twenty-third of December, she was ready to take Forest home with her in clothing that the hospital had again supplied.

The police spoke to Forest once more before he left the hospital and told him nothing would happen, seeing what the man had tried to do to him. But they would probably need to speak to him once more at a later date.

Back home, Forest's mum put him to bed and gave him a pie she had bought, before going out once more, telling him she had arranged an evening with a good friend and, seeing she could do no more, he needed to sleep.

'Don't bring anyone home tonight, mum.'

'You go to sleep, and I will see you in the morning.'

Alone with his bandaged head and body, Forest lay there and cried as the blanket flapped in the cold, windy night.

Pulling his overcoat over his blanket as the room got colder, Forest huddled under it, trying to get warm, before a noise woke him as the half-moon shone into the room, giving him anxious thoughts of who it could be.

Then he saw his mum's face as she stood there holding onto the wall, obviously drunk and with a soldier's arm around her.

'You awake, Forest?'

Acting as though he was asleep, he turned over and faced the wall, praying she and whoever was with her would not come in.

'He's asleep, Ron. Try not to wake him. Some matelot had a go at him yesterday. He's got a few cuts and bruises on him.'

Listening, Forest felt more tears spread across his face.

'Don't come in here if I fall asleep; he needs to rest.'

Wide awake, he heard the door close and sat up, listening to the two of them talking and drinking as they fell onto the bed, with the man eager to begin what he had come for. Easing himself off the bed, Forest made his way to the top of the stairs and, sitting down, worked his way down as the bruises throbbed around his body with each step. Easing his way into the kitchen, he drank a mug of water after seeing his reflection in the cracked mirror and winced at the spectacle before him.

'You look like a bloody Egyptian Mummy.' Nearing the looking glass, he peeled the bandage away from his eye and saw the dark-purple swelling. 'You made a bloody mess of my face, Lispy, but you got yours.' He replayed in his mind the events that took the man's life. In the front room, the thought of what could have happened made him shiver as he eased into an armchair. Then he realised it was almost Christmas Eve, and Danny had invited him round to his house on Christmas Day. 'Don't think I'll be able to make it, Danny. Can't see me sitting in your house looking like this.'

Sat there with his overcoat wrapped around him, he listened to the occasional screech and groan as his mum's bed earned its way.

As the morning became evident, with people moving outside, Forest needed to pee and grimaced at his pains, before heading out to the back yard. The dark morning beckoned another day, be it Christmas Eve or not, and he longed for his mum to fetch him something to eat and hoped it would be before midday. Back in the front room, he waited for movement, and at eight o'clock, the sound of someone coming down the stairs brought him wide awake. The soldier stood at the front door, looking at him, sitting there with his coat wrapped around him in the armchair.

'You all right, boy?'

Forest opened his one good eye wide, unsure of events. 'Thanks, I'm okay.'

The soldier could see otherwise in the semi-darkened room as he tried to move in the chair. 'It's bloody freezing in here. Let me light a fire for you.' With the flames catching the pieces of wood, the man knelt beside him and studied him better. 'You've been in the wars. What happened?'

Seeing the man looking concerned, Forest chanced it and told him what had happened.

'And she left you like this? Are you hungry? Don't bother answering that. I can see you are. I'll nip out and get something for you.' The military man pulled the front door behind him and hurried from the house.

The warmth gradually found its way into the room as he settled down, feeling better with the fire lit and hoping there would be food coming his way. Within the hour, the man returned and placed some hot pies into Forest's hands and a bag of something else on the table beside him.

'Where did you get food like this?'

'The dockyard Naafi; I know someone in there: she's all right.

'I got some coal for the fire that will keep you warm. Do you have to go back to the hospital? I can take you if you want me to.'

Forest bit into the pastry and the warm filling, swallowing it down, and he felt his stomach sigh with the satisfying nourishment. 'No, they told me to rest, and I should be all right in a couple of days.'

'I'll make some tea. You got anything in the kitchen?'

'There might be you'll have to look. Mum don't drink tea.'

Five minutes later, there was a hot mug of tea steaming in front of him. 'Thanks for doing this, Mister.'

'Sorry, but there's no milk in it.' The soldier pointed up to the ceiling. 'She should never have left you in this state. If I go, will you be okay?'

'Yeah, thanks again.'

The man crossed over and put his hand on his curly hair, rubbing it gently. 'I have to go, or I'll be in trouble. Do you want me to come back later?'

'No, once these pains ease up, I'll be up and about. Mum should be down soon.'

The soldier shook his head and swore under his breath. 'I must go; you watch out for yourself, boy, and don't shoot anybody else unless they are in a German uniform.'

Chapter Thirty

Being busy with chores he needed to do on Christmas Eve, Danny wondered if Forest would come round so he could remind him to be at his house at noon the next day. With no show and being unable to get away, he hoped Forest would remember. Danny's mum set about her preparations in the kitchen, with her two daughters helping. Twice, Danny needed to go out, and on the second occasion, he passed by Forest's house and called up towards his room.

'Forest, you in there?' With no answer, Danny tried once more. 'Forest, Forest, it's Danny.'

Asleep in the armchair behind the drawn curtains in the front room, oblivious to the outside world, a body was sleeping, replenishing itself from the pains and bruises, along with the tablets the hospital had given.

Giving up any hope, Danny wondered where his friend was and called out once more. 'Make sure you come around and see us tomorrow.' Then he ran off, knowing his mum would wonder where he had been.

Forest's mum came down the stairs much later and saw the fire's remains, with Forest asleep. Seeing the empty pie wrappers and the mug, she spoke to him as though he were awake. 'You can't be that bad, or you wouldn't have gone out and bought that to feed yourself. You're getting a right nasty piece of work. I'm sure that sailor never had any gun. You had it, didn't you?'

Forest, now awake, kept his eyes closed and dared not open them, or he could imagine his mum getting more irate.

'You sleep and make the most of it, sonny-boy. If you can afford that food, you can get more in for tomorrow, seeing I'm going away. It'll be Boxing Day before I lay eyes on you again, and that will be too bloody soon. Touch any of my customers again, and I'll throw you out of this house, you ungrateful bastard. I work hard to keep this roof over my head, and I don't want the likes of you getting in my way. Forest, you awake?' Seeing no response, she pulled her coat around herself and put a bit of lipstick on, facing the mirror. Seeing Forest in the reflection, she turned and kicked his chair, making him move. 'You awake?' With no movement, she left him to it and ventured out of the door, slamming it behind her.

Climbing out of the armchair and kneeling, he fed the dying fire as meagre flames found new life, and warmth returned to the room. Managing to stand and feeling a bit easier, he found the bag the soldier had brought him beside his chair and opened it. There were four lardy cakes inside, like the ones he had eaten after his first fish and chip meal disaster, and he tucked into two of them. Later, with another mug of tea and after taking some tablets, he checked himself in the mirror and decided that some bandages could come off. Removing one from around his body, he stopped and checked out the bruising covering his ribs and shoulders. Putting one bandage back the best he could, he tucked it in and looked at his face. Several bruises were changing colour, but his eye was worrying him. The bandage around his head, holding the pad over the puffy area, safeguarding it, was becoming loose, so he removed the dressing and studied his purple-blackened eye. It was still half-closed and bloodshot, but at least he could see something out of it, and he decided there was no way he could go to Danny's home looking the way he did.

Christmas Eve evening turned into a cold one, and with the front room being the warmest, Forest managed to collect some wood from the back yard to keep the fire going. He did climb the stairs to his bedroom to collect his blanket and a few coins, but the effort wrenched his aching body. Staying curled up in the armchair, he ate the remaining two cakes and washed down his tablets with another mug of tea, before going into a deep sleep, knowing the house was his and nobody would come in and disturb him. At least he prayed they wouldn't.

Christmas Day morning he sat there in the cold. He shivered with the fire gone out, pulling his overcoat around himself, knowing he needed to eat. Finding his body more operational, he made his way to the kitchen, but every shelf and drawer was empty. Going into the front room, he looked at the chair his dad sat in when he came, and wondered what he was doing. Then he remembered the one-pound note he had given him. He had put it where he had kept the gun, but further back, not with his other coins. Leaving the kitchen, he made his way to the bedroom and, wincing at the effort, searched for the money.

He tried to find it twice, with his arm stretched out under the floorboards, but it avoided him each time. 'Come on; you're in there somewhere.' Suddenly, the pain shot across his body as he touched a piece of paper. Unable to grasp it, he decided to leave it there and try another time. Besides, no shops or cafés would be open, seeing what day it was.

The few people who witnessed the body taken from the ruined building spread their gossip, along with that of an injured young coloured boy. Speculation and idle chit-chat swept the neighbourhood as to what had happened. The police held onto their assumption that the sailor was the one with the gun, so they decided to keep quiet about the incident until the New Year, seeing it was blatantly obvious what had happened – except for Forest's mum.

Danny checked the time in the front room, wondering where Forest was, when his mum walked in.

'I thought Forest was coming today?'

'He should be here by now, Mum. He knows you've cooked extra food. Is Dad still okay about him

197

coming round?'

'Of course; but right now, I need you in the kitchen to help me lift that big pot.'

Danny looked at the time once more, showing eleven o'clock, and hoped Forest was all right. At half-past eleven and still no show, Danny pleaded with his mum to let him go around to Forest's house to see why he hadn't turned up.

'No, not today, Danny. If he's coming, he'll be here. We can't go interfering in their family business. It is nothing to do with us.'

Danny thought about Forest's mum's business and what went on in that house. His mum might not want Forest at her dinner table if she knew. Deep down, Danny guessed something was wrong. Something had happened; he knew it. 'I'm a bit worried, Mum. Let me pop out for five minutes.'

'Your dad is getting up now. He's been up all last night, and he won't want to find you out of the house on Christmas Day, you know that.'

Chapter Thirty-One

Forest checked himself in the mirror once more in the front room as hunger and loneliness got the better of him. Danny's invitation for Christmas dinner brought stomach pains, knowing there was nothing to eat in the house. Securing his bandages around his body the best he could, he wondered what Danny's parents would think, turning up looking the way he did. Checking his eye once more, he noticed that it looked a lot better, but was still bloodshot and swollen. Leaving the bandage off, he washed his hands and face in the kitchen before going to his bedroom, trying to find some better clothes. Having dressed the best he could, he went to his cupboard and removed the back panel inside. The two presents he had bought were still intact, wrapped the best he could in brown paper and string. Downstairs, with one last look in the mirror, his stomach told him to eat something, and the only place was with Danny and his family. Sighing, he tried to smile, but like at other times when his face had taken a beating, it made him look worse, so he decided he must not smile at anybody.

'It doesn't look as though your friend is coming, Danny. I will give him to one o'clock and then I am serving dinner. You know your dad likes his Christmas dinner early, seeing we have something later at teatime.'

Danny's mum left the room, and his dad walked in in his best clothes. 'Danny, your mum and the girls are going to dish up dinner. I'm not waiting any longer for your friend to turn up.'

They both looked up as someone knocked on the front door. Danny hurried from the room, and his dad called out as he was about to open the door. 'If it's your friend, tell him he's lucky we didn't have our meal at twelve o'clock like we always do.'

Opening the door, Danny looked at Forest standing there, seeing the state of him. 'Christ, what happened to you? You look terrible.' Danny knew straight away he had said the wrong thing as Forest put his head down and wiped at his good eye as a tear appeared, before turning away, ready to walk off. 'Come inside, you idiot; we've been waiting for you.'

Danny's mum appeared in the passageway and, seeing Forest, told Danny to bring him into the house. Seeing the state he was in, she came and put her arm around him. 'Dear God, are you all right?'

With a wet eye, he nodded, trying not to smile.

'Danny, take him into the front room and let him sit by the fire; he looks frozen. I'll be in in a few minutes.'

Carrying his old shopping bag, Forest followed Danny, and once in the room, he felt the warmth hit him. Mr Downes studied Forest, telling him to sit in the armchair beside the fire. Suddenly, Danny's sisters came into the room, wondering what was going on. Seeing a half-closed eye and a headful of bruises, they held the door open, examining him.

'Back in the kitchen, girls; help your mother out there.'

The quick words brought them alert, and they hurried from the room, anxious to find out what had happened to their brother's friend.

With just the three of them in the room, Mr Downes crossed over and knelt beside him. 'Are you the young man they pulled out of that house with that sailor the other day?'

Forest, still holding onto his bag, nodded once more.

'Where is your mother, Forest? I'm surprised she let you come out in this condition.'

Uncertain of everything around him, Forest wiped a tear away. 'She's gone away.' He crossed his fingers at the next sentence. 'She knew I was coming here, so she went to her friend's place.'

Danny – knowing damn well who her friends were – remained quiet.

'In this state?'

Another nod came back.

Shaking his head, he left the room, telling Danny to pour a drink for his friend.

'What's all that about you and this sailor? Did you have another problem?'

'I killed a sailor, Danny. It was an accident. He tried

to do things to me, and he had a gun like that one I got rid of. It fell on the floor, and I managed to grab it. I shot him.'

'Jesus, you killed him?'

'The police know all about it. They know it wasn't my fault. The sailor did this to me. You should have seen me yesterday.'

'I can't believe your mum has left you like this. My dad will see you all right now you are with us. Let me pour you that drink.'

Forest became the interest of the family as he sat at the table. The chicken and vegetables he ate warmed and filled his belly as Danny's mum and dad spoke to him without bringing what had happened into the conversation. After a meal and Christmas pudding, one that Forest never knew existed, everyone relaxed and listened to the wireless. Danny's sisters were curious and asked Forest how he got his injuries, but were told to mind their own business. After a refill of drinks, Danny's mum pulled out the presents. Dad got a new pipe and mum a new apron, which she was thrilled about, seeing the girls had made it. Danny's sisters received new shoes and Danny a real football, something he really wanted. Next came another present, which Danny's mum passed across.

'This is for you, Forest. I hope you like it. Merry Christmas.'

Opening it, Forest found a pair of shoes, proper ones, and a pair of long trousers. He sat there looking at them, being the first Christmas presents he ever had. 'Thank you.'

Everyone saw the emotion in him and got on with something else.

'Danny told me your sizes, so if they don't fit, blame him.'

'They will. I like them.'

Danny passed Forest over a gift. 'This is from me.'

Taking it, he opened the coloured paper and found a thick warm jumper inside. 'I can do with something like this, Danny; it's smashing. Thanks.'

Forest leaned over the side of the armchair, wincing at the pain in his ribs, and picked up his bag, before pulling out his first present. 'This is for you.' Giving it to Danny's mum, he waited for her to unwrap it.

'Forest, how lovely.' She looked at the picture on the tin of biscuits showing her what was inside. 'You didn't have to do this.' She got up from her chair and kissed him on the forehead. 'Thank you. I'm sure these won't last too long in this house.'

Putting his hand back in the bag, Forest handed Danny a gift. 'For you.'

Danny's dad saw the smile that strained across Forest's face, giving the impression of Quasimodo or something like him.

Opening the brown paper, Danny found a Swiss Army penknife. 'Forest, this must have cost you.' Danny put his arm around Forest and thanked him.

'Not too hard, Danny. My ribs are still a bit sore.'

Pulling away, Danny grabbed his hand. 'That's a fantastic present. I'll always look after it.'

Danny's mum could see how Forest's gift had affected her boy and came over. 'Let me see this penknife. Very smart, but you shouldn't have spent all that money on Danny.'

'He's my best friend; I wanted to. I thought it might come in handy.'

'You bet it will.' Taking Forest's hand once more, Danny shook it with delight.

Later, Danny took Forest up to his bedroom to show him his comic collection, and while there, he once more asked about what had happened, with Forest telling him everything. 'You didn't throw the gun in the water as you said.'

Forest grimaced as he tried to explain. 'Danny, you know the sort of life I lead. I kept it should something happen. Look at me; if I never had it with me that day, Christ knows what would have happened. Are you mad about it?'

'No, suppose not, but don't lie to me again about things; mates don't do that. I understand what you said about keeping it. I'm glad you're all right, if you know what I mean, but I bet he scared the hell out of you.'

'I thought I was going to die. I spent the night in the hospital afterwards. I told the police I thought the gun belonged to the sailor. I think they believed me. Mum took me home, and she had a go at me yesterday, saying I was interfering with her customers.'

Danny felt like saying something about his mum, but held back. 'Well, today, forget all about that. Here you will find everyone on your side, but keep away from my sisters. I know what you're like with girls.'

'The way I feel right now, there's no way I could, you know.'

'So, Nancy is out of the question?'

Forest looked up from the comic Danny had given him.

'Come on, Forest, I'm not daft. I know you're still seeing Nancy and her friend.'

'Do the others know?'

'I've not said anything, but you're playing with fire there, if you ask me.' Danny pushed him gently. 'By the way, mum and dad said you could stay the night. You can bunk in with me.'

'You sure?'

'Just make sure you don't fidget too much.'

Chapter Thirty-Two

In the front room of Danny's house, all the family played games that were easy for Forest to manage. More food came out at teatime, and by the evening, it was the best day Forest had ever known. Before going to bed that night, after the girls had gone up, he and Danny washed down in the kitchen, and during it, Danny saw the state of his friend's body.

'Look at you. I think my mum should have a look at some of those bruises.'

'I could do with this bandage around my ribs tightening up a bit; it keeps slipping down.'

Allowing Danny's mum to see his wounds, Forest sat there anxiously as she put ointments and other remedies onto his body. Finding a fresh bandage in her drawer, she set about trying to make him as comfortable as possible. His eye having now opened more, she soothed it with warm water.

'I suggest you top and tail in the bed tonight, Danny. Just make sure you keep your legs still: you don't want to go knocking them against these bruises.'

Danny's dad came in as Forest tried to cover himself further. 'I've been next door, Danny. Mrs Knott has said she would give us a spare bed.'

'Is there room for another bed, Dad?'

'Come upstairs with me now, and we'll find out.'

While they were away, Forest stayed in the front room with Danny's mum, and she offered him some of the biscuits from out of the tin he had brought her. 'Go on, take one; they are nice, especially the chocolate ones. Where did you find them? They're not easy to come by.'

'One of mum's friends, he got them for me.'

'Forest, how come your mother is away, and you are by yourself today of all days?'

He sat there, with Danny's mum awaiting an answer.

'Don't you want to tell me?'

Still staying quiet, the tears came, and he put his head in his hands.

'That's all right, I understand.' She sat on the arm of the chair and put her arm around his shoulders, comforting him. 'This house is always open to you. If things get bad, you come here and see me. I mean that. Danny's dad would welcome you like any one of us would. I am going to make a cup of tea; would you like one? I'm sure Danny's dad will.'

Forest lifted his head and smiled at her, not realising the way he looked. 'Please.'

'You stay there and help yourself to another biscuit. There is some fruit on the table if you want some. It is still reasonably fresh.'

Forest listened to the movements outside the room,

thinking that whatever was happening was for him. The mug of tea came in, and still the noise persisted. Finally, Danny came in with his mug of tea.

'You should see my bedroom; it looks so different. You coming up? I'll bring the tea.' Together, they walked into Danny's bedroom.

'Is that bed for me?'

'It's all yours. Mrs Knott gave us the bedclothes as well. They look better than mine. Mum said you could have a pair of my pyjamas; that's them on the bottom of the bed.'

Forest sat down, fingering the nightwear, never having had anything like them. 'You get undressed to get dressed to go to bed? I always sleep in what I've worn during the day.'

With the heavy curtains pulled, and the warmth from the fire downstairs drifting up through the house, it made him want to stay forever.

Undressed and in bed, Danny passed out some comics to read, and together they discussed different adventures that the characters portrayed.

'I'm tired, Danny. Do you mind if I go to sleep? It's been a long day, and I still ache.'

'Sure.' Danny needed to ask a question and hoped he didn't upset Forest. 'That penknife you got me, it's not stolen, is it?'

'No, Danny. I've been saving some mud money, along with other money from the wood me and Johnny collect. I wouldn't give you a stolen present.'

'Sorry, but I had to ask. You're not upset, are you?'

'Too tired to be.' Snuggled down in the bed, he drew the covers up around his neck. 'Glad you like it.'

'Thanks again. I mean it.'

Laying under the covers with the light out, Forest listened as Danny farted and giggled.

'Glad you did that, Danny. I'm holding mine in, frightened to let one go.'

The giggles came thick and fast as the pair of them did their hardest to try and make the most noise.

After a bang on the wall from Danny's dad telling them to pack it in, the boys drifted off to sleep, with Forest being the warmest he'd ever been for this time of year.

Both boys woke with Danny's mum calling them through the door, telling them that breakfast would be ready in half an hour.

'You sleep all right, Forest?' Danny stretched and yawned, pushing his legs down the bed. 'It stunk a bit in here last night; I'd better open the window for a while, or mum will say something.' Then he laughed as he heard Forest do another. 'Don't do one of them during breakfast, or mum will say something; dad, too.'

'It was all that rich food. I'm not used to it. Are we dressing to go down?'

'No, I always go down in my jim-jams.'

'What about me? I can't sit there with these on.'

'Why, what's wrong with them?'

Forest got out of bed, with Danny holding back

laughter, seeing the state of him.

'I see what you mean! You need to pee, or is that how you wake up every morning?'

'Bit of both.' Forest looked around the room. 'You got a piss-pot or something? I can't leave like this.'

'Glad you slept on your own. I wouldn't want that thing digging in my back. Here.' Danny reached under his bed. 'Pee in that, and I'll use it afterwards. I'll get rid of it later.'

After a good breakfast, Danny's dad pulled Forest to one side and spoke to him alone. 'Son, that business with that sailor. Am I thinking your mother is prone to bringing men home with her? I'll not judge her, but if that is the case and anything happens in the future, I want you to leg it around here. That's not a healthy life for a boy being in that situation, you understand me?'

Sat there quiet, he nodded, as was his usual way when things got a bit serious.

Meeting up with Danny, he told him what his dad said and his mum the night before. 'You are one lucky human being. I wish I had your life.'

Danny realised that he was getting ready to leave and go home. 'Why don't you stay with us? I'm sure you could if I asked mum and dad.'

'No, they've done enough. I had better leave, but can I stay for dinner first, or is that being cheeky?'

'Boxing Day is Christmas Day leftovers, with pickled onions and other stuff that make you fart.'

Forest held his ribs as he laughed out loud. 'I'm still

holding them in.'

'Mum said to me that you should stay for dinner.'

At four in the afternoon, Forest said his farewells to the family. Waving him off from the front door as the clouds darkened, Danny wondered what would be waiting for him once he returned to that house. He had tried to get him to stay another night, but he knew it wasn't easy for him to do that.

With his Christmas presents in his bag and feeling a lot better with his eye opening more and more, he strolled along the pavement, in no hurry to get home. Once in his street, he saw his mum going into the house with somebody. 'Miss me, Mum?' Forest found a place not too far away in a bombed-out building. Sitting in an understairs cupboard with its door blown off, he sat and watched the bedroom curtain pull across, knowing things had just gone back to what they always were.

The rain came down, and Forest was getting wet from the leaky shelter and decided to make for his front door and stay downstairs. Reaching the house, he tried to open the door by pushing it, but his mum had shut it on the latch. He put his hand through the letterbox and felt the string attached to the key behind the door. It was gone, and there was no way to get in. Going around to the end house, Forest achingly climbed onto the back yard wall of the first house and balanced his way towards his yard. Easing himself into the messy space, he tried the back door, only to find that locked. Cursing his luck as the rain came on heavier, he opened the outside toilet door and sat there. With the presents now damp in his bag, he took them out, hanging the trousers and jumper over the cistern to dry, and stood his new shoes against the wall. Sat there, Forest pulled his coat around him as the day, already cold, became colder still.

Chapter Thirty-Three

It was dark when the kitchen light came on, and, stuffing his clothes into his bag, he moved to the window and peered in. His mum was talking to a stranger he had never seen before, and with the rain still coming down, he chanced it and tapped on the glass. The man, being nearest, saw him and spoke to his mum. The look was enough as she came to the back door and opened it.

'Where the hell have you been?'

'I went to one of my friend's house; he invited me. Can I come in, Mum? I'm getting soaked out here.'

The man came to the door and peered out. 'He yours?'

'For what he's worth.' Standing back, she beckoned him inside. 'What's in the bag?'

'They gave me some clothes and a pair of shoes.' He opened the bag for her to see. 'Danny's my friend; his mum gave them to me.'

Taking the bag from Forest, his mum pulled out the contents and looked at them. 'Don't she think I can buy you clothes? It's not the first time I've seen you in clothes that's not yours. These are long trousers: you don't wear long trousers or shoes like that. I'll sell these and buy you some decent ones. Now you get upstairs and dry out. I don't want you getting a cold – or worse.'

'Mum, those were a present.'

'So will the back of my hand be if you don't do as I say. Now go and stay in your room.'

'Can't I stay in the front room, Mum? That bedroom is freezing with the blanket over the window.'

The man intervened. 'Probably is with this weather.'

Forest saw the anger in his mum's face. 'I'll get it fixed tomorrow, but for tonight, you get under those covers and stay warm. Go on; I'll see you later.'

Wet and fed up, Forest climbed the stairs, knowing he would never see his Christmas presents again, and as for getting his window fixed, that would never happen.

The Christmas period passed, and things went back to what they were. Forest had tried several times to try and get the pound note from under the floor, but each time it seemed to move further away, so he was determined to pull the floorboards up when he knew his mum would be away from the house. It was New Year's Eve, and Danny came looking for Forest, seeing he hadn't seen him since Boxing Day. Hearing someone moving about behind the blanket, Danny called up to him.

'Forest, come down. I want a word.' Seeing the blanket lift and him nod, Danny waited on the opposite side of the street. Eventually, the door opened, and he came out.

'Hi, Danny.'

'How's things with you? You look a lot better.'

'Yeah, I'm healing, all the bandages are off, and my eye's better. It still smarts at times, but at least I can see things clearer.'

'No long trousers or jumper? I thought you might have put them on.'

Not knowing what to say, he shrugged. 'What's the visit for?'

'Later on, I wondered if you fancied a wander around, seeing it's New Year's Eve. There should be plenty going on. What do you think?'

'Why not? I can meet you at six. I'm trying to put another blanket up to that window.'

'You want any help?'

'No, I've nearly finished; besides, mum could be back at any time. You heard anything from the others?'

'Johnny came back yesterday; he said his mum got fed up with her sister's kids keep shouting and making a noise. He said he'd come out with us. See you at six, then.'

Forest did most of the guiding, pointing out the different public houses and what went on in many of them. In attempting to sneak a look inside the doors, Johnny tried his luck and got more than a sneak at the Duke of York pub when one of the regulars saw him and threw the remains of his pint at him, telling him in no uncertain terms to leave. By half-past seven, the boys were making their way past the harbour taverns, when someone tapped them on the shoulder. Turning expecting trouble, they looked into the face of Eddie.

'I thought you were away until after the New Year. Your mum allowed you out tonight. That's unusual.'

'She's gone to bed with a headache, but I can't stay out too long.'

'Johnny, you heard any more about your dad?'

'No, mum won't talk about it. She ignores the letter as though it had never come.'

'Your dad's a fit bloke. I bet he's all right.'

'Hope so.'

'I've been looking for you, Danny. Your mum told me to tell you to be home by nine at the latest. Where are you going?'

'Forest is giving us a guided tour of the pubs. Johnny had a fright earlier when some bloke saw him trying to poke his nose in the door. I'm glad you're back, Eddie. It's not the same without all of us being together.'

'What happened to you, Forest? Your face looks a bit bashed about.'

Danny came in before he could answer. 'One of his mum's friends had a go at him; he's getting better.'

Forest smiled. 'You should see the other bloke.'

Danny intervened. 'Shall we get a drink?'

'Look, over there by the Admiral pub. That's the Sergeant-Major stood outside having a pint. Let's go and see him; he might buy us a drink.'

Danny laughed at Forest's remark. 'You are joking.

If he sees us, he'll tell us to push off.'

'I'm going to wish him a Happy New Year for later. Come on, he won't mind.'

All three boys followed, making their way across the road as Forest walked up behind the gatekeeper.

'Good evening, Sergeant-Major, you are looking smart as usual. Would you like to buy me and my mates a lemonade, seeing it's New Year's Eve?'

The others stopped a little distance back and murmured to themselves.

'You cheeky pup. You've got a bloody nerve, seeing all the trouble you cause me during the year.'

'It's nearly the New Year, Sergeant-Major; go on, treat us to a bottle.'

His beady eyes twitched as he stroked his long moustache with his fingers. 'You're a cheeky one, ain't you?' Seeing the state of Forest's face, he put his hand into his trouser pocket and pulled out some change. 'If you cause me problems next year, you'll get more than lemonade, you hear me, lad? I'll be watching you and those scallywags behind you.' He put the coins into Forest's hand and pointed to the off-licence next door. 'If there's any change, I'll have it back.'

Forest saluted him. 'You're a good 'un. God bless you, Sergeant-Major, and a Happy New Year for later.' Forest called the others, seeing them stand there with their mouths open, and as they passed him, they all thanked the man for his gesture.

Inside the off-licence, he ordered the four

lemonades and asked the others if they wanted a packet of crisps.

'He's buying us a drink. He said nothing about crisps.'

'He won't mind, Eddie. I fancy a packet, don't you? And four penny packets of crisps, please.'

Coming out of the premises, he walked back to the Sergeant-Major and placed the few coins into his palm. 'We got some crisps: you don't mind, do you? I've had nothing to eat; was that all right?'

The Sergeant-Major cuffed Forest playfully behind the ear. 'Push off before you drink that and try your luck with my friend here. Don't come back.'

The man with the Sergeant-Major laughed as they walked off, with the boys looking back while eating their snack and drinking their lemonade.

'He must have a soft spot for you. I wouldn't dare ask him for anything.'

'He's all right, Johnny. It's all show with him.'

Walking through the streets, the boys finished their drinks, with Forest collecting the empties, saying he would take them back for the pennies on them.

Johnny screwed up his empty packet. 'You wouldn't think there was a war on, listening to the happiness in some of these places.'

Looking around, Eddie pointed to a street a little distance away. 'All those houses were standing back last year. How's that crack down the side of your house? Is it still safe?'

'So far. Mum keeps moaning about it, but at least dad made it secure before he…'

Forest butted in. 'Like what happened to our flat when it got hit. Imagine me being inside. I wouldn't be here with you lot now.'

The time neared half-past eight, and Eddie and Johnny said their goodnights, with everyone wishing each other a Happy New Year.

As soon as the others had gone, Danny stopped Forest from walking off. 'Tomorrow, breakfast around our house. Mum's invited you; we all have a good meal every New Year's Day morning. Be at our house by nine. I meant to tell you earlier, but I forgot.'

'Thanks, Danny, I look forward to that. How come your mum manages to get all that food, seeing the war's on?'

'Mum saves her pennies during the year, as dad does, for Christmas. He sometimes gets a gift from people who he's helped, like the butcher and others.'

'I'd better get these bottles back before the off-licence closes. See you later.'

Chapter Thirty-Four

With a few pennies in his pocket, Forest eventually found his mum in the King's Head. The packet of crisps, being the only food he had eaten since the morning, left him hungry, with his stomach aching. With the crowded pub full of merriment, Forest edged his way into the doorway, trying to get his mum's attention as people were singing and laughing as the evening gave way to the night. Deciding he had no choice, he eased himself around people, heading for the table where his mum sat, laughing with a giant of a sailor. Like his mum, the man was well tanked-up as he pulled her towards him, kissing and caressing her. Managing to get next to her, Forest whispered into her ear.

'Mum, let me have a few pennies. I want to buy something. I'm hungry.'

Not taking any notice, with the gin affecting her senses, she ignored him.

'Mum, Mum, let me have some money.' Putting his hand on her sleeve, he tried to get her attention. 'Mum, please.'

The sailor with her was sober enough to see him acting suspiciously, and reached across the table, grabbing hold of his wrist. Forest had no idea what the man said to him as he tried to pull away.

'She's my mum. Let me go.'

The drunken sailor stood up, knocking some drinks over, and pulled Forest towards him. Looking back towards his mum, she smiled, sipping her gin, not worrying what was happening around her as the man dragged him, kicking and shouting, out of the building and pushing him against a wall, giving him a gentle slap to the head. Petrified, Forest swore as the enormous matelot lifted him into the air, shaking him until the four pennies he received from the bottles clattered to the floor, while the few people around laughed at the spectacle. Moving towards a cordoned-off fenced area, the sailor spoke unintelligibly and threw him over. The splash and smell hit Forest simultaneously as the water he landed in came from a broken sewer. With his vision reduced, he felt movement about him as rodents swam past, alerted by the sudden invasion. Realising what else was around, he shoved everything as far away as possible. Trying to climb out of the disgusting ditch he was in, he fell back with each attempt. Laughter reached him, but he couldn't see anybody, as he grabbed hold of something rusty sticking out of the ground. With his head out of the filthy water, he called out for help, hoping someone would come to his rescue. Eventually, a part of the fence shifted, and a man looked down at him.

'Christ, that stinks.'

The man removed some of the fencing and it came

down towards him on its side, as the man called out for him to climb up and don't fall back.

On the first attempt, he did just that as he slipped on one of the fence slats, going under the disgusting flow of whatever was in the bomb crater. Trying a second time, he managed to pull himself up onto the pavement.

'You stink something awful. You need to wash that off of you before you come down with something serious. That's raw sewage down there, and you're wearing a lot of it. Did I see rats in there?'

Forest turned and looked down at the revolting water, spitting out whatever was in his mouth. The smell coming from him made him choke as a couple of passers-by made a detour of him, holding their noses.

'You need to get out of those clothes, son. God knows what you've picked up in there.'

Forest saw the man back away from him, as others did. 'Thanks for helping me.'

'You need to help yourself now; get home and get in a hot bath.'

The big matelot, now back in the pub, taking hold of his floosie, leant over her, trying to discover what the night might hold for him.

Making his way along the pavement, people avoided Forest, telling him how bad he stank. Several times he choked and spat out something he might have swallowed, not wanting to know what it was. He reached his street and heard the ships sound their horns in the harbour as midnight announced itself. 'Thanks, mum, Happy New Year.' Getting to the house and going out into the back yard, he peeled all his clothes off, touching things he wished he never had to, and left them against the brick wall. He turned the tap on in the house to find no water coming through. 'Great, that's just what I want. Bloody hell.' Back in the yard with an old cloth, he looked into the toilet, hoping the pan had clean water in it. Sniffing, he decided he had no choice as the new cold January weather bit into him. Dipping the cloth into the water, he soaked it and wiped himself down the best he could. Deciding he wasn't going to get any cleaner, he made his way up to his room to find his bedroom in a shambles. His wardrobe and cupboard doors lay open, and all the shelves were bare. Moving the mattress, he discovered his floorboard removed. Getting on his knees, he felt underneath, unable to find his tin. 'Come on, mum, not my emergency savings. I need that sometimes.'

Forest sat on the bed with a blanket wrapped around him, shivering from the experience and the freezing bedroom. Seeing a note on one of the shelves, he picked it up and read it. 'You little bastard, you come around me wanting money for food and drinks, and all the time you've got money hidden away.' Forest saw his savings tin lying on its side, stamped on and empty, the two shillings and nine pence, gone. 'How much more money do you have hidden away. You want some food and clothes; then you buy them.' Forest guessed his mum might have sold his clothes. Looking at the note again, he read the last few lines. 'You won't see me for a week or more, so earn your own money whatever way you can.' Now he knew he had to leave at some point. With no choice but to forgo his breakfast at Danny's, he couldn't even wash the stinking clothes in the yard, so how could he leave the house? Pulling the bed over, he sat on the side of it, looking at the covered window, and knowing the night would be cold as he huddled his blanket around him.

The following morning, he choked on the smell coming off him. Going downstairs, he tried the tap again, where water trickled out. Leaving it running, he tried to rinse his hair the best he could, before collecting his clothes from the back yard and placing them into the sink. Finding a small bar of soap, he tried to wash each item, scrubbing at the stains and marks embedded in the material. Unable to get anywhere, he left all of them to soak and climbed the stairs to his room. Wrapping his smelly blanket around his freezing body, he thought about the money his mum had taken. Was the pound note his dad had given him still under the floor? After what had happened, he had nearly forgotten about it. With the bedcover wrapped securely around him, he pulled the window blankets away from each other and moved his bed to one side. He peered under the flooring on his knees, and sitting further back was the one-pound note. Tugging at another floorboard until it came free, he wedged it with his bed leg and put his hand underneath. Bringing it out, Forest inspected it should any rodent have had a nibble of it, but it seemed okay.

'Sorry, mum, but this is mine. Louie gave me this.'

Leaning on his side, he peered under the floorboards, curious about what else might be under there. Looking in all directions, he saw a dark shape much further away, near the doorway, and wondered what it could be, as the dated wardrobe had stood there since the house became theirs. Peering once more at the shadowy shape, he decided it was worth investigating, and, putting the floorboards back, he rearranged the room, struggling with the bulky closet, weaving it away from its location. Having had years of dust and dirt rooted there, the floorboards had different fixing to the rest in his room. Not only were they shorter boards, but they were screwed down and not nailed like the rest. By now, Forest's curiosity grew stronger as he tried in vain to dislodge some boards.

'Forest, you need a screwdriver. Whatever that is under there, you're going to find out.'

Chapter Thirty-Five

Danny looked at the clock, wondering where Forest could be. He knew there was no way he would miss out on a good breakfast and guessed there must have been another incident. He knew there was nothing he could do, seeing his family were about to sit down for their annual New Year's Day breakfast. Danny's parents showed their concern, and Danny had to accept Forest was probably at home with his mother.

As midday showed itself, Danny, anxious about his friend, pleaded with his dad to let him find out if there was something wrong, only for his dad to tell him, whatever it was, he couldn't keep going around there interfering with another person's life. And if he was that worried about him, there would be time enough to go around there later. Telling his son that, he inwardly wondered himself if something once again had happened to the lad. The following day, Danny's parents took the girls to the cinema for a treat, and seeing Danny wasn't interested, it was up to him to stay home.

Eddie sat with his mum in the kitchen, looking at the newly arrived letter on the shelf.

He found out that the postman had delivered it days before, and it was only now, the second of January, that he found out about it when his mum had put it on view. It was tempting to get up and rip it open, but his mum was adamant that he did not touch it.

'Mum, don't you think you ought to open it. It could be good news.'

'Leave it alone, Edward. I'm not opening it, and neither are you.'

'But, Mum.'

'Leave it be, I said.'

Eddie kicked his ball up against the house, angry that his mum refused to see what was in the letter. He knew she thought it was terrible news, but he tried to convince her it was not. With one almighty kick, Eddie struck the ball and watched it sail over the fence. Not bothering to care about it, he squatted down by the chickens as they waited for him to feed them with any morsel he had. Suddenly, the ball came back over the fence, and Danny peered over it, seeing Eddie sitting there.

'Don't you want it anymore?'

Eddie turned and stared at Danny. 'It's mum; she got another letter and didn't tell me. Now she won't open it.'

'You want to pop out with me. I'm going around to see Forest; he should have turned up at my house yesterday, but he didn't.'

'Why not? I'm going to have a lousy day stuck in

here with mum. Let me tell her I'm going out.'

Danny waited, and together they made their way around to Forest's house. 'I tried calling on Johnny, but I think he must be out with his mum. Something has happened. There's no way Forest would miss a meal.'

'How come he stays living with her? I would have thought he would have left home by now. I would, with people keep knocking me about.'

'Where could he go? Seeing his mum lives a road away, he wouldn't come to my place.'

Eddie shuffled along beside him, not listening, thinking about his mum's behaviour.

'This new letter, it doesn't have to be bad news. It could be anything. I've told mum dad's a fighter.'

'You've got to think positive. That's what my mum would say.'

Eddie kicked a stone into the air and watched it hit a wall. 'Bloody war!'

'Too right, it is. Come on, let's see what's happened to Forest.'

Seeing the house in darkness with the curtains drawn, Danny nudged Eddie. 'I wonder if his mum is entertaining. Forest said when the curtains are together, someone is up there with her.'

Eddie held back. 'Well, I'm not knocking on the door.'

'Let me get closer; he might be in his room, seeing his covers are apart.'

Eddie looked up, imagining what it must be like in

the room. 'It must be freezing up there with those blankets up at the window. Look, that's him in his bedroom. What's he wearing, Danny? Looks like a blanket or something?'

'Forest, Forest. It's Danny.'

Both boys saw that he recognised them as he edged away from the open window.

'Forest, it's Danny. What are you doing in there?' With no answer, he waited and called up again. 'That's it, I'm going to knock, and if I don't get an answer this time, I'm going in. You wait here. I'm going to find out why he can't come down here. If anybody comes, give me a shout.'

Danny banged on the front door as Eddie moved across the road and waited. He banged on the door three times, then decided to open it with a bit of brute force. Flexing his shoulder against the rattly door, it gave way on the second attempt, and Danny found himself in the house, and an awful smell hit him.

'Forest, it's me, Danny. You still upstairs?' Putting his hand across his nose, he climbed the stairs and saw Forest sitting on the floorboards with a blanket wrapped around him. 'What's that smell? It's terrible.'

Forest looked up from his seated position and sheepishly pulled the cover tighter around his cold body.

'The state of this room, what happened?' Danny heard the sobs and decided to change the subject. 'Why didn't you come around for breakfast?'

Forest moved to answer, and Danny backed away as the smell hit him. 'You're coming with me. You got any clothes on under that blanket?'

Forest shook his head.

'What happened? Why are you in this state?'

Forest picked up his one-pound note and stood up. 'It's a long story. Let's go downstairs to the front room. That's if you can stand the stink.'

'Let me speak to Eddie. He's outside, waiting.' Crossing to the window, Danny tried to take a breath of fresh air before calling out to Eddie, saying he'd be out later. In the front room, Danny again asked what the smell was, and Forest began his tale.

'Your mum's sold all your clothes, even the ones we gave you at Christmas?'

Forest nodded, and Danny saw the pound note in his hand. 'But you've got that.'

'How can I buy any clothes? Mine's in the sink. I can't go out like this and buy any. I've tried to wash them umpteen times, but the smell won't come out, and the water only trickles out the tap. This blanket is as bad now. I'm bloody freezing, and I'm hungry.'

'When do you think your mum will be back?'

'She said in a week, but you never know what she's going to do.'

Danny thought about Forest's plight. 'Those clothes in the sink, chuck them out in the yard, and that blanket with them.'

'But I don't have anything else to cover myself

with.'

Danny saw an old throw over one of the armchairs and pulled it off. 'This can cover you until we get to my house. I'll sort you out once we're there.'

'I can't come to your house like this. What will your mum and dad think, or your sisters?'

'There'll be no one in until later. They've all gone to the picture house. Let me tell Eddie; he won't mind.'

Opening the front door, Danny saw Eddie shuffling his feet on the pavement, then looking further across the open space; he saw a navy man hurrying their way.

Chapter Thirty-Six

Eddie saw Danny point, turned, and was ready to flee when he saw the man. Straight away, he knew who the person was by the walk. Stood there, unable to move, he rubbed his eyes, not believing what he was seeing, when Danny shouted at him to move. With the man getting closer, he began to cry and ran towards him.

'Dad, is that really you?'

The smile coming back told him it was.

'Dad, Dad, you're alive: I knew you were.' Tripping and stumbling, he ran into the arms of his dad as he lifted him off his feet and hugged him to him. Eddie threw his arms around his dad's neck. 'Dad, Dad.'

'It's good to see you, son. How's your mum?'

'Dad, this isn't your uniform. I wouldn't have recognised you if Danny hadn't. Oh, Dad.'

Eddie's dad gave Danny a wave, and, taking his son's hand, they walked off together.

'Is your mum all right?'

'She's okay; the house is still there, and mum's still got some of her birds.'

'Fresh eggs, that's what I've missed.'

Eddie wiped his face, realising his dad was a little weepy as well. 'Dad, I knew you would come back to us.'

'It would take more than Hitler's boys to get rid of me, son. They had a good go, but here I am. You and mum are fighters, too, seeing the state of some of these places.'

'Was it bad, I mean at sea with…?'

'We don't want to talk about that, Eddie; these legs of mine are still trying to get the feel of walking on solid ground.'

'I bet you'll find it funny sleeping in a bed that doesn't move.'

'You're right there! Come on, let's go and see mum.'

'Let's chuck those stinking clothes out. The whole house needs fresh air coming in. Leave the back door open: no one will see you.' Danny looked at Forest, stood there naked, and passed him the throw. 'Cover yourself with that.'

'It's so cold out there; let me put my plimsolls on. They're not too bad, just a few marks on them.'

'It's no colder outside than it is in here. When I get you home, make sure you take those plimmies off before we go in, just in case. I don't understand what's happening with you, but this can't go on.'

Danny managed to get Forest back to his house and took him through to the back yard. 'I know it's cold out here, but I can't leave you indoors smelling like that. Mum will have a fit. Stand in the privy for a while until

I get some water heated, and don't sit on the seat, just in case you mess it up.' Danny put pots of water on the stove and lifted the bath off the outside wall as Forest called out, 'I think I've been here before, Danny.'

'So do I, mate! Still, let's get you cleaned up before the family get back.'

With the hot water and soap waiting, Forest stepped into the tub and yelped as the hot water penetrated his body. It took three baths to get the muck off him. Whatever was on him was more or less glued to him. It took two washes with more hot water to clean his hair before it resembled anything as it should. Danny put some iodine on a couple of Forest's nasty-looking cuts, making him jump and shout out. With that done, he sniffed him and decided on one more hot tub, and this time he put some disinfectant in and told him to soak in it until the smell was gone entirely. With an old towel, Danny waited for Forest to get out.

'You look a lot cleaner.'

'Thanks, Danny.'

'Well, you do smell a lot better than you did. Throw your plimmies in the water and let them soak; we'll dry them out later. Dry yourself and come up to my bedroom. I've left some clothes on my bed. Put them on while I sort the yard out.'

Forest climbed into the clothes in the bedroom while feeling the house's warmth around him, and thought about the state of his bedroom. He would ask Danny if he could come back and help him tidy it up;

then he appeared in the doorway.

'Here's a pair of dad's old slippers for you. I'm sure he won't mind, and there's a comb in that drawer. You might want to try and sort out that muddle of hair you've got.'

Forest found the comb and winced as he tried to pull it through his curly locks. 'I might need to have this cut or shaved off.'

'Shave it off: the barber dad knows will do it for you.' Danny smelt Forest again to make sure he was clean. 'Mum should be home in an hour or so. You want some toast?'

'Please, Danny, if you've got some.'

'There's some strawberry jam in the kitchen cupboard: you can have some of that on it if you want. You ready to come down?'

'Nearly, just about there with this comb.'

'I'll put some bread under the grill. Come down when you've finished.' Danny knew his mum and dad would say something, but at least he was presentable.

Looking at Danny's bed, Forest remembered the one he had slept in at Christmas, but it must have gone back to the next-door neighbour. In the kitchen, four pieces of toast, two with jam spread across them, slid down Forest's throat, warming his insides, along with a mug of tea.

'I expect you could eat more, but mum's bringing in fish and chips with her. There's bound to be enough for you as well.' Danny was determined to speak to his mum and dad before talking to Forest. 'Come in the front room; I've lit the fire. It will soon be nice and warm in there. Dad told me to light it before they returned.'

It was half-past six when the front door opened, and the smell of the chippy came up the passage. Danny's mum came in first, and all the family followed behind her, and he saw his mum look at Forest in his clothes. His dad told one of his girls to nip back to the chip shop and get another meal. A few moans came back, but his elder sister left without taking her coat off. His dad went into the front room, making sure his boy had the fire going, while his mum hurried past, acknowledging Forest as she went into the kitchen. Danny tried to speak to her, but his sister returned, and everybody sat down, eating their supper from the newspaper. Forest was the first to finish, and Danny's mum left a good portion of her chips, offering them to him, as everybody watched her chips slide down his throat. After a cuppa, Forest sat by the fire, and Danny nipped out to the kitchen, where his mum and dad grabbed him.

'I see he's wearing your clothes and your dad's slippers. If this keeps up, you'll have none left. What happened this time? Your father is as concerned about him as I am.'

Danny began his story, cutting it short in places, and his parents listened astounded to what he was saying.

'Don't you ever think you're hard done by, Danny?

That lad in there, God bless him. Heaven knows what his life must be like.'

'Your mum's right. I've spoken to her about his situation.'

Danny thought, if only you knew the real truth.

Forest was told he could stay the night again, but had to top and tail in Danny's bed, and the next day his dad would borrow the bed from next door. Going to bed that night, Danny asked Forest outright if his mum was coming back to the house.

Sitting in their pyjamas, Forest sat on the bed and leant back against the wall. 'Don't know. She never tells me things like that.'

'I know she's your mum, but it's not right the way she treats you. All the beatings you've had from…' – Danny thought how to phrase it – 'her friends.'

'Her customers, you mean.'

'I suppose so.'

Forest laid down on the bed, and Danny joined him. 'You're the only person I've ever known that has looked out for me.'

Danny heard the little sobs coming from him. 'You're my mate; Johnny and Eddie's, too.'

'Not too sure about Eddie being my mate, but Johnny's all right.'

'Eddie has his funny ways. His dad's come home: he'll be different now. It's his mum that makes him the way he is.'

'I'd swap with him any time.'

'Look, tomorrow I will come around to your house, and we will tidy it up a bit. I just hope that smell has gone.'

'Thanks, Danny. You saw me with that pound note, that was the one my dad gave me when he came to the house. Mum don't know I've still got it, or she would have drunk it by now.'

'Where is it?'

Forest sat up and pointed to his back pocket. 'Let me take you to the picture house, my treat. I can't say that very often.'

Danny knew he mustn't refuse and sat up. 'Thanks, I'd like that. You know what's on?'

'Not sure. We'll have to check tomorrow.'

Suddenly, the door opened, and Danny's dad came in, telling them he'd need help with Mrs Knott's bed the next day and asking if Forest was all right.

Seeing the door close, Forest choked up a bit. 'He's a nice man, your dad, and your mum's great for all the things she has done for me.'

With a pillow at both ends of the bed, they climbed in. 'Promise me one thing, Forest.'

'What's that?'

'Don't fart tonight.'

That took all the emotions away as the two boys cracked up, giggling at each other.

Chapter Thirty-Seven

The next day, after making sure there was no one in Forest's house, the boys started downstairs, tidying the rooms and cleaning the sink with what water came out of the tap, seeing it was still a mess. Although the smell had subsided quite a bit, there was nevertheless an unpleasantness hanging around. With the back door opened, Danny saw the pile of discarded clothes.

'We need to get rid of that lot. God knows what might be living in it.'

Wiping around the sink, Forest glanced out through the window. 'Mum's got a big bag somewhere, probably in her room. I'll get it when I've done this.'

Danny looked around the outside yard, seeing how dirty and grimy it was. 'Forest, can I use your loo?'

'I wouldn't if I were you; a rat was lurking in there the other day, a big one, and it chucks up a bit. Mum has never properly cleaned in there, and all her clients use it to piss and throw up in, and not everyone finds the pan. If you need to pee, use the wall by the drain; no one can see you.'

Danny went out into the yard while Forest went upstairs. Coming back, he called out, 'You found that bag?' Not getting a reply, he went up the stairs warily and saw him rummaging in a wardrobe.

'I just found some of my clothes. Mum said she'd sold them. I never thought to look in here, and the presents you and your mum gave me are here.'

Danny edged into what he knew was Forest's mum's room and studied the bed, knowing what went on there.

'That's the entertainment area.'

Surprised at the remark, Danny followed Forest into his room and watched him put his clothes into his cupboard.

'Won't your mum find them in there?'

Picking up a threadbare blanket, he placed it on top. 'Doubt it. You want to give me a hand to sort my room out?'

'It's bloody cold in here. Can't we do something with that window?'

'Like what?'

'How about putting some heavy curtains up there? We could nail them. That might help.'

'Might, but let's sort this first.'

They pushed Forest's bed over the screwed floorboards and rearranged the room, making sure the room looked all right. Retrieving a big bag from his mum's wardrobe, he gave it to Danny and, once downstairs, he used one of his mum's old dresses to pick up his clothes in the yard, stuffing everything inside while they tried not to breathe.

'I'll chuck these in the bomb-site down the road,

Danny. The weather will eventually kill the smell.'

'Do it now, and then we can wash our hands before we go to the picture house.'

Eddie was in his element with his dad being home. The shock his mum had when she saw him made him realise how much she loved him. He kept thinking about when they reached the front door, where he asked his dad to let him go in first and told him to get warm by the fire and went to find his mum. He ran up the stairs and found her in her bedroom, sorting bedding out. As she went to say something, he put his finger to his lips, before asking her if she had opened the letter yet. The look told him she hadn't, and that was when he told her he had brought something home with him and her telling him it had better not be a stray. Then he heard his dad coming up the stairs and walking into the room; his mum passed out.

The evening was wonderful, with his dad sitting in his chair, smoking his pipe, and his mum fussing around them. He went to bed early for his dad's sake, as he knew he wanted to be alone with his mum. The next morning, he listened to his mum speaking about the Navy and wondered if his dad was going back to sea when he heard her news.

'Your father has to go back to sea in a week or two when his new ship is ready, but he tells me once this horrible war is over, your dad is coming out of the Navy. He has done enough.'

Eddie could not believe what his mum had told him; his dad loved the sea.

'Your father will find a safer job.'

Suddenly, his dad walked into the kitchen.

'Are you packing up the Navy, Dad?'

'Not quite, son; the Merchant Navy will require men with my knowledge. It'll be different, but a lot safer once the war is over.'

'Eddie imagined his dad being on one of the big ocean liners, tying up at all those exotic ports around the world and telling him about it. If his dad was joining up, then so would he. He just hoped his mum wouldn't moan about it. That afternoon, they went to the park for a kick-about and he laughed when he kicked the ball at his dad, and he headed it away, or when he scored a goal against his dad, and he chased after him.

'That cowboy film was great. Imagine the fun you would have back then. Barbara Stanwyck was good in it.'

Danny laughed at Forest's reaction. 'She's out of your league: she's no Nancy.'

'That's what I'd like to do when I grow up, get involved with horses in America. I'd like anything like that.'

'For a minute, I thought you were going to say Barbra Stanwyck . You've never said anything before about horses.'

'Imagine living in America like a cowboy and

living on a ranch out in the middle of nowhere. I could visit my dad – wouldn't that surprise him?'

Danny thought, yeah, it probably would. All the way home, Forest went on about how he fancied going to America.

'Want some chips, Danny? I could eat some.'

'If you're paying, why not.'

'Come on, I'll race you to the chippy.'

Chapter Thirty-Eight

Forest slept in Danny's room and snuggled under the thick blankets in the neighbour's bed, stretching his legs out. Looking at Danny asleep, he wondered whether he ought to tell him about what he'd seen under his floorboards – but should he? What if it was something valuable, money even? If it was something important, he might want to give it up. Deciding to think about it, he needed to borrow a screwdriver from Danny's dad if he had one. After breakfast, he told Danny he had to go back to his place to make sure his mum hadn't returned and would hide the clothes somewhere else should she look for them.

'Mum wants me for a couple of errands; do you want me to meet you when I've finished to give you a hand with anything?'

'No, not a lot to do. I'll come back and meet you here. If you're still out, I'll find you.'

'Okay, see you later.'

With Danny doing his errands and helping his dad, Forest made his way home with the tool. Entering his street, he noticed the curtains hadn't changed and guessed his mum was still away. Opening the front door, the faint smell of the sewer was still evident inside the house. Pulling his bed out, Forest gave himself room to deal with the screwed-down floorboards. Attacking the first one, he managed after a struggle to loosen the tight-fitting fastenings, and eventually, just two shortened boards remained. He checked out the window to ensure no one was there and sat ready to discover whatever was underneath. About to pull the boards away, a bang came from downstairs as the front door crashed open.

Forest listened to his mum's voice and a man's vulgar laughter as they came into the house. Without further ado, he replaced the boards and eased his bed back, lifting it into position, and made his way to the top of the stairs. Recognising the voice of the man who had tossed him into the foul water, he eavesdropped on the conversation as best he could, hearing his mum laugh along with the man as they joked about something or other. Then his mum's voice approached the stairs. Forest, worried about being found went back into his room, opened his wardrobe and climbed in, pulling the doors shut behind him. With his heart beating in his ears and his body shaking, he squatted there, hoping and praying she wouldn't come in.

'Forest, you home, you little bleeder? Christ, it stinks in here. What have you been doing?'

The heavy footfall of the man came behind her as his mum looked into his room.

'Had a change around, have you? Well, that won't last, seeing I'm letting the room out.'

Forest heard her walk into the room and kick the opposite side of his wardrobe. Then the man spoke to her, pulling her away, suggesting what they came for, and they left the room, going into the other bedroom. With his knees under his chin, he listened to the noisy developments coming through the walls like at any previous time. The time passed agonisingly slowly with his hands over his ears and his body aching in the constricted space. As he shifted with the cramp, heavy footsteps came to his doorway and moved into the room. Hearing hands on the wardrobe door, Forest froze, waiting for the reaction he knew would come, when his mum spoke to the man and pulled him away.

'Come on, Bruce, I'll get the window fixed this afternoon and show you everything later before your brother arrives. Let's go out and have that drink first.'

'You wicked woman, is it my money or this body you are eager for?'

Forest heard his mum moan, and then they left, heading downstairs. Easing the wardrobe door open, he lifted his stiffening legs out and stretched, before listening to the front door slam shut. Getting to his feet, he crept to the window and watched as the two of them walked away arm in arm. Knowing he had lost his room, he pulled his bed out and lifted the boards. Below him was a blanket covering something; removing the blanket, a large biscuit tin lay on its side, tied together with string. Picking it up, he gave it a shake, but nothing moved inside. He pulled the yarn away with his hands shaking and opened the hinged lid.

There facing him was a stack of postcards. Removing some, he could not believe his eyes: crammed underneath were banknotes of sizable denominations. Not bothering to pull them out, he closed the tin and fastened the string the best he could. Putting the boards and bed back, he collected his clothes and the money-filled container, along with the screwdriver, and placed them in the bag he had, knowing he had to be careful with his find, should Danny or any of his family know what he had. Otherwise, he could lose it and his new bed. Finding a derelict building, Forest searched for a confined space inside and sat down. Opening his find, he extracted an incredible amount of money.

'Have you seen anything of Forest, Mum?'

'Not since he left this morning. He is coming back, isn't he?'

'He said he was. He borrowed one of dad's tools to do a job. I hope he's still got it, or dad won't be too pleased.'

'I've made up his bed in your room, and I've put that little cupboard there. It fits nicely in that space between the beds. You can have a shelf each.'

'Thanks, Mum.'

'Are you going around to his house to find him?'

'No, I'll wait upstairs. Dad's let me go, for now. I'll give him a hand later if he wants me.' Up in his bedroom, Danny hoped nothing had happened again; then he heard a knocking on the front door and called down. 'I'll get it, Mum. I think it might be Forest.' Hurrying downstairs, Danny opened the front door and saw him grinning at him. 'I expected you earlier. Come upstairs; mum's made Mrs Knott's bed up. You are still staying with us?'

Danny's mum came out of the kitchen. Seeing Forest, she waved at him. 'Your bed is ready for you. Did you sort your problem out?'

'Yes, thank you, Mrs Downes. I've found the clothes you gave me at Christmas.'

'That's good.'

'Come upstairs, Forest. What else have you got in the bag?'

Taking it out, Forest passed Danny the screwdriver. 'Thank your dad for me if you see him before I do.'

'You didn't tell me what you wanted it for?'

'Let's go upstairs; I need to tell you something.'

Danny pointed to the new cupboard. 'You take the bottom shelf.'

Putting his clothes inside, Forest pulled out the tin and opened it, showing Danny some postcards. 'I found these in the house. Is it okay to keep them in there with my clothes?'

'Take both shelves; I don't need them. My stuff is in the airing cupboard.' Danny looked at the picture postcards of different places around the country. 'You like this sort of thing?'

Forest, observing he wasn't that interested, put them back and placed the almost empty tin in the cupboard. 'Danny, while I was there, mum came home with the sailor who tossed me in the wastewater. She's letting my room out to the man's brother. I overheard her telling him he could stay there. I don't know what to do if I have to leave here.'

'When is she doing this?'

'Today. I was in the wardrobe in my room, listening. She didn't know I was there.'

'I can't believe she would do that.'

'I want to go back before she brings this other bloke with her. I think there might be more of my clothes hidden there, or should I say *your* clothes.'

'Do it now. I'll come with you.'

That was the one thing Forest didn't want. 'You don't have to come.'

'I'll help you find them. Let me tell mum we're going out.'

Downstairs, Danny walked into the kitchen to find his dad there. 'Me and Forest are going out for a while.'

'Before you go, I need a bit of help next door, son. Mrs Knott's got a problem with her sink. I can't get under there. I'll probably need you.'

'Okay, Dad. Forest has got something to do at home. Is it okay for him to go?'

'No problem.' Seeing him behind Danny, he spoke to him. 'You go and do what you need to, son. Is everything all right?'

'Yes, Mr Downes.'

Danny followed his dad next door, and Forest ran back to the derelict building with his bag. He went inside, found the money he had hidden, hurried back to Danny's house, and knocked on the door, where Mrs Downes answered.

'That was quick. Are you going upstairs?'

Forest nodded.

'Take these towels up with you and put them on the bed in the front bedroom: that will save my legs a trip.'

Taking the towels, Forest hurried up, before going back into Danny's room and pulling the tin from the cupboard. Placing the money inside, he covered it with the postcards as he found them the first time.

Chapter Thirty-Nine

Just after everyone had sat down from eating dinner at five o'clock, the air-raid sirens sounded, and the family hurried from the house to the air-raid shelter at the bottom of the street. Forest, anxious about his money, reluctantly left, hoping it would be a false alarm, seeing there had not been any air raids lately. Sitting in the shelter along with other residents, Danny and Forest listened to the guns firing as planes came over the city. The noise was thunderous as the guns fired, and without warning, a massive explosion sounded close by.

'That's a house or something gone. I need to get out there. Everybody stay here until the all-clear sounds,' said Danny's dad.

Danny watched as his dad ran out of the shelter with his metal warden hat on his head and looked up into the sky. 'Take care, Dad, those Luftwaffe are probably still up there.'

Forest was itching to find out it wasn't Danny's house that got hit, as he could imagine the money he had found lying all over the place. Everybody heard a couple more bombs hit, but they were further away this time. Many people in the shelter gave their views on Hitler, and then they heard a cheer go up as the all-clear sounded.

Eddie was out in the garden at home with his dad when a lone German fighter banked over the city. With the sirens going off, they watched a plane come towards them and hurried indoors. With his dad grabbing his mum, they rushed into the kitchen and dived under the kitchen table as their only means of safety. Eddie's dad told them to stay where they were and made his way out of the house after the explosion. Smoke rose high into the sky, giving him directions to the difficulties he knew he would face.

'I don't know why your father has to do that. He's not at sea now.'

'It's his job, Mum. Dad's not the type to stand around: you know that.' Listening to the unmistakable all-clear soundings, Eddie wondered where the bomb had landed. His first thought was Danny's house, but he knew they were close to a shelter. In the garden, looking at the column of smoke, he realised it must be closer to Forest's place, and that was when he decided to follow his dad. Eddie ran as the black smoke rose high into the clear blue sky, with his mum calling him back. Eddie saw it wasn't Danny's house and continued towards Forest's.

Getting back home, Danny and Forest went up to their room as Mrs Downes made some tea like she always did after a raid. 'I'll call up when I've made it.'

'Bloody war; now it looks as though someone else has copped it.'

Not really listening to Danny, Forest sat on his bed thinking about what he should do with the money, when the front door opened, and footsteps headed towards the kitchen.

Danny edged towards the top of the stairs, trying to listen as his dad said something to his mum, guessing someone they knew had copped it. Back in his room, Danny gave Forest a shake, seeing he was somewhere else. 'Looks like somebody mum or dad knows has…' Then he heard his dad come up the stairs.

'Is Forest with you?'

'Yeah.'

His dad walked him back into the room. 'Sit down, Danny, sit with Forest and let me sit there.'

Both boys knew something had happened and waited for something they didn't want to hear.

'Forest,' Danny's dad started, placing his hand on his knee, 'you live at number ten in the next street, am I right?'

Forest nodded, not knowing what else to do.

'Son, I'm afraid your house had a direct hit.'

Forest sat there as Danny stared at him.

'We found three bodies in the house, and I imagine one of them was your mother. Did she have black hair, and do these earrings belong to her?'

Forest looked at the cheap dangly earrings, knowing they were hers.

'Son, are they?'

Forest nodded once again, knowing his life had changed. 'Mum's dead?' Feeling Danny hold him, he pulled away from the embrace and sat there.

'Forest, the two other men, do you know who they are?'

With his head all over the place, he knew who they were in one way. 'I never know who mum's coming home with.'

Danny guessed who they might be, but kept quiet.

'Forest, are you all right?'

'I think so.'

Mr Downes got up from the bed and told Danny to stay in the house with Forest and not leave. Indicating Danny should leave the room, he spoke to him at the bottom of the stairs before hurrying away. Back upstairs, Danny went into the bedroom to see Forest lying on his bed, looking up at him.

'Well, things have got a lot worse.' Turning over, he hid his face in the pillow.

Danny put his hand out, feeling Forest shake, and knew he was crying. 'Dad said you're staying with us, while listening to him break his heart as he held onto the pillow. 'I said you're staying here.' Danny heard his mum come up the stairs and opened the door for her as she stood there with two mugs of tea.

She whispered, 'How is he?'

'He's crying.'

'Take these and stay with him. Have you told him

he's staying here?'

Danny nodded and took the mugs.

'I'll be in the kitchen if you want me. It would be better for you to stay with him for the time being.'

Suddenly, there was banging on the front door, and Mrs Downes hurried down to answer it.

'Eddie, what are you doing here?'

'Forest's house has caught a hit. Is Danny in?'

'Yes, we know. Forest is upstairs with Danny. Do you want to go up?'

'Can I?'

'Be careful what you say: he's a bit teary.'

Eddie climbed the stairs and opened Danny's door to see Forest lying across the bed on his stomach. 'My dad has gone around to Forest's place to help.'

Forest listened and turned over, wiping his face. 'What place?'

'I'm sorry, Forest, is there anything I can do?'

Danny interrupted. 'He's staying with us now. This will be his home.'

Forest looked at both of them, wiping the tears away. 'Mum's dead, and her fancy blokes. At least I won't have to put up with being threatened or beaten up again.'

'No, you won't, not in this house. Dad was the one who suggested you stay. Mum did, too, once she realised.'

Once Eddie had left, Danny sat with Forest, waiting for him to sit up.

'Mum hated me more than I ever realised. The things she told me, in a way I'm glad she's gone.'

Danny choked on his mouthful of tea.

'Did I tell you she wished she never had me? She told me I ruined her life. The names she called me, along with her blokes. They made me feel worthless.' Forest spoke about his life, telling some of the terrible situations he had got in with his mum's visitors. Danny sat there listening, wanting to comfort his friend, but he knew he would push him away as now wasn't the time.

As the day wore on, Danny's dad returned and sat with his wife in the kitchen, discussing Forest's future. Later that evening, Mr Downes brought Danny and Forest down to the front room when the girls had gone to bed.

'What's up, Dad?'

Forest stood there, expecting the worst, seeing Mrs Downes sitting in her chair, watching them.

'Sit down. I want to talk to you both.'

Forest gripped his hands together under the table and began to shake. Mrs Downes got up from her chair and put her arm around his shoulder.

'Are you all right, Forest?'

A nod came back as he hunched over.

'Danny, you and Forest, I've had a chat with your mum.'

Feeling his bladder would burst, Forest hurried from the room, frightened of what would happen to him.

'What's happening, Dad? He's not leaving, is he?'

'No, Danny. Tell me, do you know if he has any relatives?'

'He had an aunt and uncle in London that used to look after him, but he told me they hardly fed him and made him work hard to stay with them. When he was eight years old, they made him work in the docks, cleaning and sorting after school and at weekends. You're not sending him back to them, are you?'

'No, Danny, I'm not. Go and see if he's all right.'

Moments later, the two boys came back into the room and sat down.

'Forest, you know you can stay here with us, but I have to ask you a question.'

Forest looked up, clenching his hands together.

'Danny has told us you have relatives in London.'

'Please don't send me there.' Tears appeared in his eyes.

'Not if you don't want me to, I won't.'

Mrs Downes saw the relief in his face. 'Forest.' She waited for his attention. 'Forest, if you are going to live here with us, I cannot have you keep calling me Mrs Downes and Bernard, Mr Downes. Would you like to call me Auntie or Joyce? I don't mind.'

Danny put his hands across the table. 'And I want you as a brother, not a mate.'

Mrs Downs kissed Forest's forehead, before leaving the room with her husband. 'You think about what I said and let me know.'

Chapter Forty

In their bedroom that evening, Danny waited for Forest to come to terms with what his parents had told him. Getting undressed and into his pyjamas, Danny picked up his comic and sat on the bed, waiting for Forest to say something while trying to read his serial and not getting anywhere. Then he noticed Forest studying him.

'What do you think about what my mum said?'

Sat there fully dressed, Forest rubbed his eyes. 'Your mum's lovely, and your dad's great. I've never known anybody like them before.'

Danny reached under his pillow for his penknife that Forest had given him at Christmas and pulled out a blade. 'I think we should be blood-brothers.'

Forest looked at the knife and smiled. 'What, like cutting ourselves.'

'It's something I want to do: let our blood join together, then we can be brothers for life.'

'You serious, Danny? You want some of my blood in you?'

'Why not. You got something wrong with it?'

'After what's happened to me, I wouldn't be surprised.'

'Come on, let's do it.' Danny drew the blade across

his palm with the penknife ready and winced as the skin parted and the blood oozed out. He put a finger over it and passed the opened penknife across to Forest. Taking it and holding his palm out, Forest looked at Danny, hoping he knew what he was doing.

'You sure about this?'

'I'm sure. Hurry up, or there will be blood all over the place.'

Forest, doing the same, watched as his blood spread across his outstretched palm, before Danny gripped their hands together.

'Brothers for life. We've got our blood mixed in each other's bodies now. We may have different surnames, but brothers we are!'

'How long do we sit here holding hands? It feels a bit girlish.'

Danny shoved Forest and burst out laughing, with Forest doing the same, taking away some of what had happened and making him feel a lot better.

'Let's get downstairs and put a plaster on it. Mum's going to call me daft for doing this.'

'I think you're daft.'

'Come on, brother, before blood drips on the bedclothes; then mum will have a reason to moan at me.'

Forest pushed Danny in front of him, thinking that he would be that person if he had to choose someone for a brother. 'I might not have bought that penknife for you if I'd known you were going to slice me.'

Danny turned and stepped down the first stair. 'The amount of blood you've lost in the past, this shouldn't worry you in the slightest.'

Forest went to cuff him. 'You saucy sod,' he said, and chased him down the stairs.

With their wounds plastered, Danny answered the front door the next day to find Johnny standing there. 'We all wondered where you were. Where have you been?'

As Johnny went to speak, he noticed Forest behind Danny. 'Sorry to hear about your mum, Forest. I've just been to Eddie's, and he told me what happened.'

'Thanks, Johnny. Danny's mum and dad are putting me up.'

'No, we're not. You're living with us.' Danny held up his hand with the thick plaster on it.

Johnny looked at it and saw Forest had a similar one. 'What happened to you two?'

Danny jumped into answering first. 'Me and Forest are brothers.'

'That will take some convincing, if you know what I mean.'

'He means blood-brothers. Danny decided to slice me and mix our blood. It serves him right if he turns black. His mum thinks we're mad, and his sisters.'

'Weird, if you ask me.'

'So, where have you been?'

'Mum decided to clean the house through and change things around. I had to help her.' Johnny danced around on his toes. 'I think she is seeing somebody she met when we were away at her brother's. He's foreign and works for the government.'

'What, are you getting a new dad?'

'Don't know, Danny. Mum likes him a lot, and I know he likes mum. He's staying with us next week.'

'Hope your walls are thick.' The smile and giggles coming back made even Forest smile. 'Don't go listening if they do.'

The three boys made their way out into the street, with Forest telling them he needed to see what had happened to his house. The devastation was extreme, as houses on either side of his had collapsed in on themselves.

'Mum got more than a bang that time!'

Johnny looked aghast at Forest.

'Don't worry, Danny knows how I feel about her. She was kicking me out of the house and letting some bloke have my room. Suppose she did me a favour. That was the first, and now the last time she'll ever do that.' Turning away from the destruction, he added, 'Looks like it's going to rain; is there anywhere we can go?'

Coming home from the picture house, Johnny said his goodbyes and thanked Forest for the treat. Walking home together, Forest put his arm around Danny's shoulder. 'Must be getting taller. I could never have done this when we first met.'

'I bet you will grow a lot faster now you'll be living

at our house. You're not that much shorter than me now. Come on, mum's doing grub in an hour. I think we've got spam fritters tonight.'

'What's those?'

'Only spam in a batter. Mum makes a decent job of cooking any meal.'

'You're making me feel hungry already.'

In bed that night, Forest decided to tell Danny about when he lived in London. He came out with shocking details, revealing how he had knifed a man who was trying to strangle his mum, and she hit him with a heavy pan. He told Danny he was sure he didn't kill him, and it was his mum that did it, and how afterwards she got him to tip the body in the River Thames.

'That's why we came here; mum was worried about being found out.'

'Bloody hell, Forest, that's twice you've killed someone.'

Forest sat up and put his legs out. 'That wouldn't have happened if he had never tried to do what he was going to do. You saw the state of me.'

'Sorry, I didn't mean it like that.'

'Danny, there's something else I need to speak to you about.'

'Not another murder?'

'I don't murder people: I've just had bad luck all my life living with mum. No, this is something different. Promise me you won't say anything to your family.'

'You sure it's not anything like that?'

'Promise. When I went back to my house, I told you mum came in with a boyfriend. Promise you won't say anything.'

Danny sat up in bed and stared at Forest. 'As long as it's not about killing someone.'

'No, honest. Danny, I found something under the floorboards in my bedroom. Do you know who lived in that house before we moved in?'

'Some old bloke; he died years ago, I think. I'm sure mum said the police took him away. Why, what did you find?'

Forest opened the cupboard and lifted the tin out.

'What, those old postcards?'

Forest, ready to lift the lid, looked up. 'Is your mum or dad likely to come in?'

'Doubt it. Why?'

Removing the cards, Forest indicated for Danny to come closer and put his finger to his lips. 'Don't shout out. You ready?'

'What is it?'

Forest set the tin on the floor between the beds. 'Four thousand pounds is sitting in there. I've counted it twice.'

Danny looked at the money. 'Bloody hell, all that! What are you going to do with it?'

'Keep it. I can't give it back. The old man died: that's what you said.'

Danny fingered the top of the pile of notes. 'Why didn't you tell me earlier?'

'I wasn't sure if you would say something to your mum and dad, and I would have to give it back. This money can see me having a good life when I get older.'

'You can't keep it here; someone might find it.'

'I have no choice, but I want to bank it later on.'

'But you said you didn't want mum or dad to know.'

'I don't, but I do want to give them some of it.'

Danny studied Forest, knowing how perhaps he deserved to find the money. 'If you don't want them to know about it, how can you give it to them?'

'That's something I want you and me to think about. Your parents have been good to me, and I'll make sure they get some of this.'

'How much are you giving them?'

'Is one thousand pounds enough?'

Danny fell back on the bed and whistled. 'All that?'

'It still leaves me with three. I want you to have half, too. When I put this in the bank, and we're old enough, you can have half, I promise.'

Danny sat up and thought about what he'd said. 'You don't have to do that.'

'Yes, I do. We're brothers, remember.'

Danny got out of bed and sat with Forest. 'Who'd have thought me seeing you that day when dad was cockling that we would be here now with you telling me this? Mum and dad, with all that money, I can see them moving house one day.'

Both of them kept discussing how they would get

the money to Danny's parents, and after several ideas, they gave up, not knowing how they would do it, before drifting off to sleep in the early hours.

Chapter Forty-One

The following morning, Danny and Forest were still discussing how to give some of the money to Danny's parents when the idea came.

'Your dad, he saves lives doing his job, people in the blitz and all that.'

'He's saved dozens all over the city.' Danny smiled at Forest, 'That's it, someone's life he has saved gives him the money, but secretly, like, what's that word – anonymously. But how can we manage it?'

Forest liked the idea and grinned. 'That's it: we'll do that. We can put it through the letterbox with a note, but I will write it. I guess your dad knows your writing.'

Sitting together at the breakfast table, both quieter than usual, they tried not to think about their plan, when Danny's mum challenged them.

'You two had words?'

Danny was the first to begin giggling, and Forest followed.

'No, Mum.'

Suddenly, Danny's sisters came in and sat down, listening to the two of them, while ignoring them as silly.

'Danny, after school, your dad wants you to give

him a hand in Fence Street; there's a house down there where some trees have fallen, and he's cutting them up for logs.'

'Me and Forest will give him a hand, Mum.' Still, the giggling came from both of them.

'I don't know what is up with you two this morning. I heard you talking late last night. It's a wonder you're not both tired out this morning.'

Two weeks later, with Forest having practised many times, he wrote a note with Danny's dad's name on it. Happy with the wording and having bought a large brown envelope, Forest wrote Mr Downes name and placed the money inside. With their hearts racing, they waited for the family to leave, before placing the envelope on the mat inside the front door, crunching it a bit as though it had come through the letterbox, before disappearing themselves. Coming home later, they walked into the house, hoping their labours had worked. Going up to their room together, Danny sat on the bed and waited for something to happen, while Forest fidgeted beside him.

'What if your mum and dad don't say anything?'

Danny shrugged his shoulders. 'Don't know.'

'Danny, Forest, dinner!'

At the table with the rest of the family, Danny could see something had happened, yet no one said anything. It wasn't until afterwards that Danny's mum spoke to them, with the family sitting together in the front room.

'Something happened today.'

The girls looked up at the unusual statement and together asked, 'What, Mum?'

'Danny, you and Forest left after us. Did you see anyone come to the house?'

Danny felt Forest kick him under the table. 'No. Why should I?' He hated having to tell his mum a fib, but as Forest had said, he might very well have to.

Sat in his chair, Danny's dad sucked on his pipe and blew a ring of smoke into the air.

'There was an envelope addressed to your dad put through the letterbox today, but we don't know who it's from: the writing was a bit strange, but that's not the issue.'

Forest joined in the conversation when he decided he should say something. 'Danny, don't you remember when we were leaving. That old man, he had something like that, a brown envelope or parcel.'

Danny's dad looked up. 'Did you see what he looked like?'

'He was just an old man with a cap on his head; we didn't take much notice.'

'Is something wrong, Dad?' Danny tried hard not to smile.

'You could say that, son.'

'What happened, Mum?'

Danny's mum lifted the envelope from the floor beside her chair and placed it on her lap. This time, Danny kicked Forest as not to say any more. Without warning, she opened the brown paper packet and withdrew the bundles of notes.

Both girls stood up and hurried across the room, touching the money while asking questions. Danny, doing the same, joined them, as Forest stayed where he was, taking in the scene.

'There is one thousand pounds here. The note says your dad saved someone's life; that meant a lot to them, and he's giving him this as a thank you for doing it.'

'You save lots of people, Dad. What are you going to do with it?'

'Your father isn't sure, Danny. He will wait a while should the person come back for it. Do you know what this money could buy?'

'We can have new dresses, and you can move to a bigger house, and...'

'And this money might not belong to this man. Your dad and I are keeping it safe for a time until we find out who this person is, in which case your dad is going to give it back.'

Danny, alarmed at the news, kneeled beside his dad. 'Dad, if this man wants you to have it, you should keep it. You deserve it.'

'We will do as your mother said for the time being, and once the war is over, we will decide what to do then. Just let us hope Hitler doesn't get here first.'

As the year progressed, so did the fact that leaving school was getting closer. In April, it was a weekend when Eddie came looking for Danny and the others to tell them his news. Sat together in the park, Eddie began his broadcast.

'Dad's got another ship.'

Forest looked up at the few words spoken. 'What, that's all?'

'When the war is over, we are leaving Portsmouth and England altogether. Dad said we are going to live in Australia. He's got it all arranged, and mum's over the moon. He's not going into the Merchant Navy as he told us; he knows someone, and they've told him that with his knowledge of mechanics in the engine room of ships, the Aussies would invite him with open arms and a good wage.'

Danny could see how excited Eddie was. 'That's brilliant news. Wait until I tell mum and dad. They will be shocked.'

Johnny looked up. 'Let's hope he gets through the rest of the war.'

'Don't spoil it, Johnny. His dad survived a sinking. He'll be all right.' Danny kicked Johnny's foot as if to say 'be quiet'. 'What will you do out there, Eddie?'

Forest interrupted. 'Chase kangaroos, probably.'

Everybody laughed, including Eddie.

'Dad said I could work with animals if I wanted, once I've done my service in the Army. You know how I like anything like that.'

They all talked about living on the other side of the world and what opportunities there would be. Hours went by, and Johnny left with Eddie, leaving the two boys to discuss the news.

'Blimey, I never expected that.'

'Australia! I wonder if we'll ever get to go there?'

'With the money you found, who knows. School finishes this summer. You thought of what you are going to do?'

'Think so. I'm looking at going into the Army when I'm eighteen. There's no way I'd join the Navy, not after seeing all those sailors coming into the house. Too many memories. What about you, what are you thinking?'

'I want to join the Air Force.'

'What will your mum and dad say about that?'

'Think they'll be all right about it.'

The talk of what both boys wanted to do continued, and again in their room that night. With the month of May arriving, Danny found out that his dad had discovered something that belonged to Forest when he helped clear the rubble from his house.

'Danny, a word in private.'

'This piece of paper, we found it in Forest's old house; it was in a box with other unimportant paperwork, but this is his birth certificate. Could you give it to him? It would be better coming from you. It's his birthday on 19th May. Your mum wants to give him a birthday treat; you okay with that?'

Danny took the discoloured paper and realised Forest was almost the same age as him, just a month older. 'Sure, Dad, I'll give it to him.'

Chapter Forty-Two

Forest's birthday became a success as Johnny and Eddie came for tea with them, and he received presents for the first time, along with a homemade cake. One of the gifts was a plain-paper exercise book with pencils, a rubber and a ruler that Danny's mum gave him. She told him she had seen him drawing and pencilling on scraps of paper. It was a day he would never forget, especially with Danny's mum and dad making a fuss of him.

A few days later, near the Victory Dockyard gate, Forest found the Sergeant-Major, busy with people entering the dockyard, and he waited across the road, hoping he would soon be alone. Seeing his chance as the man came back, he took his moment and ran across the main road.

'No home to go to, son?'

Forest smiled the best he could. Coming up to the well-turned-out individual, he put on his best voice. 'Good morning, Sir.'

Straight away, the man twitched his moustache and squinted at the young lad in front of him. 'Do I have to be worried about the "Sir" treatment? It is usually Sergeant-Major.'

'No, Sir, I promise. I was wondering, could you

help me with something?'

'That frightens me straight away. Whatever it is, there is nothing I can do about it right now. Come back later, at six o'clock; I finish my shift at that time. Are you sure nothing is happening that I need to be aware of?'

Forest grinned and put his hand out, unsure if the man would shake his hand, but he just nodded. 'Until six then. Where shall I meet you? Here?'

'That public house along the pavement opposite where you swindled me out of drinks and crisps. Come and find me. I'll be in the public bar.'

'Thank you, Sergeant-Major. I call you that because I don't know your name.'

'It's Mr Perkins to you.'

'Mr Perkins, I will see you at six o'clock. Can I buy you a drink?'

The man looked at Forest and smiled. 'You sure it won't be me buying you one?'

'No, Sir, my treat.'

'Off with you now, I have a busy day ahead of me with ships coming and going.'

Making his way across the road, Forest looked back once to see the Sergeant-Major, now Mr Perkins, pointing directions to a couple of sailors as they entered the dockyard, probably ready to leave with their kit-bags over their shoulder.

Inside the public bar, looking for Mr Perkins at six

o'clock, Forest stopped when the barman confronted him.

'The bottle and jug's next door. I think that's what you're looking for. I'm not serving coloureds in here, even if you were old enough.'

'It's all right, Len. I told him to meet me in here. Get him a lemonade, please.'

'Sit him around the corner, Frank. I don't want customers thinking I'm serving the likes of him in here.'

Forest took the insult like the hundreds of others he'd always received and would have left, but he needed to speak to Mr Perkins.

'That's my pint on that table, lad. Take it and place it on an empty one over there.' He pointed to a secluded section away from any other drinkers. 'I will be there in a minute.' Stood at the bar, waiting for the lemonade, Mr Perkins expressed his feelings. 'That's a bit harsh, Len. It's not the lad's fault he's black. He seems a nice boy; cheeky, but no trouble.'

'Keep him out of sight; that's all I ask.'

Frank Perkins placed Forest's drink in front of him and sat down. 'So, what's all this about you wanting to ask me something?'

'Thank you for the lemonade, Mr Perkins. I was going to buy you a drink.'

'Never mind that now.'

'I hope I haven't caused you a problem?'

'Take no notice of Len: he's a queer one. He gets funny with people for some reason. Don't think he should have ever been a barman.'

Forest looked across at the man behind the bar. 'Is he, what you said, queer?'

'No, not that way. He just gets uppity with certain people at times. If he owned this place, Hitler would do him a favour by dropping a bomb on it, as he would never have customers. Bill, the landlord, he's a good sort. He won't mind us being in here.' Taking a long swallow of his beer, Frank wiped his moustache and turned to face Forest. 'Now, what is it you want?'

Having thought about what he was going to say, Forest sipped his drink and started. 'A member of the family has left me some money, and I want to put it in the bank. My mum died when that lone Luftwaffe dropped his load on us a while back. I was out with my mate, and mum was at home when it hit.'

Forest saw the concern on Mr Perkins' face.

'I'm sorry, where are you now?'

'My mate's mum and dad have taken me in. I'm all right, but I was wondering, could you help me put the money into a bank account or something?'

'I can do that with you, lad. When do you want to do it?'

'When it's convenient for you, Mr Perkins.'

Frank put his hand on Forest's head and ruffled his hair. 'You ought to get that lot shaved off; the few coloured lads in the Navy have their hair close-cropped, and it suits them. Seeing you've got some money, why don't you have it done?'

'Could do, I suppose.'

'Look, I'm off tomorrow at two o'clock. Meet me at the gate, and we can get this money banked. You happy with that?'

'I want to be able to put more money in when I can. Will I be able to do that?'

'You'll be able. Drink that lemonade up and shoot off, and I will see you tomorrow. Some friends have just come in, and I need to speak to them.'

Finishing his drink, Forest stood up and put his hand out, and this time Mr Perkins shook it. 'See you at two tomorrow.'

'I never thought he would help like that, and he bought you a drink in the pub?'

'His name is Frank Perkins. Can you believe it, me and him sitting in the pub together having a drink?'

'How much are you putting in?'

'I'm taking twenty quid with me, and once I've opened it, the rest I'm putting in now and again. I think we ought to do it together in different banks. I don't want it looking like I've pinched it. Don't forget, Danny, some of it is yours.'

'You've given dad that other money. You don't have to give me any.'

'Half each, I've told you. Has your dad said any more about it?'

Danny checked they were alone and no one was outside the bedroom door. 'I heard dad tell mum it looked as though he would end up with the money. He has tried to find out who gave it to him, but nobody's got a clue.'

'Let's hope it stays that way.'

Forest opened the tin and took out twenty pounds, folding it into his pocket. Finding a couple of one-pound notes, he gave one to Danny, telling him to treat himself. 'Like being a millionaire with all this. I wonder if the old man who lived there was dodgy, seeing the police became involved. It makes you wonder.'

'Whoever he was, it's in the past now. I bet you're glad it was you that found it and not...' Danny stopped in his tracks, realising what his next words were going to be.

'My mum, you mean?'

'I didn't think; sorry, mate.'

Forest laughed. 'Brothers now, remember?'

'Yeah, brothers.'

The next day, Forest headed to the barbershop. Coming out with his tangled locks gone, he waited outside the dockyard gate, feeling the warm day around his head. Not recognising him, Mr Perkins almost walked past him, then, after some comments about his new look, they headed towards the bank in town. Mr Perkins explained what he wanted to the man behind the desk and Forest handed over his birth certificate, even though there was no father's name on it. Seeing the document, Mr Perkins smiled at Forest in a fatherly way.

'Well, Master Forest Grady. You have joined the few people who have money in the bank.'

Forest's grin exceeded the width of his face as the man behind the counter handed him back the birth certificate, along with a little blue book showing the sum of twenty pounds deposited into his account. He told him to bring the book with him whenever he wanted to top it up. With his birth certificate back in his pocket, Forest came out of the bank a confident somebody and suggested to Mr Perkins that he wanted to buy him a drink, seeing he didn't before.

'Thank you. A beer would go down nice right now, seeing you can afford it.'

Chapter Forty-Three

Forest managed to put as much money into his bank account as possible without getting too many strange looks, along with Danny helping out at times. Then, at the end of July, with school finished, everybody went their separate ways. Eddie and Johnny found employment in the Post Office, delivering letters and telegrams on their work bikes. Danny helped his dad, as did Forest, until they came to find a proper job. Sitting together in the house with Danny's parents one evening, Danny's dad approached the subject of appropriate employment.

'Danny, you and Forest helping me is all well and good, but it's not a proper job. I know you want to join the Air Force, but let this bloody war finish first. Forest, I expect you want to find work, too. Have either of you got any idea of what you want to do?'

Danny guessed the question would come eventually. 'I thought about the ambulance service, Dad. I know I can't drive yet, but I wouldn't mind finding out about it. I want to learn about first aid and all that.'

'I'll speak to Mr Harper down the street; he's an ambulance man. He might be able to point you in that direction. Forest, what about you?'

He had begun to understand all kinds of subjects much better in his last years at school, especially with his drawing, and guessed he ought to find a suitable job. 'I wouldn't mind getting involved with the building game, something like that.'

'Well, there'll certainly be enough of that, seeing the places around here are flattened. You mean like a bricklayer?'

'I'd like to draw different buildings, like being an architect. You know what I mean?'

'I should think you would need to learn all about that first, like going back to school again. That might be difficult.'

'If you and Auntie wouldn't mind, that's what I'd like to try.'

'You know you will have to spend time in the Services, don't you?'

'I want to join the Army when I'm eighteen, but if I could get educated more and learn about architecture, I'm sure that would help me later on.'

Even Danny was surprised by Forest's outburst.

'You never said anything to me about all this? Are you any good at it? I've never seen you do anything.'

Forest left the room and came back with a hardback book, and passed it to Danny. 'I did that when I was on my own. Mr Davies at school saw me doodling and pulled me to one side and asked me what I was doing, so I told him. He explained to me about things. I knew you weren't keen on him, so I didn't say anything.'

'You are a sneaky one.' Danny flipped through the pages, looking at all the sketches, and passed the book to his dad.

'You did all this, Forest?'

'It's just messing about, really.'

'Well, you can draw, I can see that. Are you any good with figures?'

'When I started drawing, they seemed to open up for me more than ever. I don't seem to have any problems.'

'Then I suggest you find out a bit more about it. You've nothing to lose by it.'

Danny, working in the city hospital, began learning all about first aid while becoming reasonably efficient. Forest managed to get a position in the dockyard thanks to Mr Perkins and gained attendance at night school intended for architecture, among other subjects. Then, in September 1945, the war ended. Celebrations and parties erupted across the country. Years earlier, the money that came unexpectedly as a gift would now support the Downes family in what they wanted to do. Forest and Danny were thrilled that after all this time, their plan had eventually worked.

At the age of eighteen, both of them joined the Services: Danny enlisted in the Royal Air Force and Forest the Army, with both of them signing up for five years. Forest's bank account was more than healthy, with almost three thousand pounds safely tucked away, where he kept assuring Danny that half of the money was his. Danny's sisters were courting, and at the end of September the following year, both girls, now young women, were getting married. The money Danny's dad had received gave each daughter a wonderful double wedding together. With Danny and Forest turning up in their military uniforms, both parents stood proudly with them in the wedding pictures. With the daughters leaving the family home, Jenny going to Scotland to live with her new husband and Florence to Wales with hers, the house that evening appeared empty.

After Danny's parents had gone to bed, downstairs together, Forest explained that he was going abroad with his regiment to North Africa and asked if anything was happening with Danny.

'Not yet. North Africa will be hot. How are you getting on in the Army?'

'Some of the lads are okay, but I have to watch one or two. You know, the black thing, but we don't want to talk about that.'

'When are you going?'

'Not sure, or how long we'll be out there, but some of them think a year or two.'

'What about your architect thing? What will happen to that?'

'The Army knows what I've been doing, and they said it might stand me in good stead for when we get out there. But I have to leave this weekend. Tomorrow, I have to be back at the base, so I need to be up early in the morning to catch the train.'

'In that case, let's have one more drink together.'

The next hour turned into three as they readily enjoyed each other's company, with Forest explaining how much they had in the bank with interest paid into the account.

Danny gave Forest his news. 'Johnny moved out of the country to Holland when his mum re-married. The Government gent she was seeing, he works in Amsterdam; that's where he's based. Johnny was a bit put out at first, but I think he's all right now.'

'Did Eddie go to Australia?'

'He did. I told both of them to send pictures when they can.'

'I can see Eddie on the back of a kangaroo with one of those corked hats on. I hope he don't moan out there like when he was here.'

Danny shrugged. 'You never know.'

It was two in the morning when they settled in their room, and sleep took over as their heads hit the pillow. Six-thirty, the alarm woke Danny, with him shaking Forest awake.

'Forest, you've got a train to catch. Wake up.'

A bleary eye opened and closed again.

'Forest, get up. Mum's doing breakfast for us.'

With a nod and a yawn, he tossed his covers off and put his feet to the floor. 'My head's a bit thick. You look as though you haven't had a drink. How come?'

Danny smiled at him as he stood and scratched his head, trying to wake up. 'You know what, you really do look the part with that haircut. You look a different kind of Forest to the one I used to know.'

'Is that bad or what?'

'You know bloody well what I mean. I bet all the girls run after you, you handsome brute. Mum and dad have mentioned how it suits you. I'm glad my sisters have married and left.'

They stood on the harbour station platform at nine o'clock, waiting for the train to leave. 'Make sure you come back, and I don't mean for the money.'

'I'll come back. You won't get rid of me that easy.' Forest climbed aboard the train and put his hand out of the carriage window, gripping Danny's hand. 'I've got plans for the future, and I want you here. So, stay in this country.'

With a whistle blow, the train began to move out of the station.

'Keep mum and dad informed of what you're doing. Write when you can; mum will let me know what you're up to, so keep it clean.'

As the train sped away, Danny waved to the one person he understood and liked. Forest had a rotten childhood, but now, with the war finished, who knew what was waiting around the corner.

Chapter Forty-Four

Five years took Forest into his twenties. The Army had taken him to Egypt and many cities and other countries. His imagination in rebuilding the countries' architecture astounded his superiors, and, as his talent grew, so did their demands. With the Army approaching him to help rebuild and bring new life to areas affected by the war, Forest's reputation grew. The devilishly good-looking twenty-four-year-old came back to England with his career established for the future with the Army behind him. In his mail, he learnt that Danny was courting a woman from Oxfordshire, not far away from his base at Brize Norton, and wondered when he would meet up with him.

May 1953. Forest left the Army and settled in London with a position he had dreamed about. Making arrangements through his bank, a substantial sum from his account was made payable to Danny, before he settled into his profession. Signs from the war were still evident, and he stood ready to bring about new life to a developing capital. The letters he received from Danny explained how he and Betty, his fiancée, were going to be married and asked him to be his best man when it happened. Thrilled with the news, he returned a letter showing a picture of Keisha, a woman initially from Tanganyika he had come to know and was going out with. It took until April the following year for the two of them to plan a reunion at Danny's parents' new home north of Portsmouth, and for Forest to bring along a female friend if he still had somebody.

Sat in first class with Keisha, Forest marvelled at her beauty. Her clear eyes sparkled as she looked at him, squeezing his hand and knowing how easily she would marry this man should he ask her. Yet Keisha's anxiety struggled with the prospects of meeting Forest's blood-brother. She had heard everything about him and how he had come into his life and wondered what he looked like. She was worried that this person she had never seen would somehow cause an awkwardness between them.

'Forest, when we get there…'

Forest turned from the train window and saw the worried look. 'Keisha, what is it?'

'Nothing, I suppose. These people, Danny's parents, where will we stay?'

'No idea, but Danny will make sure we are comfortable once we arrive. I told you more than once that you will like him. His parents are lovely people. I'm sure they will take to you straight away.' Forest kissed Keisha lovingly and held onto her. 'Danny will ask me again to be his best man when he marries his fiancée, and when we get there, I'm going to do the same in asking him to be mine.'

Keisha took Forest's hands in hers. 'Are you asking me to marry you?'

Forest grinned, put his hand into his pocket, and withdrew a small velvet case. 'Open it.'

With her heart beating against her ribs, Keisha lifted the lid and looked at the beautiful gleaming stone set in the ring. 'Oh, Forest. Are you sure?'

Taking it from the box, Forest placed the engagement ring onto Keisha's finger. Then, getting on one knee, he asked those magic words: 'Keisha, will you marry this unworthy man?'

She pulled him from the carriage floor, sat him alongside her, and kissed him, eventually saying yes.

Getting off the train before it went into Portsmouth, Forest found a taxi and gave the man the address. With the car speeding into the countryside, the driver located the address and drove down the quiet wooded lane.

'This is going to be different from the old townhouse where they lived. I hope Danny's waiting for us.'

As the taxi reached the only building, Forest saw the front door open, and a familiar face came out. 'That's Danny. I'd know him anywhere.' Paying off the driver, Forest collected his luggage and, with Keisha, opened the wooden gate. 'Give me a moment; I need to give this guy a hug.'

As they embraced each other, Keisha witnessed the two men's fondness, one black and one white, showing their pleasure at being together. After what seemed like minutes, Forest pulled away as another woman approached them from inside the house.

'Is this Betty?'

Danny turned as his fiancée joined them. 'Betty, meet this black beauty; just be aware of what I've told you about him.'

'Hello, Forest, don't listen to him. It is so lovely to meet you after all this time. Is that your friend you have left at the gate?'

Forest, realising, hurried back and collected Keisha from her abandoned spot. 'I'm so sorry, baby, come and meet Danny.'

Danny looked at Keisha as she advanced towards him, seeing what a beauty she was, and he took her hand, kissing it. 'Forest, are you going to introduce me?'

'Meet my brother, baby. I realise he's not very black, but give him time. He's still got some of my blood in him.'

'You are even blacker than the guy I used to know. I suppose that was North Africa.'

Betty stepped forward to rescue Keisha from the two men and pushed Danny aside. 'Take no notice of them, Keisha. Have I said that correctly?'

She nodded and smiled uneasily.

'You come inside with me.' Turning towards the two men, she said, 'Danny, you and Forest get the luggage and bring it inside.' Leading Keisha into the house, Betty could feel how anxious she was, and then she noticed the ring on her finger. 'Is that what I think it is?'

Keisha, coming to terms with Danny's fiancée being a genuine person, put her hand out so she could see it more clearly. 'Forest proposed to me on the train coming here. He's asked me to marry him.'

'That is fantastic news. Danny, Danny, come here.'

Danny came into the room with Forest close behind him.

'Show Danny, Keisha.'

Putting her hand out, she flashed Danny the sparkling stone.

'Forest has asked Keisha to marry him.'

The four of them sat together in the old-style cottage sitting room congratulating each other, and with Danny telling Forest their parents were in the next village involved with a fete, something they had planned for some time.

'How are they, Danny? Are they well?'

'Getting older, but life for them here is so much better. There are a few shops further up the lane, and the farmer keeps an eye on them for me.'

Although total strangers, the two women walked into the garden together, leaving the men where they were as Forest questioned Danny's position at the hospital.

'Doctor Danny. I don't know if I would want you to slice me open. I've still got the scar from that penknife I gave you.'

Danny withdrew the penknife from his pocket, and

with more smiles, the two men reminisced.

Betty got Keisha to relax as they spoke about their partners and how they had met.

'Keisha, tell me, what is it you do?'

'I work with Forest in the same building. I am a secretary for sections regarding plans, giving them out to the government and other sections. Some of it is confidential, of course.'

Betty realised not to ask more. 'Danny and I have been together a few years now. I met him in the hospital. I am a nurse; I have all my qualifications, and with Danny almost a doctor now, we are going to move once he has taken another course in his profession.'

'Forest said Danny was in the Air Force. Did he fly?'

'He wanted to, but when they found out he was good at engineering and had hospital training, they kept him grounded.'

Keisha could see Betty would be a friend the way she looked after her. In their bedroom, unpacking, Keisha put her arms around Forest and pulled him to her, kissing him deeply. 'I like Betty; she's nice. I have not spoken to Danny very much. Has he said anything about me?'

'Only that he thinks you are gorgeous and a perfect match for me, but probably too good for me.'

'Am I?'

'Perhaps, but only a little bit.' Forest hugged her to him. 'We are going on a picnic together tomorrow; you will find out a lot more about him then. Joyce and Bernard will be home soon. You'll like them. I know they're not my parents, but Joyce is big-hearted. She looked after me when I had problems as a boy. I owe her a lot. Bernard, too.'

'I love you, Forest.'

Forest placed his lips over Keisha's and showed how much he loved her.

Chapter Forty-Five

Mr and Mrs Downes walked into their house to discover Forest and his friend. Joyce hurried across the room as Forest stood there, and she wrapped her arms around him, burying her head in his chest. Bernard followed and saw Keisha, a charming young black woman, sat in a chair alongside Betty and spoke to her.

'Forest's young lady, I take it?'

Keisha smiled at the man's delight, looking at her.

'This is Keisha, Mr Downes: Forest has some news.'

Hearing Betty, Joyce pulled away and looked at the lovely presentable woman sitting there. 'My dear, I am so pleased to meet you. Let me sit between you. Forest, come over here and introduce me.'

Bernard put his hand out to Forest and shook his hand. 'It is good to see you again, son. My, look at you, the Army must have agreed with you; you're so unlike that boy I used to know.'

'Thanks, I feel good. This is a great place you have here.'

'We like it.'

'Let Forest be, Bernard; there is so much I need to ask him.'

Forest sat on a wooden chair in front of her as she placed her hand on his leg.

'What is this news?' Looking from one to the other, Joyce was almost bursting with pleasure, waiting for the news Betty spoke about.

'You look well. Thanks for putting us up.'

'Your home as much as ours; now tell me, what is…?'

'Auntie, Keisha and I are engaged to be married. I proposed to her today. See the ring on her finger?'

'Oh, Forest, that's wonderful news. Danny and Betty will be married one day, I hope, and if you and Keisha…' Joyce turned to the young woman on the other side of her. 'That is a beautiful name, my dear.' She held her hand, feeling pleased for her, before turning to Forest once again. 'You could have a double wedding with Danny. Imagine it!'

The following day they sat in the countryside beside a meandering river. Forest finished his drink and sat back against a tree, with Keisha sitting between his legs as he hugged her. 'Danny, about you two getting married. When will that be?'

Putting any uneaten food away into the hamper basket, Betty stopped and waited for Danny to say something. 'Good question, Forest; Doctor Downes is a law unto himself sometimes, especially when it comes to serious matters like a wedding. Well, Danny, answer Forest.'

Danny stretched out on the blanket, leaned onto an

elbow and winked at Forest. 'You mean us getting married, love?'

Betty threw a chicken leg at him. 'Danny!'

He saw the fierce look coming his way and sat up, chewing on the meat. 'Next April sounds good, unless you have another month?'

'Betty looked at him, not believing what he had said. 'You mean it, Danny, no messing about?'

'I was thinking like what mum said to Forest about the four of us marrying together. Do you think that would work?'

Forest squeezed Keisha a little tighter. 'Danny and I spoke about it last night. What do you think, baby? Your folks, do you think they would mind?'

'Betty might not want to; this is a serious issue, Forest.'

With more talk and a few more drinks, it became clear that a double wedding could take place the following year. That became the conversation between the two women as they joined together on their own. The more they talked about it, the more the two women got to know one another, and with Mrs Downes involved, it became apparent that the joint wedding would take place at the little church in the village in the following spring. Back in their workplaces, the two women kept in constant touch as they planned for the day, and with Forest and Danny allowing them to take charge, the months quickly passed.

Meeting up at the Downes' country home at

Christmas, the talk between the women was dresses and reception matters, along with the number of people to be invited to the joint wedding. Forest and Danny made arrangements to be each other's best man, while Bernard became a third who would pass the rings to each couple.

As the wedding year arrived in 1955, Danny became an assistant surgeon, with his career becoming successful and profitable. Forest had bought a house in a predominantly white area west of London. It took a few get-togethers with his new neighbours to assure them of who he was and what he did, as being coloured could still prove problematic no matter who you were. Renovating the building's insides, Forest became heavily involved with putting his stamp within the property's established walls, leaving the outside and the curved driveway to blend in with his neighbours.

Three weeks before the planned wedding, Danny arrived at Forest's almost finished house by himself due to Betty visiting her parents, where she spent her spare time with her mother, like Keisha was doing with hers. Stood at the house entrance in front of the driveway, Danny regarded the building, wondering how Forest had changed the structure inside. The place looked like any other, and he was surprised it didn't look different.

'Are you looking for someone?'

Danny turned at the voice behind him and saw a man of about forty-something looking at him, alarmed. 'No, this is the first time I have been here. This is my brother's house; he told me he was having work done on it, but it appears the same as all the others around here.'

'Your brother? I think you have the wrong house, Mr...?'

'Downes. This is number 25?'

'Yes, but the man that has bought this property is black. His name is Mr Grady.'

Danny explained the brother bit and how they grew up as children, then the front door opened, and Forest greeted both men.

'Robert, you have met my brother, Danny?'

The man stepped back, still a little shocked at the announcement. 'That is strange. How is the house going, Forest?'

'Nearly there. You and Sylvia must come in and look around once I have finished. How are the boys getting on at college?'

'Good; the twins are into physics more than ever now. Thank you for introducing us to the college principal; it has worked well for them.'

'Danny, come into the house. I want your opinion on something. See you later, Robert.'

Walking towards the front door, Danny expressed a smile. 'A neighbour, I take it? He practically fell over when I said we were brothers.'

'That will be all around the neighbourhood by tomorrow.' Forest closed the heavy wide, wooden front door, and Danny stood open-mouthed at the modern interior.

'You like it?'

Danny walked forward, inspecting everything. The insides were so different from anything he could imagine. Everywhere, white or off-white walls and glass panels gave the place a much bigger appearance. Lighting hung in areas he would not think of putting it, giving the open-spaced rooms an immense feeling. Forest showed him all over the five-bedroomed house, where each bedroom had its own bathroom and shower units installed, having come from America, with every modern addition added.

'A bit different from the old place back when we were boys.'

Forest laughed. 'I'll show you where you can sleep tonight: it's through that doorway.'

Danny went in and whistled. 'How much do you charge for a night?'

'Depends if you brought a bottle.'

Danny looked inside another room, seeing the soft pink furnishings and extra-large bed. 'You and Keisha, I take it? You've done yourself proud. How are her folks with the wedding?'

'They're all right now; they were a bit taken back knowing we were having a mixed wedding – the black and white thing worried them at first. Keisha told them all about us and how your mum and dad looked after me all those years ago. I think they will be okay. Come downstairs; I want to show you something else.'

Stepping down the magnificent, curved staircase, Forest took Danny into the kitchen. 'How about this? You like it?'

'Wow, it looks like something out of a magazine. What are those gadgets?'

Forest tried to explain most of them, before taking Danny outside into a massive conservatory. 'If you fancy a swim, by all means, be my guest.'

Danny knelt beside the huge oblong pool and put his finger into the water. 'Warm, too, and look at the space you have outside.'

'You won't get me swimming in cold water, not after the Mediterranean.'

With the evening arriving, they enjoyed a meal out before heading back.

'This is a fantastic house. I bet Keisha loves it.'

'She's stayed over a few times. Do you and Betty really like her?'

'She's dazzling. I don't think you could have found anyone better if you tried. Betty is always on the telephone to her. Wedding issues! I'm only glad I'm not too involved. If she asks me for an opinion and tells me something about it, I always agree with what she says.'

Forest grinned at that. 'Likewise; we must be brothers. Whenever the subject crops up, like every day, I try to be authoritative, but I always tell her she's right.'

It was Danny's time to laugh. 'And there's me thinking I was the only one under the thumb.'

Forest put his arm around his brother's shoulder.

'Remember when you said to me, I must be growing when I did this the last time.'

Danny looked up at him as he stood much taller than him. 'What, that skinny kid that liked big girls and had messy hair?'

'You mean Nancy. I'd forgotten all about her.'

'It was a wonder you never made her pregnant. If her dad had ever caught you, you would have had more than a slap around the head. Nancy couldn't keep quiet about it; she told her friends a lot about you, you dirty sod.'

Chapter Forty-Six

In April, the two weddings at the little church where Joyce and Bernard lived brought people from afar, knowing that there would be a double wedding, especially with a black couple and a white one. Even a couple of neighbours from London where Forest lived came to see the ceremony, even though they had no invitation to the sit-down. It took a considerable dialogue between the grooms to bring the two families together. Danny's sister's family generated amusement playing with Keisha's nieces and nephews, which helped the situation, and by the evening, everybody appeared to get on well with one another. With their new wives, they honeymooned in Egypt, with Forest taking charge of places to visit. The Pyramids and Cairo's museum held their fascination with the relics of the past. Luxor's river journey and the temples that occupied Egypt's kings cast a spell over everybody as guides spoke of history and foul deeds that ended a prince or princess's life. On the return journey home, Danny sprang a surprise.

'By the way, I thought you might like to know, Betty and I are moving.'

Wholly taken back at the news, Forest confronted

them. 'Fine time to tell us. When did all this happen?'

Keisha, also alarmed, took hold of Betty. 'Where are you moving to?'

Danny and Betty chuckled at the response.

'Danny has found a house not too far from where you live. I hope you don't mind. We saw it in an estate agent's window when we visited a friend before the wedding, and I fell in love with it. Danny was going to speak to you earlier, but with the wedding and the trip, I reasoned with Danny to say nothing until afterwards.'

Forest asked precisely where the house was, and after much discussion, it was agreed he and Keisha should go with them to see it at some point. The following month's work became heavy for Forest as his absence had created a build-up of visits and inspections to sites and buildings across the country. Danny, likewise, was thrown into the surgery teams as patients headed into the operating theatre for numerous operations. It was the middle of summer when everybody managed to have a weekend away from work, when Danny invited Forest and Keisha to the new home he had bought. Danny asked Forest whether he could suggest something to make the house more modern.

Keisha pulled Betty aside. 'Now he's done it. Once Forest gets an open invitation to something like this, be prepared; that's all I can say.'

They all walked around the empty property, with Forest suggesting this and that as he made notes and drew diagrams of how something could look. It took hours for the men to exchange information on various walls that could come down and where an added area could allow for something else. With the women leaving the men to it, Keisha took Betty home with her for the prepared meal she was giving later. Now away from the men, Betty was itching to tell Keisha her news.

'Keisha, I'm having a baby!'

Keisha held onto Betty, thrilled for her, and asked the vital question. 'When, when is it happening?'

'I told Danny before the wedding. I never said anything to anyone else in case it upset Danny's parents. I think it will arrive in early November if my date is correct. Is there any sign of anything happening with you and Forest?' Betty saw the distress straight away. 'Keisha, what is it?'

With her head down, Keisha sobbed her news. 'I have problems down there. I told Forest before we were married, but he's a pillar of strength for me.'

'Keisha, I'm so sorry. Do you want to tell me about it?'

Keisha explained her problem that would restrict her from having children.

'There's me going on about what is happening to me and… oh, Keisha, I'm so sorry.'

'Forest and I are going to adopt a little boy. It's what he wants. We have been to see about having him.'

'Forest would make a wonderful father. That is a lovely thing to do. Yes, I imagine he would.' Betty kept quiet, saying no more on that subject, and she helped Keisha with the meal while waiting for the men to return. That evening, the news broke about the adoption without any other explanations.

Back in their old home, Betty explained what Keisha had told her. Straight away, Danny was eager to help if he could and suggested contacting Forest the following day.

'No, Danny, not yet; you know they are adopting a little boy. Keisha said he was born out of wedlock.'

'That won't bother Forest. That's what happened to him.'

'Keisha told me his name is Jamal. Forest's thrilled about having him: they have been to see him twice.' Betty decided to ask a question. 'You said Forest had a terrible time as a child.'

Danny nodded at her statement. 'Terrible was only a fraction of what he went through with his mother; she was a cruel, wicked woman with what she did to him. It's a wonder he didn't turn out different from what he is now. I can't understand why Forest has not said anything to me about all this.'

'Let him say something when he's ready. I know you want to help. If you interfere and there is nothing you could do, imagine the awkwardness it could cause.'

'You're right. It's strange how things like this happen. He was a rogue when we were kids. The girls that confronted him.' Danny decided to stop there and say no more should he say the wrong thing.

'When you and Forest get together at the London house, be careful not to say anything unless he speaks to you first.'

The London home became a minefield, where Forest removed walls and added spaces. In all, it took just over a month to get to the stage where the house was ready for decorating, and again Forest introduced to Danny to a firm of decorators that he'd worked with. With Betty's influence and requirements, the building, within another month, was almost ready for occupancy. Then, one evening, Betty picked up the telephone at home and listened to Forest's excited voice.

'Betty, get Danny; is he there with you?'

Betty called up the stairs and guessed what Forest was going to tell them. 'Danny, hurry up. It's Forest on the telephone.' She listened to the hurried footsteps as Danny reached her.

'Is it?'

Betty put her finger to his lip.

Forest poured out his news, telling them they had just brought Jamal home with them, and they were about to go out into the swimming pool. 'You must come and visit us. I'm sure Jamal would love to meet you both.'

'We will, Forest. Danny is busy at the moment at the hospital, but as soon as we are both free, we will come and see everybody, I promise. Do you want to speak to Danny?'

Betty passed over the receiver and sat down, feeling

her stomach. The last thing she wanted was to turn up at Forest's home with her pregnancy, just months away from having the baby.

With holidays put in for, Danny and Betty moved into the London home, with their old one going on the market in August. The new hospital in London where Danny had transferred was far more pioneering in its methods and procedures, something that Danny agreed had become a breath of fresh air for him. Betty had given up work, waiting for the baby while making adjustments to the new home.

Still not having visited Forest and Keisha, Betty began to feel terrible for not doing so. She had not even asked them around to see the newly finished house. Then, one day, Keisha turned up at the door unannounced.

Opening the front door, Betty saw the stern look on her face.

'Have I offended you, Betty? If I have, you must tell me.'

Betty placed her hand over her stomach, somehow trying to hide the increasing bump. 'Come in, please. I have been so busy with everything.'

Keisha walked into the large lounge area. 'Can I ask, why are you keeping away from Forest and me? Is it Jamal?'

Chapter Forty-Seven

Betty asked Keisha if she would like some tea. With a nod coming back and a demanding look, she made her way into the kitchen, leaving Keisha alone. Within minutes, footsteps approached her, and Keisha stood there in the doorway.

'Well, Betty, what is happening? What have I done?'

With her back towards her, Betty turned around, holding her stomach. 'Nothing, nothing at all.'

'So why are you keeping away from us?'

Betty saw the troubled face. 'Because I'm having a baby and…' Betty turned back and went to reach for the kettle. 'I never meant to upset you.'

Keisha suddenly realised and walked across to her. 'You stupid woman. Look at me. Do I look as though I am not happy for you? Forest is delighted with Jamal. I want you to come and see us, do you understand? It has been ages since we all got together.'

Betty put her hand out. 'I'm sorry. I know we are good friends, but with me in this shape.'

'You never know, one day they might be able to do something for me.'

Betty knew this was the chance that she should say

something. 'Keisha, you know Danny is a surgeon at the hospital now?'

'Yes, but there is nothing wrong with me physically: I just cannot get pregnant. It isn't as though we have not tried, believe me.'

Betty smiled. 'Once you have settled with Jamal, perhaps you would like me to mention it to Danny about what you have said. I know you have consulted people about the problem, but Danny knows people knowledgeable in that field. Speak to Forest first and discuss what I have said. He may not like the idea of Danny interfering with his wife down there.'

Both women smiled and gave a little chuckle at the thought.

'I want you and Danny to come for dinner this weekend. I think it will be a sunny day: you can tell Danny to bring his swimwear and join Forest and Jamal in the pool.'

'I still feel a little awkward.'

'Enough of this nonsense, woman. I hope you have us down for Godparents!'

'Where is Jamal?'

'Being pampered by the grandparents, I expect. They love him to bits. My dad is probably throwing him around in the pool right now.'

The two women sat together and drank tea for the next couple of hours, and as Keisha was leaving, Danny arrived home.

'You are early, Danny.'

Seeing Keisha sitting there, he went over and kissed her. 'How are you? Is that little boy behaving himself? I really must come and see him.'

'Jamal is doing fine. He seems to be settling in as though he had always been with us. It was a little strange for everybody at first, but he's accepted us.'

'Danny, Keisha has asked us over this weekend. Are you free?'

'Not sure; there could be a problem with one of my patients, but I will have to wait and see.'

'Please try and come, Danny. I know you are a busy man.'

'I promise to do my utmost to be there.'

Danny and Betty rang the bell, and before long, they heard Keisha shout something. When the door opened, Forest stood there in his wet blue swimwear, beaming at them.

'Come in, come in.' Looking at Betty, Forest raised his eyebrows. 'How's the baby coming along?' Then he kissed her.

'Getting bigger, Forest, and he or she doesn't like this hot spell of weather; neither does the expectant mother. September is supposed to be cooler.'

'You must sit inside; we have a fan going in the lounge. Keisha said you might want one. That doesn't apply to you, Danny. I hope you've brought something for the pool. Otherwise, you will have to wear one of my outfits. I have a lovely orange pair of bathers: they should suit a doctor like you.'

Danny realised he had forgotten his swimwear. 'That will be different, seeing me in your clothes.'

Forest clamped his damp arm around Danny and dragged him into the house. 'First time for everything, brother.'

Betty could see the amusement in both of them as they continued to play off against one another, moving into the house.

'Jamal is with Keisha in the kitchen. I left him there dripping all over the floor. I had better grab him before he begins to help her, or should I say, hinder?'

Betty came up beside Keisha and kissed her, as did Danny.

'This is our little mischief-maker. I blame his new dad for encouraging him. Jamal, come and say hello to your new Aunt and Uncle.'

Jamal stood behind his new dad, holding onto his leg. The sudden emergence of two people alarmed him, knowing how the white people in the home treated him at times. Staying where he was, he saw the fat woman look at him.

'Hello, Jamal, you are a lovely little boy. Have you been swimming with...' Betty stalled a moment before coming out with the word. 'Your new Daddy?'

Jamal stood there, not saying a word.

'Look at this wet floor; you go and sit in the other room, Betty. I will be in shortly. The last thing I want you to do is to slip on it. Forest, take Danny with you.'

Picking Jamal up in his arms, Forest carried him out into the pool area, with Danny following, while Jamal continued to look at Danny with mixed emotions.

'Hi, Jamal, can we be friends?'

Still the silent treatment, and as Forest put Jamal down, he clung to him, not wanting to let go.

Forest went to say something, but Danny stopped him and sat down in one of the chairs around the pool. 'This is a lovely place to play. I wish I had somewhere like this.' Danny looked around as though he had not seen it before. Looking at Forest, Danny said, 'If I ask Jamal, would he let me play in the water with his dad?' Danny saw the hesitation in the boy as he listened to his words. 'I would love to get wet and have a splash about.'

Forest turned Jamal to face him. 'Do you think we should let your new Uncle play with us?'

Turning back, Jamal scrutinised Danny and nodded, unconvinced. 'He is a white man.'

Forest, amused at the words, responded. 'There is some black in him if you look hard enough, Jamal. I know you can't see it, but it's there.'

Danny grinned. 'That's right; we will tell you about that one day when you are a big boy.'

'You can play with us, Uncle.'

Forest kissed Jamal on the forehead. 'You must call him Uncle Danny.'

'Who is the other fat lady? Is she his wife?'

Danny laughed at the statement. 'That is your Aunt Betty. That fat belly she has is because she is having a baby.'

Jamal tried to see Betty sitting in the room, talking to his mummy. 'Can we go into the water again, Daddy? Uncle Danny can come with us.'

'Thank you, Jamal. Let me get into these orange swimming trunks.'

Forest stared at Danny, not believing what he said. 'You really didn't bring your swimwear?'

'I forgot them. Don't say too much, or Betty will say something.'

Forest laughed at the thought of Danny wearing his bathers. 'I suppose it is a good job we are brothers. I hope you don't mind putting them on knowing what I put in them.' Forest couldn't but chuckle at the thought.

'Enough, Forest, I don't even want to think about that.'

'Come with me, and I'll find them.' Still laughing, Forest climbed the stairs with Jamal, who had now joined his dad, laughing at whatever was happening.

Chapter Forty-Eight

The two men dived into the pool, and Forest called Jamal to jump in and he would catch him. Straight away, the lively lad ran and fell into his arms, giggling and laughing as the water wrapped around him. Again and again, Forest threw him into the air and caught him as though he was a toy. Danny realised that Jamal was underweight and needed feeding-up, but he knew he would soon fill out. Eventually, forgetting about his shyness with Danny, Jamal clung to him in a throwing game between the two men.

Hearing the excitement from the pool, Keisha and Betty looked through the glass at the spectacle as Jamal shrieked with pleasure and enthusiasm.

'It seems Jamal has a new friend in Danny.'

Betty laughed, seeing the fun they were having, before noticing the swimwear Danny was wearing. 'Keisha, those are not Danny's bathers. Do they belong to Forest?'

Seeing them, Keisha laughed with Betty, not believing it.

'I told him to bring some. Nothing like sharing, is there?'

Danny turned, seeing the two women observing

them. Suddenly, he realised it was him that they were staring at, as Forest did.

Forest gripped the top of Danny's bathers. 'They must like the colour of what you are wearing, Uncle Danny.'

Danny slapped his hand away and moved to the side of the pool, trying to hide.

The rest of the day, everyone had fun with Jamal. Even Betty became a friend as he touched her stomach when Betty told him her baby was inside. It was eight o'clock when Forest's phone rang.

'It's for you, Danny. The hospital, I think?'

'Any calls from the hospital I had put through here. I hope that was okay?' Answering the call, Danny told the others they needed to leave. Betty thanked them for the magnificent meal, and it would be her turn to invite them next time.

Danny hurried to the car with everyone saying their goodbyes, and Betty drove him to the hospital. 'I cannot believe you did not bring the bathers I put out.'

'Danny squirmed in his seat. 'I've had enough from Forest, please don't say any more. I can see him going on about this for some time.'

'Goodness knows what Keisha thought.'

The following day, Danny spoke to one of the hospital's gynaecologists about Keisha and arranged for her to see him privately. Stopping at Forest's house on the way home and knowing Jamal was with his grandparents, he eagerly waited for someone to open the door.

'Danny, what are you doing here?'

'I saw Forest's car in the drive. Can I have a word with you both?'

Keisha called Forest to come downstairs. 'Is something wrong?' Are Betty and the baby all right?'

Forest came down the stairs as Danny walked in and headed for the lounge without being asked. 'Sit down, both of you. I had a word with an associate today about you having this problem not conceiving. Don't worry, Keisha; nothing is happening without your say so, but he is prepared to check you over and determine why this is happening. I know you have seen other specialists regarding this matter, but this guy is at the top of his game, and I rate him as a friend and first-class surgeon in his field. This man could help both of you, so I think Keisha should see him. Betty knows him; his name is Thomas Chesterfield, and he might be able to help, but it is up to you.'

Forest sat there, as did Keisha, unable to say anything.

'I can see this is a shock. Please think it over and phone me as soon as possible. Betty and I want this for you.'

Keisha telephoned Betty the next day, saying she would agree to see someone and could she let Danny know?

A week later, with an appointment arranged out of hospital hours, Forest walked Keisha into the hospital's private section, with Danny beside them.

Betty went into labour in November, and Danny was the one who delivered a beautiful baby girl at their home. Keisha arrived with Forest at the house the next day when Jamal was at school, and Keisha gave Danny a big kiss.

'Can I see them?'

'Upstairs in the bedroom; mum and baby are doing well. Seven pounds eight ounces and big brown eyes.'

Forest pulled out a cigar and presented it to Danny. 'Smoke it or frame it.' He shook Danny's hand, and with the bottle behind his back, he took Danny through into the lounge. 'A toast to the new baby. What are you going to call her?'

'Betty has all that in hand. I'll let you discover that when you see her.'

'Brown eyes, you said: does she take after me?'

'Just the eyes, Forest, everything else is as it should be. We can give the girls a few more minutes; then I'll take you up.'

'Did everything go as planned; you know, the birth?'

'Betty did marvellously. She's tired, but after all that work, she should be.'

Forest could see how proud Danny was as he poured him a drink. 'To the baby, Betty and Dad!'

Danny clinked glasses, when Keisha entered the room, spotting the booze.

'Leave those drinks down here. I don't want either of you smelling of whisky with that new baby in the house, Danny. I'm surprised at you.'

'Just a little one to wet the baby's head.'

Forest kissed Betty on the forehead, trying to keep any smell of his drink away from her. 'Well done, you!'

Seeing the baby in Keisha's arms, he looked at the little pink package. 'Have you named her?'

Betty, tired as she was, smiled at everybody. 'Yes, we've called her Fern Joyce Downes. Joyce after Danny's mum, and Fern after you.'

Forest, amazed at the statement, looked at Danny and Betty. 'What do you mean, after me?'

Betty continued. 'Your name is Forest, and Ferns grow in a forest, so, you two being blood-brothers, Danny and I decided Fern was a name that could link you together, seeing both of you are going to be Godparents.'

Forest sat in a chair, and everyone watched as tears clogged his eyes.

Danny knelt beside him. 'Come on; it's not like you to get emotional.'

'Danny, when you came into my life that day after seeing me in the mud cockling, I knew you were special. Your mum and dad have been like real parents.'

'They are your family: you know that.'

'I know. But the life I had. I assure you Jamal will never find himself in that situation.'

Consultations and further appointments took Keisha nearer to Christmas, with the gynaecologist finally deciding that minor surgery was the best option. The festive period proved a joyful affair, with each family visiting one another's houses and family members joining them, while visits made further afield took Forest and Danny to see their ageing parents.

Keisha went into surgery in the second week of January. Now finding the situation more manageable with her baby, Betty looked after Jamal at their home, leaving Forest free time with Keisha. With the operation over, Danny and Forest stood around the private hospital bed as the surgeon came in. Danny stood back as Forest and Keisha listened to the results of her operation. As the surgeon walked away from the bed, Danny watched Forest wrap his arms around his wife.

'Thank you, Thomas, for helping them. I am in your debt for this.'

With a pat on the back, the specialist walked away, leaving Danny at the end of the bed, knowing that in a few months there could be an announcement of a baby in Forest's and Keisha's lives, and he quietly left them in a euphoric mood.

With Keisha out of the hospital and recovering, Forest worked flat out for the military and government to rearrange drawings and plan new ones. Ever the mischievous and lively lad, Jamal began to lose his fear of the past and settled into school, becoming popular, a distinctive individual similar to his father. Some teachers took to him in his characteristic ways with his bright eyes and inquisitive mind. At the same time, another would put him through an arduous lesson, unsure why he was in such a prominent school.

Chapter Forty-Nine

In April, the news came that Keisha and Forest never expected to hear. A baby for Christmas. Danny and Betty were thrilled for them. They hosted a house party with all the immediate family and close friends attending, with delighted family members drinking and partying into the early hours. Jamal seemed pleased that such a big event was happening, although it troubled him in some way. The year progressed with the cold months edging towards the festive season after a perfect summer – along with Keisha having constant check-ups ordered by Danny regarding the pregnancy.

Jamal now sensed the household's mood changing. His sixth birthday in August had been great, with a pool party that his school friends found unbelievable. The garden was decorated and the magician performing his tricks had fascinated everybody, but now it was different, as all talk was about the new baby.

In November, Betty announced that she was having a first birthday party for her daughter. She wanted a quieter affair with Forest, Keisha and Jamal at their house, along with the grandparents attending the occasion in the afternoon. Forest turned up with Jamal on his shoulders and Keisha with presents for Fern.

Once inside the house, the atmosphere of a party had vanished, as Jamal found the excitement gone with baby talk robbing him of the fun he imagined. Danny noticed his distraction, sat by the window, looking out at the rain that had begun, while watching a squirrel run across the lawn and into the trees. Going over to him, he sat with him as the others talked about the expected arrival.

'Looks like the rain is ruining that squirrel's day.'

Jamal considered Danny's words, thinking he wished he was at home in the pool, listening to the rain on the roof as he splashed through the water, learning to swim.

'How is school, Jamal? Your daddy said you are doing well and reading a lot of books. Who do you like reading about?'

Jamal still sat there, not knowing if he wanted to talk or not.

'Jamal, are you all right?' It was then Danny saw the little tear in his eye. 'You come with me; I have something you might enjoy.' Picking him up, he walked him across the room, telling the others he was taking Jamal into the basement. Once there, he opened a cupboard door and watched the little boy's eyes brighten. 'That is a trainset I bought when I found out that Auntie Betty was going to have a baby. I thought it might turn out to be a boy, but we had a little girl, and I don't think girls will play with train sets, do you?'

Jamal wiped his eye and studied the insides of the cupboard.

'What do you say we get this out and put it together to see how it works? Would you like that?'

'Yes, Uncle.'

Danny saw the immediate reaction as he brightened, and within minutes both of them became transfixed with the trainset. It was a good hour later when Forest tried to figure out what had happened to his boy and proceeded to the basement. Peering in the room, he didn't need to say anything as he witnessed the enthusiasm in both their faces and he tiptoed away, leaving them to it. Betty called down with the table laid ready to eat, having heard Forest's report about how enthralled they were with the trainset, something she had forgotten about. The next day, a Monday, Danny phoned Forest to arrange a drink out after work.

'Thank you for coming, Forest. I know how busy you are.'

'Not a problem. You sounded troubled when we spoke. Is there one?'

'Don't know, really.'

Forest sipped his beer and looked at Danny, unsure where the conversation would go.

'Yesterday at Fern's birthday, I saw Jamal looking out of the window.' Danny hesitated before continuing. 'He was crying; that is why I took him with me. I know we never had a party as such, but I have never seen him like that before.'

'You never said anything; if I had known.'

'I think it might be the new baby coming. He may

feel he's going to be left out, seeing his past. I know he's loved, but it happens.'

'You know I am away a lot of the time, but Jamal knows how much I love him.'

'I know you do. Has Keisha said anything to you?'

'No. I'm sure she would if there was a problem.'

The two men continued their discussion, with Forest a little concerned but ready to speak to his boy when he could.

'Jamal, I have told you so many times today to behave yourself. Keep this up, and you will go to your room and stay there. I have told you your daddy is away until tomorrow, and Uncle Danny doesn't want you around at his house every five minutes. Now leave me alone and go and read a book or something.'

Jamal wandered off towards his room, knowing his angry mummy had already told him he could not use the pool until his daddy returned. Sat in his room, skimming through his comic book, not really paying attention, he tried not to think about the baby arriving. Whenever he saw his mummy, she was caressing her bump, which she called it, paying no attention to him. He longed for his daddy to come home so they could go swimming, where he would spend time practising. The next day in the pool, Jamal threw himself into his learning strokes.

'You are getting better and better. Have you been practising without me?'

'No, Daddy, Mummy won't allow me in the pool

without you.'

Forest knew Keisha enjoyed the pool, but being near her time, perhaps it worried her. 'Next week, I will be home, and we can play as much as you want to. Have you been to see Uncle Danny's trainset lately?'

'No, Daddy, Mummy said I must not keep going there.'

Surprised at the words, he decided to speak about it with Keisha when Jamal was in bed.

'Forest, he cannot keep turning up at Betty's. She has Fern to look after: she does not want him there every five minutes.'

'Betty is fond of him. She loves having him there.'

'Not all the time, she doesn't. He's not her child.'

This time he looked up at the last statement, surprised at the harsh words. 'Jamal is at school all day. Surely an hour or two wouldn't hurt.'

'You are away most weekdays and some weekends; he tires me out wanting this and that. My baby will soon be here, and I do not want him causing me problems, not after all this time.'

Forest backed down, guessing how much this baby meant. 'Our baby, Keisha. I am part of it, remember?'

Keisha gave Forest a quick smug smile as she was leaving the room. 'If you are staying up, don't wake me getting into bed.'

Forest left his chair and kissed Keisha goodnight, one she never returned.

The first week in December, Keisha's waters broke,

and fortunately, Forest was at home. He called Danny's house, but he was at the hospital, with Betty telling him she would be there instantly. With an ambulance arranged, Keisha was in the delivery ward within a half-hour. At two o'clock the following afternoon in the hospital, Jamal sat on his daddy's lap as Betty and Danny came in to see the proud parents. Seeing Keisha's attachment to the baby in not letting her out of her arms, Betty told them she would gladly look after Jamal for a while until she and Forest were ready.

Chapter Fifty

The arrival of a baby girl thrilled Forest, knowing he had become a father, but he never forgot Jamal, knowing he might be anxious. Along with their little one, Betty and Danny visited the proud parents at home, happy for the couple's achievement, with gifts and a bottle ready to wet the baby's head when Keisha was not looking. The outcome could not have proven better for the happy parents, as Forest poured his thanks and affection to Danny for them getting this far. After some time, Betty called to leave, seeing they were walking home, and left the two happy parents alone with baby Zahra. Betty suggested they collect Jamal from school and take him home to allow them more time with the new baby. Collecting Jamal, Betty asked Danny something she could not understand. 'I can't believe how dark Zahra is, compared to either of them. She's so different.'

Danny smiled. 'It happens, but I guess she will be a beauty like her mother.'

Betty elbowed Danny in the ribs. 'Jamal, what do you make of your baby sister?'

Danny, holding Jamal's hand, looked down at him, saying, 'Girls, they always cause us boys a problem.'

Jamal looked at Fern in his Auntie's arms. 'Baby Fern is good. I think she is pink and pretty.'

'Thank you, Jamal, you tell your Uncle off saying things like that. How can a sweet little thing like Fern and Zahra be trouble?'

'Wait until you grow up, Jamal; you will find out what I mean.'

Betty kicked Danny in the leg, making Jamal giggle as Danny pulled him onto his shoulders as his daddy did at times.

Forest called to collect Jamal two days later and found him with his Uncle in the basement. 'You will have to make this trainset bigger: the space you have down here, you could fit it up as a play area, seeing as you enjoy this as much as my boy.'

'Actually, that has been on my mind, but I wasn't sure if I'd be childish doing something like that.'

'Jamal loves it down here, and I can see you do, too. Life's all about enjoyment. Go for it. What do you think, Jamal, should Uncle Danny make a full-sized layout as you sometimes see on the television?'

Jamal visualised the room having a giant trainset running through it. 'Could you do that, Uncle?'

'Of course he could. You keep onto him; it would be as much for him as it would for you.'

Forest joined in with them for an hour before prising Jamal and himself away from the trainset. Betty met them in the kitchen with Fern tottering around, finding her feet, with Forest having to have a hug.

'Daddy, Uncle Danny said girls are trouble. Are they?'

Danny looked at Betty and saw the stare coming back. 'Well, he listens, doesn't he, Danny? Perhaps you should watch what you say in future.'

Forest kissed Fern before handing her back to her mother and smiled at the remark. 'Jamal, I think we should leave; Uncle Danny might be in big trouble.'

Kissing Betty goodbye, Danny showed them to the door.

'No car, Forest?'

'No, I saw the colour of the sky and hoped it might snow. I don't think Jamal has seen it before.'

'You might be in luck. That might be flakes coming down now.'

Jamal looked up into the funny-coloured sky, noticing the tiny white flakes falling around them and putting his hand out to catch one.

'You sure you don't want me to drive? It won't take me a minute to get the car out of the garage.'

'We want to walk, don't we, Jamal? If this keeps up, we might be able to build a snowman in the garden.'

Christmas arrived, and the two families came and went from each other's houses, giving presents and receiving them. Danny bought Jamal a trainset with instructions to bring it with him when he visited. The New Year quickly followed, and things settled down, with Forest busy at work and Jamal going to school. After the holidays, the first weekend, Forest needed to fly to Scotland on a significant project with the military and would be away for three or four days. With his trains put together on his bedroom floor, Jamal passed out-of-school hours watching television, reading or playing trains. He had tried speaking to his mummy and the new baby, but she always stopped him from getting near her.

On the second day of Forest's departure, Jamal passed the baby's cot when he heard her cry out. Seeing his mummy was missing, he edged to the cot and looked in, seeing Zahra had a cover over her face, and, getting closer, he went to pull the blanket away when his mummy came in and saw him. Rushing to the crying sound, Keisha, seeing the baby's face covered, stared at Jamal and struck him across the face, knocking him over.

'Don't you ever do that again, you wicked boy. I leave you alone for a few minutes, and you try to smother my child. Get anywhere near her again, and I'll have you sent back to the children's home you came from.'

In tears, Jamal ran to his room and fell on the bed, not knowing what he had done. His face reddened and sore, he buried it in his pillow and cried, wanting his daddy. He didn't know how long he had slept, but the darkness outside his window told him it was late. With his stomach rumbling, telling him he was hungry, he wondered why he had not had his tea. Getting off the bed, he crept downstairs and saw his mummy sitting in her chair and hugging Zahra. Going into the kitchen, looking around with nothing on the table, Jamal took an apple from the fruit bowl and saw his mummy staring at him.

'Yes, you know, don't you? I know what you were trying to do to this baby. Take the apple; you will not get anything from me today. Get to your room and stay there, and if I hear that train running, I will throw it in the rubbish bin. Do you understand me?'

Running back the way he came, he sat on his bed sobbing, looking at his trainset.

Jamal found his breakfast ready for him the next morning. Sitting at the table, not saying a word, he ate his cereal and quickly readied himself for school. Downstairs, he waited at the front door, wondering if his mummy would take him in the car like always. Suddenly, she came up behind him and grabbed him by the neck.

'I've got a mind to make you walk to school, seeing what you did.' Opening the door, she pointed to the garage and told Jamal to sit in the front seat, something his daddy never allowed him to do. 'Don't think for one minute I would let you sit next to my Zahra. Get in the car.'

Sat in the front, he watched his mummy secure Zahra into the car's back seat before sitting next to him. The quietness frightened him as they left the driveway and joined the traffic. His mummy leant across him as they reached the school and glared at him, opening the door. 'Out, and if your dad comes home, he can pick you up.'

Jamal did as he was told, thankful to be away from his mummy.

Chapter Fifty-One

Jamal's teacher noticed the mark across his face and asked him how he got it. Not wanting to say should his mummy be angry, he shrugged his shoulders, saying nothing. Throughout the day, individual teachers noticed how worried he appeared and decided that one of them should mention it to whoever collected him at the end of the day. Sat in the playground entrance just inside the school, Jamal fidgeted uneasily, waiting for someone to come.

'Who is taking you home, Jamal? Is it your mummy?'

Sat there, saying nothing, the teacher became more concerned that something had happened at home. Seeing the car pull up outside the school, the teacher recognised the vehicle and called Jamal to get ready.

Forest walked into the playground, and the teacher told Jamal to stay where he was until she called him. Meeting Forest, the teacher stopped him from going further and spoke to him, mentioning how his son had a mark across his face and had not been his usual self.

'I have no idea, Mrs Fischer. I have just got back from Scotland. Where is he?'

Coming into the entrance hall, Forest saw his boy

run to him, throwing his arms around him and crying openly.

'Whatever is it, Jamal?'

Not getting an answer, Forest told the teacher he would take him home and try and find out what had occurred. In the car with him, Forest cuddled Jamal and attempted to speak about what had happened.

'Did someone hurt you?' With no response, Forest drove home with Jamal in the back seat, wondering what had transpired. He did notice a mark on his cheek, but considered one of the boys in the school might have had a tussle with him, being a coloured lad. He knew it might happen one day. Parking the car in the garage, he took Jamal's hand before entering the house and felt his grip tighten.

'I don't know what is wrong with Jamal. Has something happened? The school spoke to me, asking if there was something wrong. They said he's been quiet all day.'

Keisha ignored him and went about her cooking with the baby strapped to her.

'Keisha, I said, has something happened?'

'Ask him, he knows. He tried to smother Zahra. Yes, I hit him, and I will again if he tries to do that again to a defenceless baby.'

Forest stood there, shocked at her words. Turning to Jamal, he looked down at him with his head sunk onto his chest. 'Did you do that, Jamal?'

Jamal ran up the stairs to his room with tears

flowing.

'Let me go and speak to him. I have never seen him act like this before. I don't understand him doing something like that.'

'I wish we never had him. There, I said it.'

Astonished at the outburst, he watched Keisha with Zahra against her chest, not uttering another word. 'What's going on here?' Making his way to Jamal's room, he saw him lying across his bed and went in and sat with him, placing his hand on his shoulder. 'Did you do what your mummy said, Jamal?' Forest felt him shake and curl deeper into a ball. 'Jamal. I will not smack you, but you must tell me what happened.'

The sobbing grew louder as Forest picked him up and cuddled him into his body. 'I love you; you know that.' He tried in vain to ease the sobs coming from his boy. Sitting against the headboard, he continued to hold onto him until the blubbering eased enough for him to speak. 'Jamal, daddy loves you, you know that. Please, tell me what happened.'

Jamal lifted his head with wet eyes and clung to him. 'I never hurt baby Zahra; the blanket was over her face, and I tried to pull it down, but mummy said I put it there. I didn't, Daddy.'

Relieved that Jamal had said his piece, Forest hugged him once more and kissed his face. 'I knew there must have been a mistake. Let me speak to your mummy. You stay here and change those school clothes: I will come and get you later when dinner is ready.'

Finding Keisha in the kitchen, Forest tried to take the baby from her, but she refused and kept Zahra in her wrap. 'You cannot prepare dinner with Zahra there. Here, let me take her.'

Keisha stared at him, annoyed that he ran after Jamal. 'I'm not staying in this house with that boy. You either give him back to the home, or I'm leaving.'

Still stunned at Keisha's outburst, Forest stood against the worktop, utterly confused by her actions. 'Don't you think this is getting silly? I have just spoken to him: he told me he was removing the blanket from Zahra's face, not covering it. I cannot imagine him doing anything like that. Surely you can understand.'

Keisha shouted, making the baby cry. 'He tried to murder my baby.'

'Don't be stupid. It would help if you calmed down. This is getting out of hand.'

'Calm down, is that all you have to say? Calm down! I'll calm down when you remove that boy from this house. Then I'll calm down.'

Forest realised something was wrong, but was unsure how to handle the situation. 'Jamal is in his room. I am taking him over to Betty's; he can stay there tonight.' Not daring to say another word, he left and telephoned, hoping she was at home. 'Betty, I have a problem. Could you look after Jamal for the next day or so? I will explain when I get there.'

'Is Keisha and the baby all right? Do you want me

334

to come over?'

'No, let me bring him around in about half an hour or so. Thank you, Betty.'

Betty walked into the lounge, where Danny was reading a medical magazine. 'I have just had a call from Forest; he is bringing Jamal with him, and he has asked me to look after him for a couple of days.'

Danny put the magazine aside, not really listening, and looked at Betty. 'What's that about Jamal?'

Betty explained again.

'Did Forest say nothing else?'

'No.'

'If there was a problem with the baby, he would have said something.'

Forty minutes later, Danny opened the front door. Forest stood there with Jamal and a suitcase.

'What is happening?' Seeing Jamal look sheepish, he invited them in. 'Auntie Betty has some biscuits made. Do you want to go and find her? I think she is in the kitchen.' Danny waited for Jamal to leave. 'Is he all right?'

Danny took him into the lounge. 'You look bushed. Do you want a drink?'

'Pour me a large one; anything will do.'

Danny passed the drink across and sat opposite his brother. 'Do you want to tell me?'

Chapter Fifty-Two

Forest described everything as Danny sat there, taking it all in. He told him the most distressing part was collecting Jamal from school with the teacher pointing out the mark across his face where Keisha had hit him.

'I can see he is upset, but how is Keisha?'

'Not sure.' Forest took a mouthful of whisky. 'I've never seen her like this before. She's fuming and wants Jamal out of the house. She even told me to take him back to the home we got him from. How can she say that?'

Danny knew Forest was hurting. 'It could be her hormones having had the baby. Some mothers have a problem adjusting.'

'She accused Jamal of trying to murder her baby; not *our* baby, *her* baby. She's told me that several times now.'

'Wait here a minute. I want to look at him.'

Forest finished his drink and poured himself another.

'How is he, Betty?'

'Hungry; he tells me he has had no dinner. I am cooking him something.'

'Beans on toast, Uncle. I like beans.'

Danny ruffled his thin-cut hair. 'So do I.' Taking hold of his face, he quickly scanned his cheek.

Betty nodded and pointed to the red mark, having overheard Forest's comments.

'If we have time, Jamal, I have a surprise for you, but let me talk to your daddy first.' Danny saw Forest finish his second drink in the lounge and held him back from getting a third. 'I think Keisha might need counselling, just someone to talk to her. Do you think she would?'

'Not at the moment. I have never seen her like this. She scared the hell out of me saying what she did.'

Danny suggested he go home and see how she was without Jamal being there. 'Telephone me if there are any more tantrums. You have that baby to think of. Just make sure Zahra is being looked after properly.'

Forest went to get into his car when Danny stopped him. 'I don't think so. You have had the equivalent of four or five doubles. Walk – it will make you feel better.'

Jamal went to bed after Danny had shown him the preparation he was making to build a proper railway complex, telling him that they could spend all day playing down there once finished. Sitting with Betty, Danny approached the worrying situation.

'I don't think hormones are disturbing Keisha; I think it is more than that. She has been so different since the baby arrived. Have you noticed how she speaks to Forest at times?'

Betty nodded, not wanting to say yes. 'Let's see what happens tomorrow.'

'I hope he gets home all right.' Danny thought how, of all people, Forest deserved a peaceful life.

With Jamal staying at Danny's house, Forest tried to understand why Keisha had exploded the way she had. The more he tried to find out, the more she flared at him for not believing her and telling him that if he persisted, she was leaving and going to live with her mother. A few days later, with Jamal still away, Forest mentioned what Danny had said about seeing someone, to which Keisha flew into a rage and screamed at him.

'It was me you married, not Danny.'

Forest tried to ease the situation by putting his arms around her. 'Baby, let's try and sort all this out. We had such a great time before the baby came.'

Keisha threw the bed sheet off and challenged the remark, scratching him and digging her nail into his skin, drawing blood.

'Before the baby came? Don't you mean before we had Jamal?'

Forest got out of bed and picked the baby up, that had started to cry. Seeing him, Keisha rushed across the bedroom and tried to snatch the baby from him, cutting the infant's face with her long nails. Becoming angry and pushing her away, Forest took Zahra into the bathroom to wipe the blood seeping from her ear. Another attack from Keisha provoked him to lash out as she attempted to take the baby from him.

'For Christ's sake, Keisha, what is wrong with you? Zahra is bleeding. Do you realise what you have done?'

'My baby, my baby, give her to me.'

With Keisha screaming and the baby crying, Forest looked in the mirror, wondering what was happening in his life as the infant held onto his finger. Stemming the blood flow with a towel, Forest soothed Zahra the best he could and listened as Keisha moved around the bedroom. Opening the door, ready to protect the infant, he found her searching the room for her baby.

'Keisha, I have Zahra. Come here. But please be careful with her.' Handing her over, he stood alongside them, making sure she was capable of supporting her. 'Take her and lay on the bed.' Forest, wearied with events, sat opposite and watched as she cooed and conversed with their baby, but knowing something had to happen to help his wife.

With Keisha eventually falling asleep exhausted, Forest eased Zahra from her and put her in her cot. Telephoning Danny, he apologised for the late call while telling him what had happened. An hour later, Danny arrived at the house with an ambulance before Keisha could wake adequately. Danny administered a mild sedative, and the ambulance men escorted her from the room. She meekly struggled seeing Forest with Zahra in his arms and tried to get back to her baby.

'Will you be all right tonight? There is nothing you can do for the moment. Keisha will be in the best place with someone to look after her. I know you must feel terrible, but let us get her better. I will phone you first thing tomorrow once I know what is happening. Betty can look after Zahra tomorrow, and we can discuss anything then.'

Danny went into the bathroom and washed his hands. Seeing the bloodied towel and Forest's shirt, he decided he needed to try and answer why Keisha was like she was. Betty had given him the idea, and now he was prepared to look into it.

The following day, with Jamal at school, Betty drove to Forest's with Fern to see how he was doing. Finding him busy in the kitchen trying to feed the baby and himself, she took over, telling him to wash, shave and dress before he did anything else, and to get to the hospital and see how his wife was. Betty never discussed what had happened, only that Keisha would need him by her side.

After collecting Jamal from school, Betty could see he was becoming his old self as he spoke about different things, yet not once asked about his mummy. Betty organised to look after both children until the circumstances became more apparent as to why Keisha had acted the way she had.

Two days later, Danny managed to get a sample of Jamal's blood, not having told Forest, and one from him, saying the hospital might need it. Days later, while doing his rounds there, he received the information he had asked for. Reading it, Danny slunk into his seat and put his head in his hands.

Forest took time off work to figure out his next move. Invited to dinner at Betty's for the foreseeable future, he presented a bottle of wine, seeming much happier than he had in a while.

'Keisha appears to be much better, so the hospital said. The doctor I spoke to said she could be ready to come home soon.'

'Oh, Forest, I am so pleased. Did they say why she acted as she did?'

'They are still trying to get to that. I am taking Zahra with me tomorrow to see how she reacts. The doctor said it should be all right. I just hope it is.'

Chapter Fifty-Three

Danny arrived home and noticed Forest's car parked there. He had not had the chance to speak to Betty about what he had found out and decided it could wait until later. Opening the front door, he greeted Jamal as he ran up to him and grabbed his hand.

'Uncle Danny, come and see what the man has made in the basement. He has done lots of things. Hurry, Uncle.'

He dropped his case on a chair with his car keys and followed the excited youngster. Hearing Jamal's enthusiasm, Betty smiled as Danny was pulled through a doorway, disappearing into the basement, and she turned to Forest.

'Danny is as bad as Jamal with that trainset. He has had the man from number five sawing, building and painting a new layout downstairs. Ron, that's his name, told me he would finish it this week, then he will begin to put together the tracks and all the other things. Whatever that will be, I have no idea. Do you want to join them? I can look after Zahra.'

'No, I'm fine. It is nice to sit quietly with her.'

'She is no trouble; not like this one, she always wants attention.'

'You are so good to me, Betty. I do appreciate everything you are doing: you know that.'

'Don't be silly. You and Danny are brothers, be it by blood or not.'

A good hour later, when Betty called for the others to come up for dinner, Jamal was still full of excitement, leading Danny into the lounge.

'Jamal, go and let Auntie Betty get you a drink while I pour one for myself.' Danny headed for the glass of wine Betty had poured for him. 'Are you drinking, Forest?'

'When this little one is asleep, I will.'

Danny watched Forest with Zahra in his arms and could see how much he loved her. Shaking his head, he sat in his chair as Fern crawled, making her way to Forest. Watching her as she tried to climb his leg, Forest one-handedly lifted her off the floor, hugging her opposite Zahra.

'You were made for children. I can see you will always have a friend with that one. She dotes on you for some reason.'

'It could be the good looks or the tan.' Forest gave a generous smile. 'At least she has taste.'

Danny thought about that word and emptied his glass as Betty called them in for dinner. Getting up, Danny lifted Fern from Forest's arm and took her into the other room, placing her in her highchair. Betty told Forest to put Zahra into the small cot she kept close by, and everyone sat down. By nine o'clock, with Jamal and the girls asleep. Forest poured himself another drink and made a couple of telephone calls that he needed to make while Danny spoke to Betty in the bedroom.

'I got the results today about something that has concerned me with all this Keisha business. Something you mentioned some while back.'

Betty stood there, trying to understand. 'What did I mention?'

Danny put his finger to his lips and crossed to her. I had Zahra and Forest's blood tested at the hospital. They are different.'

'Betty sat on the bed, beginning to realise where Danny was going.'

'Zahra is not Forest's child?'

Suddenly, Forest knocked on the door, and Danny told him to come in.

'I have to go to Portsmouth tomorrow; that should bring back some old memories. Betty, is it all right for you to have Zahra and Jamal a few days more?'

'You know I can.'

'Thanks. They want me involved with a new Navy building in the Dockyard.'

Danny waited for the right moment.

'I might bump into our old friend, the Sergeant-Major.' Forest saw the look on Betty's face. 'I haven't walked in on something, have I?'

Regaining her composure, Betty stood up and hugged Forest. 'Of course not.'

'Steady on. I don't want your husband thinking something is going on.'

With that, Betty quickly left the room, not saying a word.

Forest turned, watching her hurry away, before turning back. 'What did I say?'

'Sit down, Forest. Let me close the door and remember the children are asleep up here.'

Forest, now concerned, waited to talk to him. 'I've had enough worries lately. What's going on?'

'I don't know how to tell you this, but there's no easy way for me to do it.'

'Tell me what? Is it about Keisha?'

Danny nodded. 'I'm afraid so.'

'She's not become worse, has she? When I saw her earlier, she seemed a lot better.'

Danny pulled his chair nearer Forest.

'Christ, you're frightening me now. What's happened?'

'What I am going to say will hurt, but if it were the other way around, I would want to know.'

'Know what?'

Danny took a breath and spoke. 'Forest, Zahra, she is not your child: you are not the father.'

Forest sat there dumbfounded. 'That's crazy. I'm her father; she's black like me, isn't she? Danny, what are you telling me?'

'You have different blood types: there is no way Zahra can be your child. I'm sorry.'

Danny put his hand on Forest, but he pulled away, angry, and stood up.

'You're supposed to be my brother. How can you say something like that? It was you that suggested Keisha have an operation to correct her down there, and now you are telling me my baby isn't mine.' Forest left the room, hurrying downstairs and grabbing his coat. He left the house, jumped into his car, and screeched it out of the driveway.

'Go after him, Danny.'

'I had to tell him; he had to know.'

'I know you did. Just make sure he's all right.'

Chapter Fifty-Four

The drive through the streets flashed by as Forest forced the car to answer. All he could think about was his brother telling him his baby belonged to someone else. Tears ran down his face, blurring his vision as horns blared at him, and people shouted whenever the car came near the kerb. The whole thing was a nightmare. Keisha was his wife. Could she have done this to him? A grinding sound brought him back to reality as the wing mirror flew off the car's passenger side, and sparks flew from the bodywork as the car scraped a wall. Pulling into a lay-by and stopping, Forest slumped across the wheel, his heart breaking. Suddenly, his door opened without warning, and a policeman grabbed him, pulling him out of the vehicle.

'Having some fun, are we, matey?'

Forest fell against the bonnet and tried to balance himself as the policeman pulled out his handcuffs.

'I suggest if we want to play chase in our car, we go to a fairground, and with the alcohol I can smell, are you in trouble. My sergeant will love you. He has a thing for people like you.'

Forest could only make out those last few words. 'People like you.' Turning, clenching his fist, he swung it at the policeman as another car pulled in behind.

'Forest. No!'

Too late, Forest's fist hit the middle-aged policeman, laying him out on the road surface.

'What have you done, you idiot?' Danny knelt beside the prone man, attending him.

'I am a doctor. Are you okay?'

The policeman looked at Danny and towards the black face beside the car. Rubbing his jaw, he struggled to his feet with help and clipped his handcuffs onto Forest's wrists as he stood there, allowing it to happen. Danny straight away spoke to the policeman, explaining what had caused Forest to react the way he had.

'That may be, sir, but striking a uniformed man doing his duty. A night in the cells will do him no harm. Follow me, and perhaps his situation might change if he behaves himself.' The policeman escorted Forest to his car, ensuring he was secured. Turning to Danny, he watched him lock the damaged car and put the keys in his pocket. 'Please follow me, sir.'

The following morning, Danny arrived at the police station to find out Forest's circumstances. The policeman who had brought Forest in was at the station and saw him arrive.

'Doctor Downes, this way, please.'

Danny followed, unsure of Forest's predicament. Seeing the time he had spent talking to the policeman the night before, he had tried to convince him that Forest was a person of standing within the community, and nothing like this had happened before. Nearing the cells, Danny stood behind the uniformed man as he unlocked the cell door. They stared into the bleak room as Forest sat on the mattress, feet up and his head in his hands.

'If I come in, Mr Grady, am I going to be safe?'

Forest looked up at the policeman and stood. 'I apologise, Sir. My fate is in your hands. I deserve whatever you throw at me.'

The policeman listened to the words and approached him. 'I am sorry for the circumstances in your private life, but let me warn you now if this should ever happen again…'

Danny stood by the cell and saw the state of Forest, with his clothing in disarray.

Forest put his hands together towards the policeman. 'Am I being charged?'

'If it wasn't me, I might say yes to that question. You have to thank this gentleman for convincing me otherwise. Put your shoes on and tidy yourself.' Coming out of the cell, he spoke to Danny. 'Take him home and make sure he's aware as to how lucky he is, especially being a coloured gentleman.'

Forest looked at the man saying that.

'I have no problems with people of a different race or colour, but there are many in this place that does. I hope he appreciates what you have done for him, Doctor.'

Joining them, Forest put his hand out to shake the

policeman's hand, understanding what he meant. 'Thank you, Sir. Can I leave now?'

'You can, but make it fast before I change my mind.'

Sitting in Danny's car, having had hours to think about what he said to him, he realised he needed to say something. 'Danny, turn the engine off.'

Danny sat there, unsure what he was going to say. He had told Betty everything that had happened and was anxious about how things would turn out.

'Yesterday, I wished you had never told me about Keisha having an operation, but thinking about things, what she did could have happened at any time, and when you told me about the blood, I was so angry. If I had stayed, I might have hit you like I did the policeman.'

'I'm glad you didn't. You put him down so easily; you have one hell of a punch there.'

'I realise why you told me, Danny. It must have been horrible for you. Does Betty know?'

'Yes. She's worried about you, like me.'

'I'm worried about me, too. Jamal and Zahra, what happens now?'

'Jamal, he's yours and always will be. Betty and I know how much you love him. Zahra, that's another question.'

'Do you know who the father is?'

'I have no idea. That is something you are going to have to ask Keisha about.'

'Not today, I won't. I am supposed to be in Portsmouth. I guess I'll have to telephone someone and sort that out. Danny, can I count on you and Betty to look after the children? I will need time to find out what Keisha has been up to.'

'You don't have to ask. I'm always here for you.'

Forest put his arm around him and hugged him. 'Blood-brothers – see what blood can do?'

The following month, Keisha revealed how she had found Busara, a Mozambique national visiting London when Forest was away. She explained that he had never been to the house, and they had only been together when Jamal was at school. But Busara wanted her to live with him, and when the baby came along, she knew it was not Forest's, especially with Zahra being almost jet black and her features so like Busara's. Telling him she was sorry about Jamal, but with Busara's child and the way she felt, there was no way she could live with him anymore. Between them, it was agreed they separate, with Keisha taking Zahra with her. It was a painful situation, but Forest knew it was for the baby's sake as much as it was for him and Jamal. Keisha came back to the house and packed her belongings, along with the infant's. In the lounge, Forest waited for his wife to come down as the taxi arrived, and he spoke to her.

'Keisha, why?'

'It was nothing you did, Forest. I'm sorry.'

Chapter Fifty-Five

The trainset in the basement that Danny and Jamal escaped to, increased in size with landscaping, tunnels and rails. The actual trains operated from a central opening through a crawl space within the set-up, with liftable sections should a breakdown happen. With the basement walls decorated to reflect the train's features, Danny allowed Jamal to occasionally bring a friend to run the trains, enthralling the other youngster. Meanwhile, Forest had his house altered and repainted after all the unpleasantness, hoping to eradicate some of the past. His work continued to take him away at times. With Jamal approaching his next birthday, Betty, who was still looking after him when Forest was away, suggested he give Jamal a party in the pool and invite all his school friends. Putting in for overdue holidays, he arranged for as many children to attend as Jamal wanted. Betty and Forest organised the forthcoming event, and Danny ensured he had that weekend away from the hospital to give support.

The summer's day arrived, and Jamal, with his many friends, jumped, swam and played in the warm water with Danny and Forest in their own swimwear, taking their lifesaving duties seriously as the all-boy assembly shrieked and hollered with laughter. Chasing one another in and out of the building, Forest could see he would need to have the pool cleaned as bits of grass and food managed to find their way into the water. Betty's entertainer for the party proved a delight with his magic and antics, giving the boys a fantastic time. With parents arriving to collect their children by six o'clock, Betty began clearing away some of the spent food and decorations that had fallen or become broken in the excitement. Danny changed into his clothing, leaving Forest in his bathers to watch the remaining children as parents continued to arrive. It was with the last five boys still playing when she came. Forest, alert, studied the woman and went around the pool to approach her.

'Who are you waiting for?'

The woman turned and looked up, trying to recognise the face, but unsure. 'Peter, Peter Hathrow.'

Forest called out for him, and the youngster came running towards them in his bathers, and Jamal pushed him back into the water, with both of them squealing with laughter as Jamal jumped in with him.

'Jamal, enough, Peter's…' Forest stopped, unsure how to proceed as the woman was black and the boy white.

'I am Peter's kind of nanny. I look after him when his parents are away. My name is Lisa.'

Forest's ears pricked up, trying to think where he had heard that name before. 'I'm Jamal's daddy, or dad

353

now is what he calls me, seeing he is growing up. My name is Forest.'

'I know you, or I did. You were that boy on the piece of linoleum on the hill above Portsmouth when I met you; you had cut your ear, and I wiped the blood away.'

'Wow, you remember all that! How many years ago was that?'

'I'll try not to think.'

Forest stood there, totally engrossed with this woman. 'Lisa, not, Sas, am I right?'

'I have not heard that in years, thank goodness. Please don't start calling me that. It took a long time to get away from that name.'

Forest forgot all about Peter and Jamal and sat down, asking Lisa to do the same. The more he looked at her, the more he felt something tug inside him. She was like a breath of fresh air as she smiled and communicated with him. There was no ring on her finger, making him fluster around her, and he asked her if she would like some birthday cake or a drink.

'I should take Peter home soon. Knowing him, he has probably swallowed a lot of that water.' Lisa went to stand as Forest held her back.

'Could I see you some time? We could go out for a drink or a meal?'

'You're not married, are you?' Lisa looked around her. 'This house is beautiful.'

Forest shook his head. 'Once, but that is history.

Jamal is my adopted son.'

Lisa, surprised at the revelation, said nothing.

'What is it you do?'

'I'm an architect. I work for the government and the military. You say you are a nanny?'

'Kind of. I was married young; it didn't work between us, but no children, luckily. I began training as a nurse but had to give it up. The flat we had was too expensive for me to take on when William, my husband, left me. So, I took up looking after children like Peter.'

Forest took hold of Lisa's hand, feeling the softness and the rougher surface in her palm. 'I cannot believe this is you from all those years ago. Please say you will consider coming out with me?'

Lisa beamed at Forest, taking in his physique and capturing his attention. She took a piece of paper from her handbag, scribbled a number down, and passed it to him. 'You think about what you have just said. You might change your mind. That is the number at the house where I am, should you still want to go out. Now I must leave with Peter; his parents are due back tomorrow, and I don't want them finding him tired out.'

Forest called Jamal and Peter to get out of the water. 'Can I phone you tomorrow?'

Lisa gave a small laugh. 'Only if you want to.' She put a towel around Peter's shoulders and looked for somewhere to dry him.

'Take him through that door at the end of the pool; there are more towels should you need them.'

Moving away, Lisa held onto Peter and quickly went to the room indicated. Within minutes, she had Peter dressed and escorted him out, to see Forest talking to another woman. Giving him a wave, the two made their way out, heading for a car parked in the driveway. Pulling into the road outside, Lisa looked in her mirror as Forest opened the front door, watching her, and she wondered if a man would be coming into her life who could love her after all these years.

Taking his time in the bathroom, Forest ensured he had the right cologne and his hair trimmed to perfection. He looked at his body in the full-sized mirror, smiling at himself and nodding. 'Not too bad, Forest; let's hope this one can stick to one man.' Getting dressed, he readied for his date with a woman he last saw in the 1940s. He remembered how lovely she was in her old clothes, but guessed he must have seemed rough, especially with the mop of tangled hair he had in those days. With Jamal at Betty's house, he took the car out into the warm summer evening, ready to collect Lisa from the address she had given him. Turning into the road, he knew the houses were money straight away and deliberated Lisa's role in the home. Having felt the slight roughness in her hands, he imagined she was more than a nanny to Peter. Finding the house, he rang the outside bell, listening to it chime inside, and waited. Moments later, a well-dressed woman of about fifty answered, seemingly offish that he was on her doorstep.

'Yes?'

'I have come to collect, Lisa. Is she ready?'

The woman gave Forest a disparaging glare and told him he needed to wait in his car, and she would be out soon. Doing what the woman wanted, he knew he had brought trouble. He could picture the woman challenging Lisa about what she intended to do, giving concern for her role there. Suddenly, the front door opened, and Lisa came hurrying out. Opening the passenger door for her, he noticed how flushed she was and realised he was right.

In the driver's seat, he turned. 'Have I brought trouble, Lisa?'

'She'll get over it. They have had a row in there. Mr Hathrow has stormed out, and Mrs Hathrow will be unbearable for days now. I feel sorry for Peter when it's like this.'

In the expensive restaurant, Forest, with Lisa's permission, ordered the meal and the evening became delightful as they drank champagne and danced to the band that performed there. He complimented her on her dress and held her hand as they swept across the dancefloor. Much later, as people began to leave and the band members slowly drifted away, Forest knew what he wanted to say.

'Lisa, this is the best evening I have had in some time. Can we do this again?'

Lisa touched his hand and pondered a moment,

before saying, 'Forest, I like you a lot, but is this a casual thing?'

'I don't want it to be casual, not at all.'

Chapter Fifty-Six

After some months, Betty and Danny realised that love was developing between Forest and Lisa, especially when he mentioned her moving in permanently. Giving notice, telling Mrs Hathrow she would be leaving at the end of the month, Lisa hoped they would soon find a replacement. In response, Mrs Hathrow exploded with displeasure at the news, telling her in no uncertain terms to leave immediately. Lisa packed her suitcase in tears as Peter held onto her, knowing she was going. She hurried from the house, and when the taxi arrived she sat in the back seat, watching Peter crying at his window.

After hearing a vehicle in his driveway, Forest opened the front door to see a distraught figure hurrying towards him. 'Lisa, what has happened?'

Falling into his arms, she told him everything as he tried to console her.

'Have I done the right thing coming here?'

'You should have done this a long time ago.'

Forest kissed her and, picking up her suitcase, took her inside the house. With the door shut, she kissed him in a way no one had ever kissed him before. Feeling the wetness from her eyes, he knew how much he wanted this woman. 'Jamal is sound asleep. I will tell him everything tomorrow.' Outside his bedroom, he looked into Lisa's face. 'I'm beginning to love you so much.'

Lisa became a firm favourite with Betty and Danny as their relationship grew. Jamal gradually became accustomed to Lisa at the house and, over time, found he liked her so much that he would snuggle up with her when they watched the television. Fifteen months into their union, Forest proposed to Lisa, asking her to marry him before Christmas. Out having a drink one evening at the local golf club, where Danny was a member, Forest gave him the news.

'Danny, I have asked Lisa to marry me.'

'Betty and I were wondering when this might happen. Congratulations are in order. Have you asked mum and dad to come?'

'What do you think I should do? I've not told them about her yet.'

'Let me sort that out; you concentrate on the wedding. I hope you have me as Best Man?'

Forest finished his first drink and picked up a new one, clinking glasses with Danny. 'What are brothers for?'

'It's about time you made an honest woman of Lisa. Have you met her parents?'

'No. Her father she doesn't talk about; he left. Her mother passed away a few years ago.'

'Betty dotes on her; she is so much like you in

specific ways. Where is the wedding going to be, our local church?'

Forest nodded. 'I haven't been there since…'

Danny halted Forest's comments. 'Don't talk about it; you have a new life emerging.'

'Lisa's pregnant.'

Danny grinned. 'That didn't take you long.'

'I feel as though a weight has suddenly lifted, allowing me to breathe. She is so different. Betty being fond of her has helped enormously. You've met Lisa before, but you don't remember, do you?'

'I've never met her.'

Forest gave a small laugh. 'You have. She was the girl on the hill we met when we were kids. You know, the one that talked to me.'

Danny sat back in his chair, dumbfounded. 'The same girl?'

'The same one; she's turned into a fine-looking woman.'

'Small world. Wait until I tell Betty; she will be upset she didn't find this out first, but she will be so happy for you.'

The days passed, and preparations were made for the wedding in November before Lisa began to show signs of the forthcoming event. Forest explained to Jamal about the wedding, whilst telling him about the baby, and Lisa told him she would love him as her own and never treat him differently.

The day arrived, and the wedding took place, with

the elderly parents meeting Lisa for the first time and making her feel welcome. Danny proved to be the joker at the small reception, making everyone laugh while giving out information about how they met the first time. With the baby beginning to show a month later, Betty confided in Lisa about what happened to Forest with his first wife when she asked her one day. Lisa promised she would never say anything, but explained how Forest would not talk to her about it.

June arrived, and so did Ruthy, weighing eight pounds three ounces. Danny spoke to Lisa in the hospital, having had problems that required surgery after a difficult birth.

'Lisa, how are you feeling today?'

'Tired, Danny, but Ruthy's well.' Studying him, she suddenly asked the question. 'She is, isn't she?'

'Yes, she is doing great.' Danny watched as Forest came into the room. 'Here comes Dad!'

'How are my girls today?'

Lisa greeted Forest with a kiss, and he presented her with a massive bunch of flowers.

'Tired, but Ruthy is asleep, so don't wake her. Thank you for the flowers; they're lovely.'

'This just a check-up, Danny?'

Danny sat there a moment before speaking. 'Lisa, you know you had some complications at baby's birth.' Danny saw Forest's concern. 'Mother and baby are fine, but…' Danny felt terrible having to come out with it. 'I'm afraid you will be unable to have any more children.'

Forest gripped Danny's arm. 'Why?'

He began to explain the best he could, watching Forest's distress, yet knowing that Lisa had problems some time in her past. Lisa took hold of her husband's other hand.

'Forest, we have Ruthy now, that is a wondrous thing, and we have Jamal. We can live with this. It won't stop us from being together, will it?'

Forest sat beside her. 'No, I'll always love you.'

Tears appeared, and Danny left the room, leaving them alone.

Jamal's ninth birthday was in September. With time on her hands, Lisa went through the few photographs she had kept from her childhood. The black and white pictures showed children and their parents sitting against a tree somewhere in the countryside. Forest came into the room, saw Lisa looking at them, and walked over, sitting beside her.

'I haven't had these pictures out in years.'

'Forest took the first one and smiled at the picture. 'Is that you, skipping?'

Lisa laughed and pointed to another girl. 'That was my little sister. She died.'

Forest hugged her to him. 'I'm sorry.'

'This is my mum and dad.' She passed the next

photograph across, and Forest looked at the man in the picture, not believing what he was looking at. The man sitting next to the woman was his father.

Chapter Fifty-Seven

The shock deepened as Lisa showed another picture with his father kissing her mother. Forest left the room, ran upstairs to Ruthy's cot, and looked at her. Inspecting the baby, he tried to find something that shouldn't be there, when suddenly the door opened, and Lisa came in, worried about what was wrong.

'Forest, why did you leave like that?'

Facing her, tears appeared in his eyes.

'What is it? You are frightening me.'

Handing the photograph back, he held onto her. 'Your father, I know him.'

Lisa became worried and confused. 'How do you know my father?'

'He's my father, too!'

They both held one another, fearful for what they had done, and clasped one another tightly, knowing he could lose another wife, and he felt Lisa cry, huddled against him. The next day, Forest explained how he thought his father lived in America with what he had told him as a boy. Lisa explained how he had come to this country years before the war, where he had met her mother, but they never married. The day became a confusion of thoughts of what they should do. Lisa reminded her husband that Betty and Danny were due to arrive that evening, and perhaps they should tell them.

Eight o'clock, the knock at the front door brought misgivings as they answered. Betty, seeing the concern, squeezed Danny's hand.

'Come in; it's getting cold out there,' said Lisa. Seeing Fern was asleep in Betty's arms, Lisa told her she could put her in Ruthy's room.

Jamal, dressed for bed, kissed Betty and Danny before going up, and after some awkward talk with drinks poured, Lisa checked that the children were asleep. Stood at the top of the stairs with her heart thumping, she took a breath before coming down.

'You two are not selling up and leaving, are you?' Danny wanted to say more, but refrained from doing so.

Coming into the room, Lisa smiled an uncertain smile. 'No, Danny, nothing like that.'

'So, what is happening?'

Forest took a long gulp and drained his glass. 'Lisa had some pictures, and two of them were of her mother and father.' Forest took hold of Lisa's hand. 'Her father is also my father. She's my half-sister.'

Betty put her hand to her mouth, and Danny stood up.

'The American?'

'A lot of what he said was lies. He was with Lisa's mother all that time. Show them the photos.'

Lisa handed over the square black and white

photographs.

'That is my father, and Forest's, too.'

Everyone went quiet, staring at the picture, trying to think.

'Will Ruthy turn out all right, Danny? You know what I mean?'

'She's perfect.'

'Now what do we do?'

Betty comforted Lisa as she sat there, agitated and concerned.

'Isn't it an awful situation? How could this happen? We love each other so much.'

Danny interrupted. 'Then that is what the two of you should do.'

'How can we? He may be your blood-brother, but he's my half-brother.

'Neither of you knew anything about all this, or you would never have married. Your baby is a beautiful child, and she has wonderful parents. Look, you two love each other. Why should it be a problem now? You have Ruthy up there and Jamal. You know you will not have any more children together, so why can't you stay as you are.'

Lisa pulled away from Betty. 'How can we? What if people discover that we are…?'

'If I were you, I would put that picture away or burn it. The culprit in all this is your father. Forest, believe me, nothing good will come if the two of you part because of this. Don't let this destroy your future together.'

'Why is this happening, Danny? Haven't I proved myself enough times?'

'You have. Take Lisa and love her. She's your wife, not a half-sister. Try and forget all this business.'

Forest sank his head.

'You need to take this wife of yours and treat her as such. We are leaving now, and I'll see you and Jamal tomorrow evening for the park's firework display. I do not want to hear any more of this; let it go.'

Having sat for ages with Lisa, Forest pulled her from the sofa, not speaking as the two tried to understand the situation. 'Danny's right. We have each other, don't we?'

Lisa nodded and held onto the man before her with tears in her eyes. 'We must put this behind us for the children's sake, or it will destroy all of us. You know how much I love you. Please say we will never part over this.'

'Never.'

'I cannot conceive now. Please say you will still want me?'

Forest ran his fingers over her wet face and kissed her as Lisa pressed her body against him. 'I'll never leave you, I promise.' But deep down, his gut feeling was: how the hell were they going to sort all of this out?

Chapter Fifty-Eight

The next day, both Lisa and Forest spent the day pouring their love out to the children. Several times, while inspecting Ruthy, Lisa made her follow her finger as she drew it past her face. Forest, in the meantime, spent the day with Jamal in the pool, telling him about the forthcoming firework display. Two weeks later, with Forest at work and Jamal at school, Lisa was putting the ironing away when she opened a drawer by mistake and saw a folded birth certificate. Opening it, Lisa looked at it and fainted as Forest drove his car through Scotland, heading towards the airport and home.

Lisa had no idea how long she had been there. It was Ruthy crying that brought her back to consciousness. She ran into the other room with her heart thumping and lifted her from the cot, feeling her wetness. Changing the nappy, she watched her hands shake as she cuddled her. As the day wore on, Ruthy napped and Lisa returned to the drawer in the bedroom. Taking the birth certificate out, she studied the paper and put it in her apron pocket. It was midday when the doorbell rang for her to find Betty there.

'This little one fell asleep on the way round. She's been active most of the night and this morning. Let's hope she stays sleeping for a while.'

'Put her in Ruthy's room. She has just gone down after her feed.'

Betty, seeing Lisa was hesitant, approached her. 'Are you and Forest okay after what happened?' Betty saw the tears and took Lisa downstairs with her. 'Are you going to tell me?'

'Will you promise me you will not tell Danny or Forest what I am going to say to you? I have to tell someone, or I will go mad.'

'It depends on what you are going to say.'

'You mustn't tell anyone, Betty. Promise me, please.'

Seeing how upset Lisa was becoming, Betty said, 'All right, I promise.'

Lisa sat quietly for a few minutes, gathering her thoughts, then began her story. 'Ten years ago, I was raped.' Lisa saw the shock on Betty's face, and as she went to speak, she stopped her. 'I was visiting my mother in Portsmouth. It was late in the evening when I went to bed in my old room, and about midnight, I heard noises and my mother shouted something. Then my bedroom door opened, and he stood there looking at me – my father. I guessed he had hit mum as he stood at the bottom of my bed, drunk and angry. Mum told me he would come around to see her when he was broke, looking for her to give him money. He gambled and drank as he aged, but he could be an ugly man when he didn't get his way. I remember his words that night, calling me a tart and what was I doing back home? The next thing I knew, he was pulling the bedcovers and my nightdress off me. I pleaded with him to leave me alone, calling him dad to try and see if that made a difference, but being determined, he raped me.'

Betty sat there, holding Lisa's hand as she continued.

'I screamed and screamed, but mum was lying across the floor outside my room. I can feel him now pressing me down. It was horrible. He used me like an animal would rut another. I know I passed out, and the next thing I knew was two policemen were pulling him off me with mum screaming at him. It was a terrifying experience. He fought and fought them, hurting me in the process. I woke up in the hospital with mum sitting alongside me. I withdrew into myself and ended up in one of those hospitals, locked doors and all that, with them eventually telling me I was pregnant. When the baby was born, they took it away. I knew it was a boy because I heard one of the nurses say he was. I lost almost a year of my life with what happened. They jailed my father, and mum passed away not long afterwards. I got married later, but it didn't last, and since then, I have nannied for people.'

'Oh, Lisa, I'm so sorry.'

'Mum said he was sexually virulent. There could be dozens of his children out there.' Lisa wiped her face in her sleeve. 'I wish it ended there, Betty.' Lisa collected her apron from the end of the sofa and put her hand in the pocket, withdrawing the piece of paper. 'I found this today. It's Jamal's birth certificate.'

Leaving the airport having picked up Forest from an earlier flight, Danny hurried homewards through the ominous, threatening skies, with the massive bouquet he had bought for his brother laid on the back seat. Having gotten over the shock of his father, Forest talked about the future, explaining to Danny that he wanted to adopt another little boy later on.

Danny, hearing the news, said, 'Good for you. Fill those bedrooms with children! You and Lisa are so good together. I'm so proud of you both.'

Lisa laid it out on the coffee table so Betty could see it. 'That name there, Rosie Barker. That's me.'

Betty checked the paper. 'But your name is Lisa.'

'That's right. Rosie Lisa Barker. I dropped the name Rosie when I was a child – nobody ever called me by it – and I took the "r" out of my surname long before I met Forest. See the date on the certificate?'

Betty saw it and stared at Lisa.

'Yes, that's me. See who the father is?'

Betty looked at it, not wanting to know.

'Louis Winston Wells. Known as Louie or Lou, Forest's father. Can you see the baby's name?' Lisa pointed to the writing. 'Jamal Barker. I never knew that was his name, but he's my son. When I first saw him, I thought of the child they took away from me, but I never presumed more than that. Forest isn't his adopted father. He's his brother!'

Betty stood up, putting her hands to her face. 'Oh, my God.'

'I cannot tell Forest, not after what has happened. I'm so frightened, Betty. What do I do?'

Betty opened her hands, ready to embrace Lisa. Looking in the mirror, she saw a bunch of flowers. 'Forest!'

Danny stood there with his brother, having listened to those dreadful words. Forest dropped the flowers to the floor as his legs gave way under him. Lisa screamed, with Betty holding onto her, while Danny tried to recover his brother from the floor.

'Forest, get up.'

With utter shock on his face, he stared at Danny and openly cried. 'How do I sort this mess out?'

Danny held onto him. 'There has to be a mistake.' Turning to his wife, Danny watched her shake her head.

'You should have sliced me across the neck as a kid. It would have saved Lisa and me a lot of heartaches.'

Danny felt devastated for him as he managed to stand him upright. 'Whatever happens here, I will make sure you all come through this awful situation. I'll not let your father, like your mother, ruin your lives. I promise.'

Forest looked through teary eyes and held onto his brother. 'Why, Danny, why me?'

Chapter Fifty-Nine

Danny spent many evenings at Forest's home reassuring him, as did Betty, that he still had a wife and two children to look after, no matter what had happened in the past. Forever fearful of how Forest reacted the day he came home, Lisa kept Jamal and Ruthy by her side as her husband stayed away from his family, trying to get his head around the turn of events. Sat with Forest in his study as they grappled with the consequences, Danny confronted the situation, wondering how to alleviate the tragic circumstances.

'Danny, my half-sister, my supposed wife, was raped by our father. My son is my young brother, and Christ knows what else is about to happen. Every time I look at Lisa, I can see him doing that to her. I try not to, but deep in here' – Forest thumped his chest – 'it hurts like hell. You know how much I love her, but...'

'Forest, if I could remedy all this, I would, but I can't. Lisa is as worried as much as you. She's told Betty she thinks she's losing you.'

'Ruthy, what is she in all this? I have sex with my sister, and...' Forest swung around in his swivel chair, facing away from his blood-brother. 'I'm destroyed inside, broken, because of that bastard.'

Getting up from his seat, Danny crossed the room and pulled Forest back around, facing him. 'Then why the hell don't you fight this? You know your mother is dead.'

Forest gripped the side of his chair, digging his fingers into the soft material. 'She might be, but what of him? He's probably out there screwing another woman, not giving a shit about what he's doing. If I ever find him, I'll kill the bastard.'

Danny considered those words, knowing Forest probably would.

'All those lies he told me about himself, and I fell for it.'

'Of course you believed him: anyone would. You were a boy back then. As much as this hurts, you have to carry on. Jamal keeps asking for you, and Lisa needs you to comfort her in all this. Imagine how she is feeling. She never asked for this to happen. She's had a rotten time of it.'

Forest eased off the chair and knelt before Danny. 'I don't know what to do.'

On the third evening, Betty and Lisa played with the children, trying to act as though things were normal. 'I think this has gone on long enough, Lisa.'

In the study, Danny turned on Forest at another sudden outburst. 'What do you mean, we're not really brothers? Damn you for saying that.' Danny clenched a fist, wanting to hit Forest. 'Are you saying after all these years we're no longer together, blood or not?'

'Why has all this happened? What have I done to deserve this?'

'Well, get it sorted, you stupid black bugger.'

Seeing the anger rise, Danny backed away as Forest fumed with hostility.

'Stupid. Black.' Making a play towards Danny, he bunched his fist, ready to strike him as the door opened and Betty stood there.

Seeing Forest move towards her husband, she shouted at him, 'Is this what you want, Forest, to turn out like your father? You've not spoken to Lisa or the children since this happened; don't you think it's time you did? She is still the woman you married, like Jamal is your little boy, no matter what happened beforehand. You are a family, like it or not. Put that aggression away; you did enough damage when you hit that policeman.'

Alarmed at Betty's outburst, he sat down in the chair, ashamed of what he was about to do.

She walked over to him and pulled his hands away from his face. 'Three days you have been acting like this. Yes, I know it is a terrible thing that has happened, but downstairs there is a woman who loves you and needs you, besides a little boy wanting his dad. Ruthy probably wonders what is going on, even though she is a baby.'

Listening to the telling-off, Forest sat there, reflecting her words as she stood over him.

'Well, are you coming down, or do I drag you?'

Danny had never seen Betty like this before and spoke to Forest. 'I think you ought to do as she says.'

Forest smiled for the first time in days. 'Guess I don't have a choice. Sorry, Danny, this black bugger needed sorting out. Will you help me if I promise not to make a spectacle of myself again?'

Lisa looked up as Forest came into the room, not saying a word but thinking the worst as he sat down in his armchair.

Betty broke the silence. 'Forest, say something.'

Lifting his head, he saw Jamal looking at him oddly, anxious that everything was all right. Giving a smile to him, Forest put out his arms, and the child ran into them. Sitting next to Betty, Danny sighed and grabbed her hand.

'Dad, are you feeling better now?'

Forest openly cried and cuddled Jamal into his body. 'Yes, son, Dad's almost there.'

Lisa looked at them, fearful another anxious moment from her husband might transpire. Betty stood up and took Ruthy from her, encouraging her to go to Forest. With Fern still asleep in her pushchair, she held onto the little one as Lisa walked over to her husband.

'I'm sorry, Lisa, it all hit me like a thunderbolt. I…'

'I love you so much, Forest.'

Putting Jamal down, he stood, pulling Lisa to him. 'I think I'll be all right now.' Seeing Betty looking at him, he kind of smiled. 'I know I've been an idiot.'

'You have Betty and me, besides your family. We

are brothers, remember, and always will be.' Seeing the situation improving, Danny and Betty left, allowing the Grady family to deal with everything.

Chapter Sixty

Betty began a search using a friend she knew for something that could perhaps repair some of Lisa and Forest's worries. Meanwhile, Danny ensured they were coping all right by phoning or calling at the house, knowing his brother might need him at any moment. Two weeks later, Danny walked into the kitchen after a trouble-free day at the hospital and found Betty anxious to speak to him with a glass of wine waiting.

'Wine this early in the day?'

Betty put the casserole in the oven and picked up both drinks. 'I've found some news about Forest's father.'

Danny sat there and sipped his drink. 'And?'

'Christine, at the hospital, her husband's in the police force. I asked her if he could find anything out about Lisa's father. Her husband made enquiries and told her he died in prison in a dispute with other prisoners. Someone stabbed him.'

'I know I'm a doctor, but that's excellent news as far as I'm concerned.'

'Are you going to tell Forest?'

'Yes, it might help them to go forward. This policeman, he doesn't know anything about their circumstances, does he?'

'No. I told her it was something a friend needed to know.'

That evening, Danny rang Forest and asked if they would like to bring Jamal and Ruthy for a spot of lunch on Saturday in the garden's summer house he had built, seeing he had time owing him and with the weather being mild for the time of year. With everything arranged, Danny laid out the table and chairs he had put away. At noon on a mild November day, Betty answered the door to an excited Jamal, who stood there alone.

'Jamal, on your own? Where is your dad?'

'Coming,' called out a voice from behind the driveway. 'I think he's anxious to see the trainset.'

After a filling lunch, Jamal set off with Betty into the house and down into the basement.

'Not you, Danny? I thought that was your territory?'

Danny refilled everybody's glasses and spoke. 'I have some news for you. I hope it doesn't come as too much of a shock.'

Forest held Lisa's hand. 'Carry on; you might as well.'

'Your father died in prison. I thought you ought to know.'

Forest sat up and picked up his glass of wine. 'Well, here's a toast to that. I hope the Devil has words with him.' Draining his drink, he watched Lisa cry. 'You're not crying for him, are you?'

'No, it just feels as though a great burden has lifted from me. How did you find out?'

Danny guessed someone would ask. 'Betty's friend. She asked her policeman husband, and he explained everything. Nothing else was said.'

Betty returned with Jamal, holding a new train engine, ready to show his dad.

'Look, Dad, Uncle Danny's got another train. You should see the other things he has.'

Forest stood and kissed Betty, before shaking Danny's hand. 'Thank you both. Jamal, come here a moment.'

Running over, Forest whispered into his ear, and turning towards his Uncle and Aunt, Jamal burst out his words. 'I'm going to have a new brother.'

Both Betty and Danny sat there, a little shocked.

'Lisa and I are going to adopt another little boy. We've talked about it, and we think it would help us with what's happened. And if that goes well, we intend to adopt another child later, seeing we have space for four children.'

Betty stood and wrapped her arms around Forest. 'What a wonderful thing after…'

Forest kissed Betty. 'After all that turmoil.'

Danny congratulated Lisa on the news. 'Does this mean I have to build a bigger trainset for Jamal and his new brother?' Turning, he saw Jamal turn to him.

'Uncle, a bigger one?'

Forest released Betty. 'He shouldn't have said that.'

Rubbing Jamal's head, Danny knelt to him. 'If you are going to have a brother, I suppose I might have to.'

Jamal wrapped his arms around Danny's neck. 'Thank you, Uncle.'

Later, Danny walked Forest around the garden. 'You know where we are if you and Lisa ever need us.'

'Danny, as a brother, blood or not, you are one impressive, extraordinary guy. How can I ever not love you like one?'

Epilogue

With Forest's children all grown up with their own families or partners, the early years had been removed and hidden away. Since that time, Christmas, like always, became a joyous occasion as the big house became filled with happy voices and children's laughter. 1987 had proved a year unto itself, with Forest and Danny having taken retirement. Having married Rachael, a young woman he met in America, Jamal now lived with his two sons. His work at a London investment firm, where he thrived and flourished, had years earlier placed him in a commanding role on Wall Street, where his success and drive held the company in awe of his achievements.

With her husband Ryan, a fireman, Ruthy appeared more homely in her way as she worked from her craft room producing miniature sculptures, besides having four children with another on the way. With two more boys that had grown into men, Forest's youngest, Rusty, at the age of twenty-three, was a single guy who loved the nightlife and the ladies that frequented those places, but on occasion still lived at home when it suited him. Samuel was the sensitive one, being gay and handsome; he had moved in with his partner Todd, but like at any

Christmas, he, as they all did, looked forward to seeing their adopted parents.

Having only had one child, Fern, Danny and Betty kept a bedroom open for her. Like her father, she took to doctoring, but in the form of assistance in some of the world's most neglected countries, where famine and disease were rife. Not having married, Fern was happy with how she met people, like when an occasional relationship developed or until she moved to another country. Betty and Danny were always concerned about her and tried to maintain a distance with their concerns as she moved into worrying regions, where fighting and lawlessness were a way of life.

It was the Christmas of 1988 when she came home to see her parents and join the season's celebrations. The wonderful time produced laughter and reunions as she joined in with what made her smile, her father's blood-brother's family. With Jamal over from America, she remembered him for the trainset he played with her father in the basement. The trains' layout still took many delightful hours as Forest's grandchildren disappeared there with her father. She often looked at Jamal and wondered what it might have been if she had made a play for him before going along the path she did. He had always loved her father, so perhaps that was why she trod a different path, and she knew Jamal was her father's favourite as being Forest's first adopted son.

With the New Year over and everyone making their way home, the two houses calmed down, leaving Forest and Lisa alone for the time being. At the same time, Fern packed her bags, ready for another trip to Africa. Danny stood with Forest, waving off his daughter, watching as Betty drove her to the airport, still wishing she had found work in this country.

'You have to hand it to her, Danny. She is a strong woman doing what she does. I applaud her for her work out there; she has saved countless lives.'

Danny knew all that, yet he still ached for her to stay. 'I thought she might have settled with someone by now. I know Betty would love to dote on a grandchild. You don't know how lucky you are, Forest, with what you have.'

'Christmas is expensive, if that's what you mean.'

'You know what I'm talking about.'

Forest put his arm around Danny's neck. 'Thirty-odd years ago, they started coming into our lives. It took a while, but thanks to you and Betty, look at how it all worked out.'

Together in Forest's study, Danny sat with him, discussing a walking holiday they were thinking about, when Lisa came in, distraught and weeping.

'Lisa?'

Forest, I need to speak to you.' She looked at Danny and hurried from the room.

'I had better go; I just hope it is nothing one of the family has done.'

Watching Lisa hurry down the staircase, he followed, seeing how she fell into an armchair and cried with her hands covering her face.

'What has happened?'

Parting her hands, she looked at him. 'I had to go to Danny's for the recipe Betty gave me. The phone rang while I was there.' Lisa's tears flowed openly. 'Betty and Fern, there has been an accident on the motorway. They're both dead.'

Dumbfounded, he knelt there, taking in her news before listening to Danny come onto the stairs. Looking up, he imagined how the news would hurt him.

'Is everything all right, Lisa? Forest, your family, nothing has happened, has it?'

As Danny reached them, he gripped Forest's arms.

'There has been an accident, Danny.'

'Can I help?'

Forest shook his head. 'It's Betty and Fern.'

The funerals took place the first week in February, as Danny watched his family lowered into the damp soil as the rain came down. Supported by Forest and Lisa, he stood there as people who attended the services gradually made their way from the graveside towards the awaiting cars. The quietness of the motor and the unspoken words took Danny back to Forest's house, where a gathering of Betty's and Fern's friends awaited them. Ruthy, organising the layout of food and drinks, had pictures of Betty and Fern placed around the room, allowing people to remember them for the kind people they were.

'Are you ready for this, Danny?' Forest could feel how on edge he was as he opened the front door. 'If you want to leave, just say the word, and I'll take you up to your room.'

Following on, Lisa wondered what Danny would do now he was on his own. Since that day, he had stayed in the guest room, not wanting to go home, but now she had news that Jamal could be returning and would probably live with them, seeing his boss had retired, and he was the one most likely to take over the London position. The rest of the day saw its way through as people expressed their condolences, and then the door closed on them.

'Danny, let me make you a cup of tea. I could do with one.'

Sat in the armchair, Danny tried to smile. 'Thank you, Lisa.'

Ruthy and her youngest roamed about the room with Faye, her toddler, making a course towards Danny. 'Hello, precious, do you want a cuddle?' Lifting the child, Danny fussed with her as Lisa and Forest watched from a distance.

'That's what he needs, Forest, something to occupy his mind. He will be devastated in that big house on his own. I wish he and Betty had more children.'

Forest watched his brother sit there with Faye, and Danny began to wonder about something, something he wanted to keep to himself for the time being. A week later, having been back to his house twice with Forest, he had wandered around somehow lost as he opened cupboards and drawers. Now, sitting in Lisa's kitchen, he brought forth his news. 'I'm putting the house up for sale.'

Forest turned to him. 'In that case, you are staying with us.'

'What, like you did with my family when we were boys? Thank you both, but it wouldn't feel right after everything. I cannot explain it, but I need to find myself now Betty and Fern have gone.'

'Find yourself with us, Danny. Forest is right; there is plenty of room here.'

'I love you both, you know that, but tomorrow I am going home on my own. I have to think about my future. I might even go back to the hospital.'

'Danny, no. You know how difficult the last few years had been there; that's why you retired. Talk some sense into him, Lisa.'

The following day, Danny made his way home and, driving his car into the road, he parked to one side, looking at the house he had shared with Betty all those years. Fern had grown up there, but now it was just an uncluttered concept with furniture placed here and there. Pulling into the driveway, Danny stayed in the driver's seat, contemplating what to do. Five bedrooms, three of them hardly ever used except for visitors. Yes, he was going to sell. He still had his memories: that is what counted.

Over the next month, Danny set about looking for

a smallholding, somewhere not too far away. Forest and Lisa had repeatedly asked him to live with them, but as much as he loved them, how could he? In the first week of April, having visited three properties in the nearby area, he found a small, detached bungalow about two miles from Forest's home, in a quiet residential area, where most of the neighbours were in their seventies or over. Giving the estate agent his thoughts on the building, he told him he needed time to make sure it was the one he wanted. Back home, it was a Saturday morning when the front doorbell sounded. His footsteps echoed through the house as he opened the front door. He found Forest and Jamal stood there.

'Jamal, what a lovely surprise. Come in. Forest, you never told me this young man was coming. Are Rachael and the boys with you?'

Jamal put his arm around Danny, giving him a manly hug. 'Just me today, Uncle. They are in the city now, living in one of the plush hotels and enjoying it. I can tell by my bank statement. How are you?'

'I'm getting there. Has your father told you what I'm doing?'

'That's why I'm here. Dad told us you're selling up. I guess he didn't tell you I'm back in London working.'

Forest walked into the lounge area, noticing how cold everything looked. 'Jamal's the new boss at the London firm.'

'Congratulations, that is some achievement.'

'Financially, too, Uncle. Now that I am over here permanently, I will need a home for all of us.'

Forest stared at Danny, hoping he would see why the visit had occurred. 'I think he would need a fair-sized home, at least with four or five bedrooms.'

'Do you know of any going like that, Uncle?'

Forest walked into the kitchen, calling out, 'I think a cup of coffee, guys; you want one, Danny?'

'Was this planned? Knowing your father, it probably was. My home is your home, Jamal. Your two boys would love it here.'

'They would also love to have you here with them, Uncle. You would do me a big favour if you lived here with us. I could do with a babysitter at times and someone who knew how to run a trainset.'

Forest brought in the mugs of hot drinks.

'Forest, you bugger, this is all your doing.'

'It might be, Uncle, but what I have just told you is genuine. Besides, imagine the times we could have with dad's swimming pool; that is until I have one put in, if you allowed me. One other thing you might want to know, Rachael is pregnant. This time, we believe it is a girl. If it is, we want to call her Betty, after Auntie.'

Danny choked up a bit on the words. 'That would be nice. Your Aunt would have liked that.'

'Please say I can buy the house from you and stay here with us. The boys love you; we all do.'

The hours passed as Danny realised he still had a family. 'Let me talk to Jamal alone, Forest. You are too cocksure of yourself sometimes. Go and play with the trainset, or better still, go home and come back later when I phone you.'

The afternoon passed, and eventually, Jamal shook his uncle's hand on a deal that suited both of them until the day arrived for Danny to join Betty and Fern.

'You can phone your father now. I imagine he's sitting by the phone waiting for it to sound.'

An hour later, Jamal answered the door to Forest and Lisa, along with Rusty, who had come home for the weekend.

'Has he seen sense?'

'Dad, tread carefully. You may be blood-brothers, but Uncle's not daft.'

'Jamal, you and Rusty pour the drinks, seeing this is a celebration moment. Forest, I heard that remark.'

'By the way, Danny, you had left this in your room at the house. I thought you might want it back.' Forest pulled out Danny's old penknife from his pocket and crossed to him. 'This is yours, I think. Just don't go cutting anyone in the family with it.'

Jamal passed his uncle his drink and put out his hand, palm up. 'Uncle, you don't have to, but I would be proud to have some of your blood in me.'

The End